Shadow Invasion

SHADOW
DEMON

T.P. BRYSON

Gotham Books

30 N Gould St.
Ste. 20820, Sheridan, WY 82801
https://gothambooksinc.com/

Phone: 1 (307) 464-7800

© 2024 *T.P. Bryson*. All rights reserved.

No part of this book may be reproduced, stored in a retrieval system, or transmitted by any means without the written permission of the author.

Published by Gotham Books (November 29, 2024)

ISBN: 979-8-3304-4159-4 (P)
ISBN: 979-8-3304-4160-0 (E)
ISBN: 979-8-3304-4161-7 (H)

Because of the dynamic nature of the Internet, any web addresses or links contained in this book may have changed since publication and may no longer be valid.

The views expressed in this work are solely those of the author and do not necessarily reflect the views of the publisher, and the publisher hereby disclaims any responsibility for them.

To Alana, the love of my life, and to my fantastic children, Amanda, Rachel, Joshua, and Christopher. All are my best friends.

TABLE OF CONTENT

Prologue 1
Chapter 1 4
Chapter 2 8
Chapter 3 15
Chapter 4 18
Chapter 5 30
Chapter 6 35
Chapter 7 41
Chapter 8 54
Chapter 9 59
Chapter 10 63
Chapter 11 68
Chapter 12 73
Chapter 13 83
Chapter 14 89
Chapter 15 95
Chapter 16 102
Chapter 17 106
Chapter 18 114
Chapter 19 116
Chapter 20 122
Chapter 21 124
Chapter 22 133
Chapter 23 136
Chapter 24 144
Chapter 25 146
Chapter 26 154

Chapter 27	157
Chapter 28	160
Chapter 29	168
Chapter 30	172
Chapter 31	184
Chapter 32	186
Chapter 33	194
Chapter 34	206
Chapter 35	208
Chapter 36	210
Chapter 37	218
Chapter 38	222
Chapter 39	231
Chapter 40	236
Chapter 41	238
Chapter 42	248
Chapter 43	253
Chapter 44	258
Chapter 45	269
Chapter 46	274
Chapter 47	280
Chapter 48	281
Chapter 49	291
Chapter 50	297
Chapter 51	298
Epilogue	301
Author's Final Thoughts:	303

Prologue

Fifty-five-year-old Professor Gerald Feinstein sat at his office desk, deeply absorbed in research for his next book, <u>Modern Monster Mythology (1800 to Present Day): History of the Nightmare</u>. Wall-to-wall and floor-to-ceiling bookshelves lined the perimeter of the windowless office. Gerald had removed several books from the shelves, now lying on his sizable desk. Gerald specialized in Modern Cultural Mythology in the Department of Sociology, University of California - El Palmar.

He obsessively read each line of text in the nearest book, occasionally marking passages and writing notes in the margins. These were his books, so it didn't matter that he defaced the pages. No one else would ever be allowed to read, let alone borrow one of his precious books. He held a cup of coffee in his left hand while using his right-hand index finger to follow each word on the page. Setting the cup down on the desktop, he turned the page and continued reading. Absentmindedly, he reached for the cup, grabbing nothing but air. Gerald looked up from his reading and saw the cup was missing.

Confused by this strange moment, he looked to the floor. No coffee had spilled—no broken cup.

"What the hell," he said.

Right where he thought he had placed the cup, Gerald discovered a strange-looking crack in the desk surface. The open crack made a hole about the size of his coffee cup. It seemed to vibrate and randomly change shape before his eyes. He blinked. The crack changed shape again and increased in size.

"Did my cup fall into that?"

Upon further inspection, he saw that the crack continued down the desk's front to the floor. Even more bewildering, the crack continued through the floor. Beyond, he could see the light shining back at him. This light came, not from the floor below, but from some other place. It felt like sunlight.

Gerald got on his knees and bent over to look through the crack. He heard waves and smelled salty air wafting through the crack. It smelled like peace and freedom. It made him think of heaven. Suddenly, he wanted to go to the beach and run through surf. He wanted to be anywhere but his office.

"Why am I working on this damnable book in my office?" He shouted to no one. "I'll quit my job," Gerald said as he sat up straight. "Screw this job and screw this stupid book. I'll buy a ticket to Hawaii tomorrow morning. Then I am out of here."

This insane outburst took Gerald by surprise. What was he thinking? He could not quit his job and head to the Hawaiian beach without notice. "It is the smell," Gerold said to himself. "It's like a spell of some kind."

He felt compelled to be where that smell came from, not Hawaii, but through the hole.

Gerald stood, took a pen and paper, and wrote, *"I am going to the beach on the other side. Bye, bye"* He set the note on top of the open books on his desk. Then he stood over the hole and said, "How do I get there?" After a pause, he added, "Come and get me."

The sunlight coming from the other side of the hole suddenly blinked off. Gerald backed away cautiously. He no longer felt tempted by that smell. The crack began to expand until it opened wide enough to step through. He backed away further, all the way to the office's wall behind him.

"What do you want," Gerold asked. "No, I won't..."

Without warning, glossy black, suction-cupped tentacles sprung from the open hole. They lounged toward Gerald, who screamed.

"Good Lord, someone. Help me."

He tried to fight the monster, but it easily thrashed him around. Bookshelves collapsed, lamps toppled, and a file cabinet fell over when it slammed Gerald into it. He yelped in pain. The monster threw him up to the ceiling causing the ceiling lights to flash with sparks, setting books on fire. The fire sprinklers flooded the now-dark room as the beast violently pulled Gerald into the dark hole. Then the hole disappeared.

The campus police were stunned by what they found inside Prof. Feinstein's office. The only undamaged item in the room was a note conveniently covered by a piece of ceiling tile that had fallen on top of it.

The handwritten note said, "*I am going to the beach on the other side. Bye-bye.*"

"What the hell does that mean." the campus cop blurted out in bewilderment.

Chapter 1

―――――・・・◆・・・・―――――

CENTER FOR INTERDIMENSIONAL PHYSICS

UNIVERSITY OF CALIFORNIA, EL PALMAR

The project coordinator, Dr. Al Marshall, called out, "HGC event number 736.24 is ready to launch."

Dr. Eugene Miles, Marshall's boss, kept up an anxious, back-and-forth pace at the back of the room. A familiar itch had formed inside his head, nagging at him without mercy. This always happened whenever an important discovery lay within his reach. The itch started somewhere deep inside his head. It then crept to the top of his forehead, almost close enough to scratch. He could only scratch the itch by pushing himself and his team harder. Something fascinating was about to occur. He could tell. He could feel it. The itch seldom lied.

"Ten, nine, eight, seven, six, five, four, three, two, one, and engage," Marshal continued.

"Engaged," the systems engineer responded.

The Hyper gravity Chamber (HGC) throbbed with energy. The smooth ten-meter sphere and the four massive gyroscopic rings that encircled it gently floated up off its base into a position equidistant from four arched pillars made of reinforced concrete. Attached to the inside edge of each pillar were four electromagnetic coils that now pulsed and sparked with visible power. Each gyroscopic ring rotated in a different direction, slow at first, then faster and faster. The rotations increased until the sphere and the rings blurred into one vibrating object.

The team of twenty-three scientists and technicians watched from the rows of monitoring stations in the control center. This high-tech facility looked more like launch control at NASA than a university's physics lab. The giant screen at the front of the room gave everyone a clear view of the HGC chamber, inside and out, where an interdimensional rift, the target of many years of hard work, would hopefully appear.

As the executive director of the University of California, El Palmar, Center for Interdimensional Physics, Dr. Miles provided his team with the best technology the Twenty-first Century offered. Under his leadership, billions of government and private dollars flowed into the project. Miles had personally hired each member of his team. These people represented the best in their fields, and he expected the absolute best from each of them. Miles' team respectfully addressed him as Dr. Miles. His peers in the field called him Miles. Those he considered close friends called him Eugene.

Miles' team had advanced far ahead of the competition in Germany, Japan, and China. It took an astonishing amount of power to produce and create an interdimensional rift. The system's new, advanced and top-secret power source promised far greater control than previously possible. Miles hoped for another breakthrough even more significant than the event achieved three years earlier. They had produced rifts, but taking control of a rift remained a far more challenging accomplishment.

After a tense pause, Marshal announced, "We have an open and stable rift." The room erupted with cheering and applause.

"Is this even possible," someone said. "I mean, look at these numbers. This new rift is huge."

This small rift was quite large compared to all previous events. Although too small to see with the naked eye, the system confirmed its existence. Within seconds, the sensors collected a fantastic amount of new information.

Dr. Miles held a physicist's dream position for almost ten years. The generous funding exceeded all expectations, but for good reason. Interdimensional rifts generated energy. Of course, interdimensional rifts came in tiny packages. It took far more energy to achieve a rift than an individual rift could produce. But they had gotten better at creating rifts. During the first controlled event, his team created and held an individual rift for 1.362 millionths of a second. Since that first event, the team had reproduced the experiment 364 times. They had failed 374 times. The best event duration to date had been a hold of 1/2500th of a second, a significant improvement.

Recently, there had been a few false readings. The system declared it had opened a rift when no rift existed within the chamber. Even after double and triple analysis of the data, the system still insisted a rift had been formed somewhere. No one had an explanation for these anomalies.

Capturing and controlling best described what they wanted to achieve. Interdimensional rifts occur naturally in the universe. The team aimed to maintain a rift long enough to collect the energy created. The accumulative power would be limitless if scientists controlled the energy from a series of connected, open, and stable rifts. Of course, finding a reliable, inexpensive way to harness rift energy is decades away.

Miles grunted at his moment of idealism. Recognizing his primary funding source, the Department of Defense, he had to admit his project's goals would bear deeper and darker fruit. Miles didn't enjoy working with the DOD or his assigned guardian, General Andrew (Hellraiser) Bates. But it paid the bills and kept his playground going and growing. He had decided not to worry about how others might use his discoveries. Philosophers and historians would debate the morality of his research long after he was dead and gone.

Miles' gray hair had thinned, and he had developed a well-deserved reputation for being grumpy and demanding. The mental and physical pressures caused by years of mind-boggling research into the unknown, and in many ways, the impossible, had taken their toll. For better or worse, he had become an obsessed man.

The spherical chamber was a complex instrument. It amplified gravity and focused it onto a single point at the chamber's center. The device sat at the center of a large, shielded containment room, which in turn sat dead center of the larger main building. The nondescript building and its adjacent power plant looked more like industrial warehouses than a cutting-edge science facility. A fenced green buffer zone surrounded the building and kept all non-personnel away. The HGC control center where Miles and his team watched the system take control of another rift was housed in a separate building about a block away. Tunnels connected all the Center's buildings to the university's underground tunnel system. Safety concerns made it necessary to build the main HGC building at the edge of campus in the wooded endowment land.

Miles raised both arms to quiet everyone down. "Everyone. I'd like to say a few words." The room went silent. "I'd like to thank you for your hard work, especially those of you who worked on the needed upgrades."

"As you can see, it made a difference. I couldn't ask for a better team than you folks. Again, thank you all." There was a round of enthusiastic applause. Everyone continued to chatter in congratulatory mirth.

Dr. Marshal followed the data stream as the boss gave his little speech. He watched the monitor with ever-growing excitement. The rift should have collapsed by now, but the data stream continued. When Miles finished his little pep talk, Marshal ordered: "Everyone, back to your posts. I need reports. Now."

One by one, the project leaders reported back. Not only had the rift remained open, it showed no signs of closing any time soon. The team monitored the rift for the rest of the evening and into the following day. The rift remained unaffected by anything they did, even after rebooting the entire system. It seemed as though they were no longer in control of the rift. Dr. Miles's itch proved right again, but no one had considered what to do should an interdimensional rift get a mind of its own. Neither did anyone know what to do should the rift grow larger. Dr. Marshal reported the unexpected situation to Miles the following morning.

"Some unknown element has stuck its foot into our open rift, keeping it from closing," Marshal said. Dr. Miles' itch got a lot itchier.

Chapter 2

---·•·•·◆·•·•·---

A SHADOW OF A SHADOW

Little Toe could not believe his eyes. A new crack had formed on the back wall of his sleeping chamber. Frequent ground shakes caused cracks to appear in this world's dark stone all the time. But this one boggled Toe's mind. A light shined through it. That made it a special kind of crack. Toe's bed lay in the furthest part of his residence, deep in the rocky landscape, which made his sleeping chamber extra dark. Little Toe liked sleeping, hiding, in total darkness. When he awoke this morning, he found a dim glow filtering into the chamber. In a moment of confusion, he wondered if he had fallen asleep in the front chamber near the entrance to his residence. But no, he was in bed as usual.

Toe grunted and sighed mournfully. "Residence, chambers? Who am I trying to fool?"

Referring to his rustic home as if it were some grand residential property was ridiculous. In reality, he lived in a boring old cave. There was no way he ended up the owner of a property grant. He had no lineage that afforded him rights to property. Because of his small stature, he lacked the prowess to take anything by force.

"I'm as poor and worthless as the black rocks around me," he muttered. Yet, as dreary as this place appeared, Toe was lucky to have it. He was better off than many others.

This world, called Tiarnas, made a slow orbit around a red sun. The sun's red light filtered through dark clouds that, more often than not, shrouded the ground below. Even at midday, the light cast a dim red glow. The sun had long since stopped providing sufficient light for the Shadow population that eked out a life on Tiarnas. The days were long. Then came the long, cold, dark nights. Toe shivered, and his shadowy body blurred ever so much.

Little Toe was an insignificant creature on the best of days. Elite Shadows often refer to low-class beings like Toe as a *shadow of a Shadow*. The insult was a crude joke. A Shadow's vague body, made of mist-like particles held together by magic, didn't cast much of a shadow. Unless the shadow wore armor like warriors or robes like the rich and influential, the sun's dim light tended to diffuse through the body with no substantial shadow created. So, to put it another way, to call someone a *shadow of a Shadow* meant that he or she had little to no substance. Everyone knew that poor Little Toe was a *shadow of a Shadow*.

Two years ago, Little Toe discovered his crude stone cave. He moved in, and since no one objected, he stayed. Later, he made an official claim with the local Magistrate, Fire Claws. Fire Claws told him that the original owner had disappeared without a trace. The cave had sat unclaimed for years. Ultimately, the Magistrate granted the cave to Little Toe, but with a humiliating caveat.

"Until someone else wants it," Fire Claws had told him.

Toe doubted that anyone else would ever want his cave. The Magistrate only granted the claim because the cave lay in a worthless corner of the farthest and darkest part of a village called Far Edge.

"Better than nothing," he thought, trying to cheer himself up. He lied to himself a lot these days. Then he thought, "This crack just might make this cave much better than nothing." The glimmer of light coming through it meant this was no ordinary crack. The crack was a rupture of some kind. If one believed the legends, ruptures led to other worlds.

A loud crunching sound rattled the cave. "Oh... my...," Little Toe thought in excited wonder. "The crack just got larger."

Ruptures have always existed but are relatively uncommon in recent times. His life may take a turn for the better. Light, a precious commodity in his world, had many magical properties. This rupture could be worth a fortune if it didn't disappear as quickly as it had appeared. A sharp, loud crackle startled him again. The rupture grew more. It was now about the length of his forearm and the width of two fingers. Toe's excitement increased as more bright light flooded into the cave.

Tiarnas hadn't always been a dark world. Long ago, many sources of light existed. Natural fire pits, glowing rocks, phosphorescing plants, and animals filled the world with beautiful colors, especially at night. When Toe was an imp, the elder Shadows taught him about the old-world from years ago. Toe had only known the dark Tiarnas.

Toe thought back to the stories of the elders. He and the other imps gathered around to listen, eager to hear exciting stories. Back then the elders were much wiser and more intelligent than elders today. Toe noted that his world had lost much knowledge over time. The old ones used to talk about magic and about natural elements like light and the black mist that covered his world. No one cared about such things these days - except for him. According to the old legends, black mist had combined with the natural flow of magic millions of years ago to form the building blocks of life on Tiarnas.

Before the creation began, only a dark and empty void existed. Molten black mist poured into the void through massive ruptures. The smoldering black mist filled the void. As the molten matter cooled, it formed the four essential elements - air, liquid, rock, and fire. Combined with heat, light, and energy, the byproducts of magic, life sparked into existence. Whether natural or magical, energy was the source of sustenance for all living things on Tiarnas.

Shadow creatures ate energy, which made them strong over thousands of generations. Eventually, the prehistoric ruptures disappeared, and the world cooled. The creatures evolved and prospered. Then darkness came. Darkness led to a slow decline of the Shadow species.

Survival for the weak and poor wasn't easy in places like Far Edge. The population in the poorest districts had grown too large, and resources began to dwindle. Desperate times made Shadows meaner and more dangerous. If this rupture in the wall became a permanent fixture, maybe Toe could bring light back into his world. That would be nice.

Toe remembered another exciting part of the creation story. In the beginning, the black mist brought light into existence through the sun, which took powerful magic. The elders told him that light seeks out dark places to fulfill its purpose, which made Toe think, "Can light exist without darkness?" He had contemplated such things for years.

Then he thought, "Can darkness exist without light? If you have no reference to compare dark and light, how can you truly understand either?"

Magic existed everywhere, so even though their sun was slowly dying, magic remained constant. It flowed through everything, animating life. It gave life power. A Shadow proverb said, "Whoever controls the magic controls the world." Powerful magic enabled the royal family to rule the Shadow Empire for almost a thousand years. Few Shadows grew up learning world history like Little Toe, but his curious and clever nature allowed him to learn by listening and observing. He had no formal education. Knowledge had proved most valuable, a means for survival. On many occasions, it had saved him. For Little Toe, smarter meant safer. Smarter meant stronger.

"The important thing," Toe thought, bringing his attention back to the crack in the wall, "A beam of light shining on these black rocks can produce tons of new energy, and since Shadows are energy eaters, I will no longer be a shadow of a Shadow. I will own something of substance."

The problem? How to hold onto this priceless windfall. Little Toe would keep the rupture secret for now, but it needed to remain a secret until he knew the law would protect him. Since this cave now belonged to Toe, the rupture inside also belonged to him. But the ruthless Magistrate Fire Claws dispensed law and justice in Far Edge. Fire Claws decided all legal matters. Unfortunately, whatever served Fire Claws' interests the most constituted the law of Far Edge. If the Magistrate wanted this rupture for himself, he would take it. Little Toe had endured years of such abuse. Bullying, beatings, and cruelty of every kind chronicled the story of his miserable life. Plenty of other Shadows would kill to get his cave once they realized it had value.

All through the long day, Toe watched as the rupture grew. Toe pressed his fuzzy face against the cold stone wall and sniffed the opening. Whatever existed through the rupture smelled wonderful. He drooled. Intrigued, he stuck out his long tongue and gave the rupture a deep, satisfying lick. A multitude of exotic flavors hit his taste buds all at once. His glowing green eyes roll back in their sockets. The muscles in his cheeks froze into a grotesque grin, and he drooled uncontrollably. Slimy goo dripped down his chin and fell in strings of goo to the cave floor, making globs and puddles. An involuntary shudder overtook his body. The pleasure seizure sent gooey saliva out of his mouth. Long strings splattered on the walls, ceiling, and all over him.

Since Shadows weren't completely solid, the explosive reaction left his body temporarily misshapen. His semi-formless dark-colored body had a preferred shape. Magic controlled how his body grew and matured. Depending on its needs, a Shadow could make its body as hard as a rock or as thin as a cloud. Unfortunately, such changes could happen as voluntary or completely involuntary reactions. Toe couldn't control his response to tasting new exotic flavors - primarily a male Shadow problem. Females of his species possessed more extraordinary magic by nature and, therefore, more significant control over their shape. Unfortunately, that also made females a lot scarier and far more dangerous.

Magic pulled Toe's body back to normal. "What was that," he thought. "One thing for sure, it is the most delightful, yummy goodness I've ever tasted." He wanted more of it, a lot more of it.

The rupture expanded again with another loud crack. Without thinking, Toe stuck a hand through the larger opening, hoping to get a handful of the delicious nectar on the other side. However, he forgot the most important of all Shadow rules. Every Shadow knows from imp-hood to not stick your hand into anything unless you know you can get it back out. The crack held Toe's hand firmly in place. As one of the smartest Shadows on Tiarnas, making such a stupid mistake frustrated him to near tears. If his enemies found him in such a compromised position, Little Toe would be in serious trouble.

For most Shadows, intelligence was not on the list of essential attributes. Most male Shadows were not that smart. Size, physical strength, and fearsomeness served them far better than cleverness, but Little Toe had been small from birth. Even as a full-grown Shadow, he remained small in stature. Toe hated his name. The Magistrate had given the name in jest.

"Yeah, funny," he thought. "The neighborhood bullies laugh as if it is the funniest joke ever. You would think after a while; the bullies would grow tired of the joke." Toe sighed. "No such luck."

Toe observed that when a someone possessed strength, size, wealth, and cleverness simultaneously, enjoyed a much better life. Such creatures ruled this world. Fire Claws, a giant creature, stood twice as tall as Toe and possessed some level of cleverness. He and his gang of thugs ruled Far Edge. They hurt and killed others for fun and profit. Little Toe hated such Shadows.

One of Fire Claws' gang members, a Shadow called Broken Fang, frightened Toe the most. Cleverness made Broken Fang far more dangerous than even Fire Claws. Toe suspected Fang tried to hide his actual cleverness, which Fire Claws would perceive as a threat to his position as the alpha male.

"It's probably a good thing that there aren't that many clever male Shadows," Toe thought. That would make Tiarnas an even scarier place. After all, smarter did not necessarily mean better or wiser."

Toe looked at his hand stuck inside the rupture. He wondered what made the rupture taste so good. "It might be the light itself or some other element common to whatever exists beyond," Toe thought. "If another world existed, would it be better than this one?"

Then, it occurred to him that if the other world differed, it might have different natural laws. "Maybe I can't get my hand out because the law about size and shape is different on the other side. My hand may have grown more solid or maybe even larger. Yet, why has the rest of me remained the same? Different natural laws," he thought.

"Another interesting idea." Toe tried to see through the rupture, but his hand was in the way. "What if I went through the rupture and became bigger? Would it not be great to be big as, or bigger than, Fire Claws?" He smiled.

For a minute, his thoughts turned to revenge. Then reality came crashing down. If the rupture didn't get larger, pulling his hand free might not be possible. He might be stuck here for a long time. Making things worse, he felt the other side pulling him further into the rupture.

"I should call for help." He sighed. "Better poor than dead."

He imagined the sarcastic remarks he would encounter. "Well now, you sure got yourself in trouble, didn't you?" they'd say. "What will you give us to get you out? Saving you from starvation is worth something."

"No!" Toe thought out in frustration. "I won't let that happen!" One thing he knew for sure: You could never trust a Shadow. He wouldn't allow his enemies to take advantage of the situation. This rupture and the light it brought promised him a ticket out of this hellhole. He needed to file a proper claim with the Ministry of Ownership in the capital city. Then, the Shadow Lords would protect him, he hoped.

Toe made a mewling sound. For now, he would wait for the rupture to get bigger. Tomorrow, he will get his hand out. He sat down, his hand still stuck, and leaned against the black stone wall. He dreamed of what he could buy with his newfound fortune.

Chapter 3

TAKING A STROLL

Alarms blared in the control center.

"What's happening now?" Dr. Miles barked as he entered the room. The euphoric feeling of success had ended two days ago.

"Reports," Al Marshall ordered.

"It's the rift, sir," a technician reported. "It's drifting."

"What do you mean drifting," Miles barked.

"It's moving away from its central position inside the chamber." He stopped to consider the data. "It has moved sixty centimeters in the last five minutes alone."

"You've got to be kidding me?"

"Uh... no, sir."

Marshal appeared at Miles's side. "Since it couldn't go back to sleep, it decided to take a stroll."

"This thing has a mind of its own," Miles added. First, it decided to grow larger, and now this. It's drifting. If it keeps this up…"

"The chamber wall should contain it," Marshal said. "Right?"

Miles rubbed his forehead. "If it doesn't, it will end up outside in the parking lot."

"Twenty-four and a half hours," the technician said.

"What?"

"At this rate, it will break free of the building in twenty-four hours."

"Crap. Double crap. Any sign of it decreasing in size?"

"No, sir. It's still growing. Sir, it's now large enough to see with the naked eye. Would you like to see it, sir?"

"Hell yes," Mile said, astonished. "Bring it up on the main screen."

The technician opened a video channel inside the HGC sphere. Zooming in, he focused on the rift. A fuzzy black spot shuddered and wiggled at the center of the screen.

"Not quite what I expected," Marshal said.

Miles watched the screen with fascination. "Doesn't have to be pretty. Just astounding."

Years ago, a much younger Dr. Miles developed a general theory of interdimensional rift formation. His theory affirmed the existence of naturally occurring fissures in the fabric of space. Such fissures, now referred to as interdimensional rifts, rip open when and wherever the pull of opposing gravitational forces overwhelmed the boundaries of space. He published his ground-breaking treatise in *The Scientific Journal for the Advances in Physics*. He entitled it "The Universal Theory of Interdimensional Rift Formation and Rift Elemental Properties."

The existence of such boundaries sparked considerable mind-boggling speculation, but Miles had chosen to focus on the nature of the rifts themselves - the what and why. He left the study of multiple universes for someone else to beat their head against. Beating one's head against a wall best describes the true nature of this kind of research.

His paper said, *"Interdimensional rifts appear when the gravity of heavenly objects (stars, planets, galaxies) warps, folds, and stretches the fabric of space. Rifts are the spaces between the woven threads of that fabric. When our universe's boundaries stretch, interdimensional rifts form. Why?"* Miles speculated, *"Just as the pores in our skin expand and contract as an essential function of a healthy body, rifts allow a healthy universe to breathe, to exchange elemental properties from this universe and another."* Dr. Miles believed that, as quantum mechanics changed our view of the universe in the Twentieth Century, interdimensional physics would change scientific thought in the Twenty-first Century.

"Miles," Marshal said. "I was thinking. We need to inform General Bates about this." Miles grimaced. "If this worsens, the general will want his team on site."

"The last thing I want is to have the Department of Defense looking over my shoulder."

Marshall continued, "If the rift breaches the building, the situation might attract attention. Dealing with nosey reporters will be far worse than dealing with Bates."

"Humph. I suppose you're right." Miles turned, heading back to his office. He yelled, "Someone, get me a cup of coffee." But then he said, "Never mind. I've got something stronger in my office."

Chapter 4

UNEXPECTED TRANSFORMATIONS

Bobby Williams' summer vacation sucked. It sucked worse than anything he had ever experienced in his sixteen years of life. At the end of last school year, his two best friends, Jeff Sasaki and Sam (Samantha) Thomas, announced that they would leave him friendless for the whole summer. This life-shattering news foreshadowed a monumentally dull summer vacation. He couldn't think of anything worse except maybe death. Although, in retrospect, near death best described his summer.

Sam's mom had planned a trip to Florida to visit a friend. She wanted Sam to come with her. Sam said goodbye on the last day of school and left the next day. Jeff's parents had planned a trip to Japan to visit family, many of which Jeff had never met. Family obligation required his presence.

"Sam couldn't wait to get out of town," Bobby grumbled. "At least Jeff felt bad about leaving me alone."

Although excited to go to Japan, Jeff at least offered sympathy for Bobby's situation. That's when Jeff got a great idea. He asked his parents if it would be possible for Bobby to come to Japan with them. Surprise, surprise, Jeff's parents said yes. Not only that, they offered to pay Bobby's way. Bobby now had a once-in-a-lifetime opportunity. The boy's mood lifted and filled him with great expectations.

At least, until Bobby's parents said, "NO."

"What do you mean, no," Bobby had protested. "You can't possibly want to keep me from such an amazing opportunity?"

"Sorry. I know it's a great opportunity," his dad said. But it wouldn't be right to ask the Sasaki family to take on the extra responsibility of another teenage boy. It's too much."

"I promise. I won't be any trouble."

Bobby's dad sighed. Too often, parents face the burden of making hard decisions for their kids. Mr. Williams knew his son would be no trouble for the Sasakis. But Other factors, essential factors necessitated his son staying home. Issues concerning Bobby's age and their family history weighed into his Dad's decision. "Sorry, son. Maybe next time when you are a little older."

Bobby tried everything to get his dad to change his mind. First, he refused to accept no for an answer. He threatened, begged, bartered, and sulked as surly as possible. Nothing worked. It felt like going through the stages of grief - denial, anger, bargaining, depression. There would be no relief until he hit bottom. so Bobby accepted it.

In frustration, he almost let loose a few bad words in his parents' presence. Luckily, he didn't. That blunder would have made things worse. Besides, he sucked at profanity. When short guys used profanity, it always sounded like they were overcompensating. Bobby had always been short for his age. Now, at sixteen, he only stood five foot three barefooted. Besides, over the last couple of years Bobby had discovered far better ways to compensate for his height issues. In fact he had become an expert at compensating.

In the end, his fate boiled down to the fact that his dad had said no. That was that. No matter how unfair, he would have to accept it. Acceptance... the final stage of grief.

Several times throughout the summer, his mom suggested that he grow up. "It's about time you learned that life isn't always fair. If you want us to treat you as an adult, then perhaps you should act like an adult."

Bobby grumbled to himself, "Yeah... well... growing up sucks too." Growing up meant submitting to unreasonable demands and obligations. Obligation was in part responsible for his abandonment in the first place. Family obligations dragged Jeff to Japan and Sam off to Florida without him. At least now, with the summer over and school starting, the never-ending boredom would end.

Bobby leaned against his school locker. From the corner of his eye, he saw Jeff coming down the hall. Renewed excitement transformed his glum expression into a giant grin. He watched his tall, skinny friend snake through the crowded school hallway.

"Bah beee," Jeff yelled.

Bobby yelled back, "Jeff reee!"

To yell out like that was quite uncharacteristic of Bobby. He tended to avoid anything that called attention to himself, especially at school. However, this occasion called for whooping and hollering.

"Dang, Jeff," Bobby said. "I'm glad you're back."

Jeff was a unique kind of friend. The type of friend you could count on in a zombie apocalypse. Everyone needed a friend or two like that. Jeff's arrival at school was the first hopeful sign that life would be back to normal. Jeff loved to have fun. Yet, his craziness had resulted in an unfortunate reputation among his peers. He had earned the title of El Palmar High School's official oddball. Bobby didn't think Jeff was that odd - more eccentric than anything else. Nearly everyone at school called Jeff by his full first name, Jeffrey, at least those who cared to know his name. Unfortunately, most said it in a mocking, condescending way. They pronounced it *Jeff-Ray* with an emphasis on the *Ray*. Last year, Bobby launched a concerted effort to help his friend establish a more respectable persona. It started small. More significant gestures would have to come later. He began referring to his friend by the manlier version of his name, Jeff. Despite this subtle contribution, Jeff remained a Jeffrey, but Bobby knew that Jeffrey had it in him to become a Jeff.

Bobby took a good look at his extravagant friend. Jeff had acquired a new hairstyle while in Japan. His normal dark hair was now white and black. The asymmetrical cut looked eccentric. He spiked it forward, upward, and sideways, much like a particular character from a favorite anime. When Jeff embraced change, he went all the way. That described Jeff in a nutshell - he went all the way. Sometimes, Bobby envied Jeff's fearlessness and willingness to be different, but that wasn't Bobby.

Clothing-wise, Jeff typically wore a fan art tee shirt and, depending on the weather, cargo shorts or cargo pants. Cargo pants defied the style norm, but Jeff remained an ardent fan of the baggy pants. By his logic, one could never have enough pockets for stuff. In addition, even though it was hot today, he wore his favorite red leather jacket. Two years ago, Jeff found the red *Akira* jacket while shopping online. The jacket, fashioned after the one in the 1980s anime poster hanging on Jeffrey's bedroom wall, represented the ultimate coolness. So, he purchased it. Even though the jacket was too big back then and too small for him now, he wore it to school often. This red jacket mystified everyone. Assuming he meant to mimic the famous costume from the eighties music video *Thriller*, people would ask, "Michael Jackson... right?" Millions still watched the late and infamous rock star's video on Halloween, so it was a reasonable misunderstanding. Still, its frustrated Jeff that they kept getting it wrong.

"It's an *Akira* jacket, not a *Thriller* jacket," he'd say. It amused Bobby that Jeff didn't realize how that obscure 1980s anime reference escaped most people.

Bobby believed that Jeff's style choices resulted from an anime addiction. Jeff loved anime and watched it obsessively. Jeff wanted desperately to be like the handsome hero from a harem comedy, but the boy's cool factor didn't quite match his aspirations. Jeff acted more like the hero's comic sidekick. Bobby had always thought that if Jeff tried harder to control himself, he might be able to pull off that cool, *Asian* male look often seen on TV. Sadly, immaturity kept his good looks from shining through. Jeff's personality did more to annoy than endear. Although Jeff did many crazy things, he had always been a loyal friend. Bobby liked that about him.

Unlike Jeff, Bobby always wore conservative clothes, both in cut and color. His hair was well groomed, neither too long nor too short. He looked as average as any other teenage boy, which helped Bobby blend into the high school crowd.

"Good to have you back, man," Bobby told Jeff, reaching out to give Jeff a sideways handclasp.

"Good to be back," Jeff said, raising his hand for a high-five.

In that moment of awkwardness, Bobby flinched. He had every reason to expect a possible head smack. Jeff tended to be way too physical. Bobby managed a smooth recovery and raised his hand to Jeff's with a smack.

Jeff laughed. "Ha. You flinched, dude." He slugged Bobby on the arm.

"Owe," Bobby protested, rubbing his arm. Are you still in junior high? And Jeff, no one says 'dude' anymore. People will think you're a dork." Bobby hated anyone calling him a dork, and he didn't like anyone calling his friends dorks either.

"Ah, but I am a trendsetter," Jeff replied. "Just wait. Soon, everyone will be saying, "Dude."

Bobby continued rubbing his arm. "So anyway, how was your trip to Japan? Was it cool?"

"Man, I had a blast. My cousins were cool. They kept me happy and busy. There was so much to do. It helped to speak a little Japanese, and they spoke a little English."

"That's cool. I wish I had had a place to go this summer."

"Sorry about that. So, your summer then?"

"It sucked without you and Sam."

Sam played an essential role in this trio of friends. She kept Bobby sane. She was smart, bold, and fun. Sam embraced her geeky, tomboy nature to the fullest. That made her the perfect girl, at least in Bobby's mind. He understood her, and she understood him. This connection with Sam transcended the normal friendship boundaries. Something special connected them, not romantic or anything like that, but definitely special.

Like Sam, Bobby embraced his true nature as EPHS's number-one geek. In general, he got along with most of the kids at school. Most non-geeks tolerated geeks and nerds, but that didn't mean everyone wanted to be his friend. Being a smart geek did little to help him make friends. It did, however, help him avoid enemies, people determined to be antagonistic. You know the type - stupid bullies. People generally excelled at only one thing: being tough, throwing a ball, being popular, or just being smartasses. These individuals, especially the entitled ones, believed that Bobby and his geeky friends sat at the bottom of the school's social hierarchy and deserved to be there. Bobby needed to exorcise such demons from his life before they became a problem for him and his friends. Bobby had a unique talent, Sam called it his sixth sense, which helped him defuse confrontation. He saw people as puzzles. Contentious people were puzzles that required a quick solution. He seemed to know just what to say or do, to stop an aggressive adversary and send them on their way dumbfounded. Yet, after his clever and insightful nature had confounded his opponent, the individual would brush him off with, *"Whatever, dork."*

That made his blood boil. The terms geek and dork are completely different personality types. Everyone knows that, or at least they should know that. Although he supposed it was possible to be a geek and a dork simultaneously, that wasn't him, not Bobby Williams. He loved games, anime, sci-fi, and fantasy. That made him a geek. He loved computers and the sciences. Not enough to want to be a scientist, but he liked the sciences all the same. His dad was a physicist, which influenced his interest in the sciences. Computers and science made him a geeky nerd. But the term dork refers to stereotypical attributes, none of which apply to him. As someone had once told him, he was an average, good-looking guy. His face flushed as his mind backtracked.

Okay, he thought. *That was my mother, and she said, 'Cute.' But Sam enthusiastically confirmed that assessment. Thus, two separate females confirmed that I am in the cute category but not a dork.*

Sam, also someone he could count on in a zombie apocalypse, returned home yesterday. Even with their houses being backyard to backyard, Bobby hadn't even caught a glimpse of her. He looked forward to seeing her today. With the return of his two best friends, he looked forward to many weekends of playing games, watching anime and horror movies, or whatever else they could find to keep themselves happy and busy.

Bobby's sixth sense enabled him to understand and solve problems. He solved puzzles and games with unusual clarity. He saw what others overlooked and perceived solutions far faster than any opponent. The competitive strategy came easily to him. This gift made him number one among the high school gamer crowd. Even the local college-aged gamers had heard of Bobby Williams.

Bobby's parents moved to El Palmar thirteen years ago. That same week, Sam's parents moved into the house behind them. Most little boys shied away from little girls, but Sam was different. She wasn't girly at all. Bobby and Sam were three years old at the time. When the two kids discovered they shared the same birthday, July 21, they became inseparable. Every year since then, Bobby and Sam celebrated their birthdays together - except for this last summer. She ended up on the opposite side of the country.

"I gather we're waiting for Sam," Jeff said, breaking into Bobby's thoughts. Bobby nodded. Then Jeff said, "Sorry you couldn't come with me this summer. I'm glad I went, but I wish you had come along. You would have loved Japan."

Bobby shrugged. "I survived. That's what we geeks do, right? Besides, the gang of three can get together this weekend." They did a high-five. "I got this great new game. You'll love…"

"Hold… that… thought, dude. Who is that girl?"

Jeff had trouble staying on track in any conversation, but when a pretty girl appeared on the scene, he lost all ability to focus. Not that he expected the girl to give him a second notice. Jeff was merely an admirer of God's handy work, and this girl was a great example of divine design.

Bobby checked out the subject of Jeff's ogling. She wore a yellow and white sundress that accented her near-perfect bronzed tan. She had gathered her sun-bleached, light brown hair behind into a soft bun that bounced and swayed at the base of her neck. Two long bits of hair hung down her cheeks, framing her beautiful smile. Bobby watched with interest as the girl walked toward them. Jeff was right. She was pretty. All down the hall, guys stopped to take a second look as the new girl passed. She raised her hand to brush her hair back behind her ear. That was when Bobby saw those two familiar green eyes, which confused him.

Jeff said, "She must be new. No way I missed seeing her last year."

Bobby shook his head. "I don't... think..."

At that instant, she turned and looked straight at Bobby. "Hey, nerd-head," she called out, throwing him the biggest smile—a smile that said there was no one in this world she wanted to see more than him. Bobby instinctively glanced behind him. No, she was talking to him. It couldn't be. Only one person had ever called him nerd-head.

"Sam," he said.

Her kelly green eyes seemed to flash as if magic had made them that green. Everyone in Sam's family had eyes like that, but Bobby and his parents had pale blue eyes.

"And hi to you, Jeffrey." Sam giggled, enjoying all the attention. Bobby's and Jeffrey's reactions amused her the most. She loved her new look.

Jeff was speechless for the first time in his life. Bobby couldn't think of what to say. Unfortunately, what came out of his mouth was,

"You're wearing a dress." He quickly rephrased, "Is that a new dress?" In his defense, Sam hadn't worn a dress in ages. Then, it was only on occasions like going to church or funerals.

"Do you like it?" she pirouetted, making the hemline dance. "I bought it in Florida. Florida was so much fun," she exclaimed. I can't wait to tell you everything. I spent the whole summer either on the beach catching sun or in a store buying clothes, shoes, and stuff!"

Sam, the last true tomboy in So Cal, had just admitted that she spent her vacation shopping for 'clothes, shoes, and stuff' and that, for some reason, she had enjoyed it. Bobby felt he had fallen into a parallel universe. Everything appeared to be the same - except for Sam. Someone had replaced her with this girly creature.

"What's your schedule like," she asked. She approached Bobby to unfold his class schedule from his shirt pocket. She jumped up and down with delight. "Oh, that's right, I remember. We have English II first hour, and Computer Science II and Drawing I in the afternoon. Come on, let's walk to class together." A crowd of gawking boys stood in stunned fascination. Why was this girl talking to Bobby Williams?

Sam led a one-sided conversation extolling the merits of her incredible Floridian vacation as they walked down the hall to their classroom. Then, the bell rang, and the teacher entered the room. Bobby sat down directly behind Sam. She had already turned her attention forward.

Over the next hour, Bobby heard nothing the teacher said. He stared at the back of Sam's head the whole time. Her hair looked so soft. He had the oddest urge to reach out and touch it. Had Sam's hair always looked this nice?

"No," he thought, "It's lighter, probably from the summer sun, and she let it grow out a few inches."

Since the fifth grade, Sam had worn her brown hair shoulder length with simple straight-line bangs cut off just above her eyes. He didn't remember it smelling this good, either. It smelled like peaches and cream or something. Her lighter, longer, softer hair looked sexy, which made him blush, thinking of his long-time friend that way.

Bobby didn't see Sam again until the fifth period. As he entered the computer lab, Sam was in an animated conversation with a friend. Once again, Bobby became captivated by Sam's uncharacteristic girlish behavior. He watched her lean forward to let a friend whisper something in her ear. This gossip, or whatever, caused Sam to throw back her head and shoulders. Sam laughed out loud. The forward and back body movement and the somewhat revealing sundress drew unexpected attention to his friend's shapeliness. Bobby's brain exploded as it tried to process one more startling revelation. Sam had boobs.

He mumbled to himself, "Did she have boobs before she left for Florida?" Rolling his eyes at his stupidity, he sat at the nearest computer and covered his face with his hands. "Of course, she did, you idiot." Yet, for some reason, he hadn't noticed Sam's figure before now. This particular revelation that his best friend had a real girl's body agitated him. Things would change between them because of this. "What on earth happened in Florida," he grumbled.

After the final class, Bobby walked Sam back to her locker. Once again, she did the talking. He had not had trouble talking with Sam before. Something was different. The tone of her voice unsettled him. It wasn't just the girly thing. She sounded more self-assured. She had transformed. He continued listening as they walked.

Jeff showed up and interrupted Sam's never-ending tale. "Hey Bobby, did you ask Sam about getting together this weekend to play games?" Jeff snapped his fingers. "Hey, I've got an idea. Friday is a half day, right? Why don't we meet on Friday afternoon and catch up on our shows? The third season of *Double D Dragons* is available for streaming. That character, Hattori, is awesome in ways I struggle to describe. Then we could get back together on Saturday to play games. What-do-ya-say?"

Happy that someone had saved him from Sam's strange conversation, Bobby said, "That sounds great. How about you, Sam?"

"No," she said without even a pause for thought. We can't on Friday." The boys, shocked by her immediate rejection, stared at her in confusion. That's the night of the school's annual beach party," she explained. Remember? There will be food, dancing, and a bonfire. I want to go. Besides, we can watch anime anytime, right?"

"You want to go to the school beach party," Bobby asked. "You spent the whole summer on the beach."

"Please, Bobby." She grabbed his arm and pulled him close. "Take me to the beach party. It'll be loads of fun, you'll see! Please, please!"

"Oh... kay." His thoughts swirled. "I guess."

"You too, Jeffrey."

"I don't know," Jeff said. "The beach is cool and all, but I'm not a beach party kind of guy, at least not with the popular populace coming. I am not sure that geeks are invited."

"Don't be ridiculous. The party is for everyone. I'm as big a geek as you and so is Bobby. If the two of us are willing to go, you should also go."

"Well, I'll think about it."

"Great," Sam said. "It's all settled. I'm so excited. It will be so much fun. You'll see. Okay, see you guys tomorrow. I've got a club meeting to attend." She waved and walked away, her hair bouncing and her dress swishing as she walked.

Jeff shrugged his shoulders and walked away without another word. Bobby stood alone, sorting out the day's strange events. His mind whirled like he had taken a direct hit from Sam, the tornado.

"Wait," Bobby said, panicking. "Did she just ask me to take her on a date? She said, 'Please take me to the beach party.' What did she mean by that? No, she must have meant going together as friends, that kind of thing. Crap, this is so weird. I can't date my best friend."

As he walked home, he thought about Sam's transformation. As a gamer, he knew that wise tactical decisions and good moves were essential to a player's survival, but Sam's unprecedented transformation left him at a loss. He didn't know what to do. He was a total newbie in dealing with real girls and their real girl games. He had survived the most challenging and extreme game scenarios. If Sam had returned to El Palmar to announce that she was a powerful mage, an extraterrestrial, or a dangerous supernatural creature, Bobby felt confident he could survive the shock. As her closest friend, he would accept her for who she was without question. That's what friends were all about. But she had returned home transformed into the one thing with which he had little understanding or experience. *Sam returned home as a real girl.*

Chapter 5

A SORT OF DATE, BUT NOT

Friday came. The half day of school ended. Exuberant students fled the confines of their academic prison and headed for Cove Beach for the annual EPHS Beach Party, a well-honored end-of-summer, start-of-the-school-year kick-off event. Bobby begged Jeff to come with him. At least with Jeff by his side, he would have one trusted male ally. Not that he didn't trust Sam, but her recent transformation left him wondering if the standard buddy code applied. But Jeff had said no way. Although Jeff was as fun-loving as anyone, he didn't relish stepping outside his comfort zone. A school party with the jocks and the uber-popular was far from comfortable. He preferred the company of like-minded friends doing geek-minded pastimes.

Bobby understood completely. School events like this often resulted in some gross personal embarrassment, if not total humiliation. The witnesses of his humiliating event would consider this as confirmation that all geeks were hopelessly weird. Sam knew this as well. So, why had she insisted on going to the beach party? Why had she made him promise to go with her?

Sam volunteered to drive since Bobby still lacked a driver's license. Sam's dad had purchased a cute little royal blue car while she played her life away on the beach in Florida. The birthday present sat waiting in the driveway when Sam returned home. She passed her driver's test the next day. Bobby envied her and hoped Thomas' generosity would inspire his mom and dad. Thus far, Bobby's parents have avoided the subject.

Bobby wondered if having Sam drive him to the party would look weird. Of course, the only other choice was to have his mom drop him off. Then, he would have to wait in the parking lot for her to pick him up when the party ended. He and Sam had always gone places together, so he soon realized it didn't matter. Bobby tended to over analyze things - a byproduct of his sixth sense. He knew his perceived impending embarrassment tonight defied basic common sense. His imagination had gone wild. It had always been like this. Sam boldly moved forward while he held back - always cautious. Yet, he couldn't ignore his sixth sense. Something felt wrong. Tonight, trouble waited for him.

"I'm just being paranoid," Bobby said under his breath.

When Bobby got home, he ran up the stairs to his bedroom and changed into his beachwear. He threw a towel and a jacket into a small duffel bag and ran downstairs to wait for Sam on the front porch. He just wanted to avoid his mom, who would likely make a big deal over Sam's dramatic change in appearance. His mom loved Sam. She fawned over Sam like she was the daughter she always wanted. Bobby wondered if his mom didn't like Sam more than him. When she pulled up, he would dash for Sam's car to avoid embarrassment. They would be on their way before his mom could say a word. That made him feel slightly guilty, but it was for the best.

Soon, Sam pulled up out front. Bobby stood, ready for his dash, when his mother, Sarah Williams, stuck her head out the front door and said, "Bobby, before you go, I need you to take the garbage bin out to the curb. Garbage day tomorrow."

"But Sam's here. I don't want to make her wait."

"I don't think taking the garbage out will take that long. Besides, I haven't seen Sam all summer. Tell her to come in and say hi."

"But Mom, we need to get going."

"Robert James Williams, the garbage, please," she said as she returned to the house. "Don't forget the garbage in the kitchen."

He turned to wave for Sam to come in, but she had already skipped her way up to the porch.

"Hi, are you ready," Sam said.

Bobby was glad she no longer wore a dress like she had every day that week. Tonight, she wore capris pants and a Mickey Mouse t-shirt. She looked more like the Sam he knew.

"Yeah, just wait a minute. Come on in. I've got to do something for my mom."

Mrs. Williams came back to the foyer. "Hi, Sam," she said. "Oh, I love what you have done with your hair. It's so cute."

"Thanks, Mrs. Williams."

"Cute," Bobby mumbled as he entered the kitchen to get the garbage sack. Sam isn't supposed to be cute." He glanced back at Sam. She did indeed look cute. Grabbing the kitchen trash bag, he opened the back door, tossed the bag into the big green curb bin, and rolled it out to the curb. Bobby could hear his mom and Sam laughing - giggling like girlfriends. Sheesh, he thought! From the front yard, he could hear the conversation.

"You've turned into such a pretty girl. I will start calling you Samantha from now on."

Sam giggled and replied, "Lately, I have been feeling more like a Samantha, but I guess I will always be a *Sam* to you guys." Mrs. Williams hugged her.

"Why such a big deal," Bobby mumbled. "Sam's cuteness only makes me nervous."

The whole situation concerned Bobby on many levels. Did Sam think of this as an actual date or not? How should he act? How should he treat her? It was all too weird. Sam's emotions had always been straightforward to read, but since she returned home, her mind had become a bundle of conflicting, unrecognizable emotions.

"Well you two better be on your way," Sarah Williams said. "And be careful." "We will," they both replied. Sam laughed as she climbed into the driver's seat of her car.

"Bobby, wait," his mom called out. "Your bag!" She carried it to him.

"Uh... thanks," he said, taking the bag. He had just climbed into the car's passenger side when his dad pulled into the driveway. "We better go," he told Sam, "or we will be stuck here all night." To his relief, she agreed. They waved as they drove off.

"Hey, honey," Bill Williams said, walking up to his wife. "Was that Sam driving?"

"Uh-huh."

"Wow, I almost didn't recognize her. What a little cutie she's becoming."

"She sure is."

"I wonder what Bobby thinks about that?"

"I got the impression he's in a state of shock. His face turned red as soon as she arrived. The tomboy he grew up with turned into a beautiful young woman."

Bill laughed. They kissed. "I know that feeling all too well."

"What do you mean? I wasn't a tomboy."

"Maybe not, but you were an adventurous soul. That was what caught my attention. Then I fell in love. To this day, I can't take my eyes off your face and body." He smiled.

"And what about my mind?"

"A beautiful mind as well," he said. "But I can't kiss your mind."

"Maybe." She kissed him again. "Can You Read My Mind?"

"Yes, I believe I can." He smiled. Then he kissed her back. "Bobby and Sam are going to a school party instead of staying home and playing games. I wonder what tonight will bring."

"Perhaps Bobby will find out that Sam has a crush on him."

"Bobby won't know what hit him," Bill said. They both laughed as they walked to the house, holding hands.

"This is nice, isn't it," Sarah slipped her arm around Bill's back and rested her head on his shoulder.

"Nice?"

"Our life here. No fear, just peace."

"Yes, this is a good life... perfect."

"Bobby better not hurt Sam's feelings," Sarah added as they walked through the front door.

Chapter 6

A NEW WORLD

Little Toe awoke from his nap to discover the rupture had grown. Unfortunately, his hand had also grown. Toe was still stuck.

Toe grumbled, "No one knows I am stuck in here, and I am hungry."

He thrust his long tongue into the rupture and licked around his sore hand. The energy coming through the rupture made Him feel better for now. At least he didn't go into convulsions this time. Again, he thought about calling for help. Instead, he confirmed his earlier resolution.

"I'm not sharing this with anyone. Why should I? I'll chew my arm off before I let another creature steal this from me."

Toe hated Far Edge. Over the years, the Shadows of Far Edge had tormented him without mercy. This newfound fortune would save him, and he would no longer live at the mercy of others. His world would change if he could get his hand free. Examining the opening, he could see his hand. Swollen far beyond normal, toe realized that chewing off his hand wouldn't be easy. He wasn't even sure the hand would regrow under such unusual circumstances.

"I know why others mistreat me. It is because I'm clever." Toe looked at his arm stuck in the stone wall. He didn't feel so clever at the moment. His thoughts drifted to the possibility of a self-inflicted hand ectomy. A glum thought went through his mind. He licked his wrist. The moist goo from his tongue soothed the soreness, and the energy from the rupture lifted his mood.

Not counting Toe's present predicament, he was undoubtedly more intelligent than other Shadows. Toe had a head much more significant in size than any other Shadow he knew. As an imp, the elders assured him that his body and head would end up normal-sized once he grew up. Instead, as his body grew, his head grew even more. It made him look out of place in his world, giving bullies another reason to hurt him.

"Since my head was so large, why didn't Fire Claws name me Big Head?" he mewled again. "That would be as dumb a name as Little Toe. Someday, he would get a new name."

Toe had a head three times the size of the typical Shadow. An oversized head would give room for an oversized brain. Shadows' heads often got ripped open during fights, so he had seen what a typical brain looked like. Those brains were smaller than his fists. By comparing his head, relative to his body size, and to the other Shadows, he deduced that his brain was likely three times the size of other Shadows. Unfortunately, he would have to crack open his head to prove his hypothesis. Toe had no intention of allowing that to happen.

Another loud crunch. The rupture suddenly moved sideways, dragging the unprepared Little Toe off his feet. "Stupid. You got into this, so think of a solution before it's too late."

The rupture moved again, then again, and again. With every shaking of the cave, the rupture moved closer to the cave's side wall.

"I don't think the rupture will turn the corner when it reaches the side wall. It will likely disappear into the solid stone with my hand still stuck," Toe calculated. "At least I will not have to bite off my hand. The wall will do that for me." Still, no matter how the hand gets severed from his arm, it will be painful. Toe braced his feet against the wall and pushed with his legs. "It needs... to expand... faster," he grunted in pain. The rupture was now as long as he was tall, but his hand continued to grow along with the crack. Despite the pain, he pulled hard on his arm.

Another loud crunch and the rupture surged to the side. Excruciating pain came without warning. Toe's hand scraped across something hard on the other side. The rupture opened wider. Open enough to see what had happened. His hand had passed through some kind of wall. He watched with great relief as his hand reformed. Toe also caught a glimpse of the other world. He gaped in wonder. On the other side of the rupture, Toe saw a gigantic cavern. Nothing in it looked like his crude, rocky cave. He saw many strange-looking objects. Everything looked smooth, shiny, and full of light as if made by wondrous magic.

Toe gave an agonizing groan and hit his head against the rock wall.

"Why did I not pull my hand free before it reformed?"

Mystified by the open rupture, he had missed his chance to get free.

"Wait a minute. Why did my hand go so hard? Why can I not relax my hand?"

Concentrating, he thought. *Go soft*. He could soften his free hand, but not the one stuck in the rock. His mind screamed. *The other world has different laws of nature.*

Another loud crack echoed through the cave. The rupture moved more, but this time, it opened far wider. Little Toe's enlarged hand fell free and immediately returned to its regular size. The opening was now as big as him. Little Toe looked at his hand and wiggled his fingers. It ached but otherwise showed no sign of damage.

The unequal pressure between the two worlds increased and pulled at Toe's body. The pressure threatened to suck Toe through to the other side. That is when his troublesome curiosity got the best of him. How could he resist the compelling scene before him? So, instead of moving away from the gaping hole, he stepped straight through it.

As he stepped through, his body parts dramatically swelled: first, his leading leg, then his head and shoulders, then his arms, hips, and trailing leg. The transformation left him disoriented and quite nauseous. Wobbling with dizziness, he paused and waited for his head to clear.

He glanced around at his new surroundings and down at his body. Everything about him remained the same, as far as he could tell, yet something had changed.

A shining sphere encompassed by an array of gigantic rings filled the vast room. Toe reached up and touched the surface of the sphere.

"Hard like stone," he noted. "Yet, not a stone."

A jagged hole in the side of the object caught Toe's attention. A cold mist vented out of the hole, and intermittent sparks of fire flashed around the sphere. He peered through the hole. The sphere was hollow. Unlike the smooth surface outside, ribs and spikes covered the interior.

"This hole looks familiar."

Toe looked back to the hole he had stepped through only minutes earlier and saw his escape route had shrunk to not much larger than his forearm. The rupture now floated in midair.

"Oh-oh," thought Toe. Sniffing the rupture, Toe smelled like home. He licked the rupture. It tasted bitter, like home.

"So, either the rupture has gotten much smaller, or I have gotten larger," Toe concluded.

Toe circled behind the rupture. The rupture was not visible from the back. Panicked, Toe moved back to the front, and there it was. Not that it mattered much. At least for now, it was too small to use as a way back home. Toe had heard the legends about Shadows traveling to other worlds. Ancient explorers told of strange encounters and odd distortions in reality. He had always dismissed such stories as tall tales to scare little imps, but maybe not.

Toe contemplated his situation. "Once again," he said, "curiosity has worsened things. The second most important Shadow rule is to *never go through a rupture unless you are sure you can return home again.*" He groaned in frustration.

Completely stuck in a strange new world, he considered his options. He could sit and wait for the rupture to grow larger, which may or may not happen, or he could explore this new world. A solution could wait."

A banging noise echoed through the chamber. A bright light flooded into the room. In a panic, Toe jumped up onto the ringed ball and did his best to hide behind it. It's not that easy for a dark creature in a bright room. It surprised him at how easily he moved. He felt so light.

"Why," he mumbled. "Since I have grown larger, should I not feel heavier? Maybe I am stronger, not lighter. Interesting."

From his perch, Toe watched as three white, bulbous beings walked through an opening on one wall. The three beings had big heads with one big, shiny eye. Inside the eye was another vague object. Perhaps the creatures' brains. Their skin hung loose and baggy and crackled as they walked. He could hear them vocalizing, but neither seemed to have a mouth, at least none he could see. Perhaps they communicate through thoughts and gestures like he did. Toe could vocalize, but Shadows had no spoken language. Mind to mind, thoughts were a far more effective way to communicate. Shadows used vocalizations and body language to emphasize a growl and a punch in the face.

"These creatures may wish to know I am here," he worried. "But, as an uninvited guest, this is probably not the right time to introduce myself." He didn't want any trouble. If the beings in this world were like Shadows, his presence would cause them to overreact.

As the beings moved closer to examine the rupture, Toe darted behind the giant sphere and snuck out the open doorway to a much larger space. The ceiling was high overhead. High above Toe, hanging torches cast light downward. Toe had to shield his eyes from the bright light. A shield above each torch cast dark spaces up overhead. Toe vaulted up to the ceiling with surprising ease. No one had noticed his presence.

In this new hiding place, Toe found several cubical structures made of a material so shiny he could see his reflection. The reflection both surprised and intrigued him. He had seen his vague reflection back home, but this was the first time he had seen himself with such clarity. Raising a hand to the metal surface, he touched his reflection gently. For the first time in his life, he saw that he was a unique individual. That pleased him.

Louvered panels covered several openings in the square and tubular vent system that spread across the ceiling. Toe pulled on the panel cover nearest to him. It came loose quickly. Balancing the cover panel on a nearby structural beam, he squeezed through the opening. Inside, he found a junction that connected to a larger horizontal tunnel. He wiggled his squeezed body onward to investigate. At that moment, the panel cover Toe left, balancing on the structural beam, slid from its perch and hit the floor with a loud clatter. Afraid, Toe hurried further into the vent system. At the far end, it turned straight upward. He climbed up until he ran into another cover. Light sifted through the vented panel. He pulled on it, but it didn't budge. So, he pushed instead. It swung open to the side.

Toe wriggled out into a box attached to the building's roof, where he encountered the Sun for the first time. It was the brightest light he had ever seen. It strobed through a spinning fan built into the side of the box. The light was so hot it hurt. With a degree of caution, he carefully peered through the strobing fan at the world outside. The fiery ball of light hung low in the sky, just above the horizon. Tarinas' red sun was nothing like this Sun. The light made everything look so bright and colorful. He wanted to see more, but fear overpowered his senses. He retreated into the open vent, remaining until the sun went down.

******

Two people in clean room suits, holding helmets under their arms, looked up to where the vent panel had fallen fallen from. They saw nothing unusual. Later, they reported the mishap to the building maintenance crew.

Chapter 7

BEACH PARTY

Bobby relaxed when Sam's friends, Delia Bowen and Amy Ross, joined the party. Although hanging out with the three girls intimidated him, at least the three-to-one ratio made the night feel less like a date.

Sam first met Amy back in elementary school. Back then, the painfully shy Amy tended to disappear into the schoolyard background. As a result, she didn't have many close friends. Since the girl needed someone to look out for her, Sam decided she and Amy had to be friends. From that day forward, they were best friends.

Amy had grown into a simple, sweet beauty. Her straight, silky, brown hair reached down to her lower back. Then there were those big, brown anime eyes, which spent most of the day avoiding eye contact. To whoever she granted a short but friendly gaze saw in those eyes a sweet soul. This demure personality made Amy easy to like, but it also made her easy to overlook. Bobby had decided that Amy represented Sam's soft alter ego.

Why the anime eyes hadn't caught Jeff's attention by now remained a mystery. After all, Amy was that shy friend to the heroine in a typical *slice-of-life* anime series but without the schoolgirl uniform. Jeff liked pretty girls, yet Bobby hadn't heard Jeff mention Amy's understated cuteness even once. Maybe Jeff just needed a little nudge in that direction. Then again, perhaps matchmaking was for professionals.

Unlike Amy, Delia didn't have a shy bone in her body. She and Sam became friends back in the eighth grade. Delia had striking red hair, freckles, light blue Celtic eyes, and a boldness to match. Delia represented Sam's more aggressive side. Today, Delia wore a 1960 vintage two-piece swimsuit with a knee-length wrap tied around her waist and a bow in her hair. She nailed the 1960 pin up girl look so well. Bobby liked Delia because she was always there for Sam. The trio of girls had formed a fiercely loyal friendship rivaling his relationship with Sam. He was cool with that. Sam needed them in the same way he needed Jeff.

To Bobby's surprise, Sam stripped off her tee shirt and capris pants to reveal her cute little red swimsuit hidden underneath. The swimsuit made Bobby's head spin, not so much the swimsuit itself, but how fantastic Sam looked. He flushed with unexpected male approval.

From the moment they arrived at the beach, Bobby's sixth sense nagged him. He couldn't shake the feeling that something unusual was about to happen. Assuming the uneasiness centered on Sam's recent transformation, he did his best to ignore it. His only goal for tonight was to keep Sam happy. Unfortunately, he still couldn't sense her feelings. Girls are way too mysterious, at least those who act like regular girls. If something bad happened between him and Sam tonight, every girl he knew, including his mom, would be mad at him. As the designated stupid guy in this scenario, innocence wouldn't matter. No doubt he would take the blame for every mishap. Then again, maybe his uneasiness came from something completely unrelated. If he was going to have any fun tonight, he needed to relax.

The three girls grabbed Bobby and playfully dragged and pushed him across the hot white sand into the cool surf. They laughed and teased him all the way.

"Hey, no fair," he whined. "Three against one."

"Oh, you poor boy," Sam taunted. She then scooped up water and splashed him right in the face.

He coughed and spit out the salty water. "Thanks a lot. I got sand in my mouth."

Before he could recover from Sam's splash attack, Amy and Delia surrounded him and did the same, engulfing him in a deluge of water.

"Alright then," he growled in mock disdain, "If you wish to play this game, don't assume I will spare you just because you are girls! My powers will show you no mercy!"

"Oh, we're so scared," they said in eerie unison. They laughed.

Bobby broke character. "Okay, that was creepy. How did you do that, saying the same thing, in the same way, at the same time? It's like you three think with one collective mind."

They looked at each other and said in unison, "It's a s-e-e-cret." They laughed with delight at Bobby's reaction.

"Enough of your female mind tricks," Bobby said, returning to role-playing. Then, rotating in a full circle, he splashed his three opponents aggressively. The girls squealed and ran along the shoreline, giving him a reason to pursue. They ran, played, and laughed until Vice-Principal Mathers and the Student Council leaders showed up with hundreds of pizzas. The crowd of teenagers devoured every slice. Then, right before the sunset, someone lit the traditional bonfire, and the music and dancing began.

Bobby didn't like to dance. He thought it made him look stupid - which it did. Sam didn't press him to participate even though she wanted to dance. The truth was, she wanted to talk more. It was important for Bobby to understand what was happening to her. She just didn't know how to start that conversation. She sat with him on a beach towel, contented to listen and watch. Amy and Delia came and sat down next to them. Occasionally, the two girls would glance over at Sam and Bobby and smile. Then they whispered to each other. Bobby's nerves spiked as an unsettling feeling gave him the chills.

Delia jumped up. "Come on, Amy, let's go dance." They ran off to join the dancing young bodies.

Bobby said, "There is a perfect example of the difference between boys and girls."

"What are you talking about?"

"Jeff would never jump up and say, come on, Bobby. Let's go dance. And I mean never!"

Sam laughed. "Don't be silly. I have seen a lot of boys dancing together." She glanced sideways at him. She had so much to say.

******

It got darker outside, so Toe slid out of his hiding place into the crowded ventilation box. An access panel on the side of the box provided him a way out onto the roof. It swung open with a clang. Toe sniffed the air, stuck out his long tongue, and tasted it. He smiled. There it was, diluted by the open air, but still delicious.

From the darkened rooftop, Toe could see a considerable distance. In every direction, he saw light. Even after the sun had disappeared, the amount of light in this world fascinated him. Countless tiny points of light filled the sky above him.

"Magical," Toe thought. Tiarnas' sky stayed dark all the time.

Colorful flowers, trees, and bushes surrounded everything in view. It astounded Toe. His world lacked this kind of color and lushness. During the spore season, the vegetation of Tiarnas became quite beautiful. Dark, barren limbs and vines became phosphorescent overnight. Bright leaves and flowers sprouted, and the air filled with glowing multi-colored spores. Toe liked the spore season. It was a festive time. Unfortunately, it only lasted for a few weeks each year. The rich Shadows on Tiarnas had vegetation and color year-round, but nothing like this world. Far Edge had little to brighten a Shadow's life.

Several creatures walked along lighted pathways outside the fenced area. Their appearance surprised him because they looked nothing like the beings he had encountered inside the building. These were small, thin beings. Unlike a Shadow's head that rose slightly above the shoulders, these beings had a distinctive, oval-shaped head that sat precariously on top of the shoulders. How the creatures kept the head from flopping around baffled him.

"Funny-looking creatures," Toe thought.

There were a few similarities, such as two arms, two legs, two eyes, and a mouth, but that was about all Toe could observe from this distance. He wanted a closer look, so he climbed down the side of the building and hurried closer. Climbing up in a tree, he gazed out at the passersby. Each creature had distinctive facial features that allowed for considerable expression. Shadows tended to have only one or two expressions. Grumpy and angry are the most common. Toe looked at his vague, fuzzy arms and legs. Unlike him, these beings appeared to be completely solid. And they wore garments as well. The wealthy and powerful on Tiarnas often wore robes to signify rank and status. Warrior witches always wore body armor. But most Shadows saw no need to cover themselves. Clothes just get in the way

The creatures made cooing, barking, and screeching sounds as they walked. They made quick, elegant moves and touched each other continually. They were playful—Toe liked it.

He focused on the couple nearest him and tried to see their thoughts, but it didn't work. The creatures' thoughts jumped around too much. After watching their interactions longer, he concluded that communication was more about vocalization and body movements than a mind-to-mind connection. Physical movements seemed to add clarity and intent of purpose to their communication. Its surprised Toe that the physical interactions were entirely peaceful. On Tiarnas, two or more Shadows getting together almost always resulted in violence. Of course, they considered violence fun. At least, the winners thought it was fun. Toe found this new peaceful environment quite remarkable. He felt a new kind of peacefulness for the first time.

"Maybe this world has found a way to avoid violence." That thought pleased him.

In the distance, he could hear the sound of thumping, chattering, and chanting. When no other creatures were nearby, he climbed down and hurried to explore more.

The sounds led him to the beach and the ocean. Tiarnas had no vast open waters like this. The ocean left him stunned. He sat on the sand and watched the soothing, rhythmic roll of the waves. Scooting closer, he touched the water with his fingers. It felt cold and squishy as it swept around and through his feet. Sticking out his tongue, he tasted the water.

"Disgusting," he thought with a grimace.

To the south, he could see the dark silhouette of more creatures gathered around a fire. From this distance, Toe thought they might be a group of Shadows. Excited to meet his own kind from another world, he hurried along the beach, moving through the darkness near the water. To his disappointment, he only found more of the creatures from before. Most were moving and jumping to rhythmic thumping noises. No doubt an important ritual. Those who had chosen not to participate in the ritual watched from the sidelines. They sat on the ground in groups of two or more.

Watching the festive participants, he realized this group had two different body types. Many of the creatures had already paired off according to those two types, but not all.

Toe almost stumbled over two creatures hidden in a darker area away from the fire and the main group. The two must have been in a fight because the victor had his opponent pinned down while he ate the others energy through their mouth. Although he sensed no hostility between the two. This time, Toe had no difficulty seeing mental images. These creatures' emotions didn't display anger or fear but rather a sense of excitement and pleasure. Toe thought the victor of this match would end up licking and sucking every bit of energy off the loser's body. The couple's actions generated a lot of energy. Toe sniffed the air. The energy generated by all the creatures was significant. The drool began dripping from his lips.

"Everything smells delicious," he thought.

******

"Are you having fun," Sam asked Bobby.

"Believe it or not, I am."

"See. I told you." She gave him a slight punch on the arm.

"So, this is what you were doing in Florida?"

"Yup, pretty much, and shopping with Andrea."

"Andrea?"

"She's the daughter of my mom's friend."

"And you went shopping. You told me you hated shopping."

"I never said that!"

"Yes, you did."

"Well... I don't like shopping with my mom, but Andrea, is eighteen and she showed me the exciting possibilities shopping offers. It was fun. I have been forever converted."

The conversation dried up, and they fell silent. Amy and Delia looked at Sam and Bobby, making strange hand signals at Sam. Bobby noticed. "What are they doing?"

Sam jumped to her feet. "Never mind them. You need to tell me about your summer. Let's go for a walk."

"It will be a short, boring walk. With you and Jeff taking off on me, not much happened."

"I'm sorry," she replied. "If it makes you feel better, I missed you. Come on, let's walk along the surf." She reached for his hand.

Bobby looked over at Amy and Delia and saw them giggling and whispering. The same uneasy feeling washed over him. He looked up at Sam, who still extended her hand. He sighed and took it. She pulled on his arm, but once on his feet, he let go and stuck his hands deep into his pockets.

"Oh yeah," Bobby said. "I forgot to tell you, I got a new Power Play Box XPro for my birthday."

"Awesome," she replied. "We can play some new games."

"And get this," he lowered his voice so only she could hear the next part. "My dad got me a beta copy of The Aliens' Revenge IX."

She turned to him, her eyes big. "No way! That's not even supposed to be available yet."

"You know my dad. He's got connections."

"I guess so."

"It's awesome. I played it this summer, but it's meant for more players than one. We can play it tomorrow."

"Sure." She stopped talking again because she didn't want to discuss computer games. "What else did you do."

"Like I said, nothing. A total washout."

"Did you miss me then?" She giggled.

"No kidding. I missed you so much."

Sam beamed at that confession. "Really?"

"I sure did - and Jeff too." Sam turned her head to cover her disappointment. "But I have to admit I missed you the most."

Sam's smile returned. "Really?"

"You are the best gamer I know."

She tensed in frustration. Bobby kept missing the point. After another pause, she said, "Things changed for me this summer. I suppose you've noticed."

"Uh... yeah," he agreed. "I guess. You changed your hair, and you sure upgraded your wardrobe."

"So, what do you think of the new look," she asked, flipping her hair.

"Uh... yeah," he muttered. He realized that question was a minefield. "I like your hair," he said. "You look great."

"Thank you."

So far, so good, Bobby thought.

She continued in a more flirty tone. "Okay, be honest. Which is better, the old me or the new me?" She gave him a coy smile.

Bobby felt the pressure plate of a landmine click under his foot and froze. One wrong move, and boom. He thought, what does she want me to say? "Uh... well... like I said, you look great. You have been my best friend forever, so I like you no matter what." Sam dropped her eyes. Crap. She didn't like that. "I'm sorry," he said. "Did I say something wrong?"

"No, Bobby." She appeared to be wiping her eyes.

Is she crying? What the heck, Bobby thought.

She continued, "It's... just that... How you feel about me is important. Ever since we were kids, you have been important to me."

"That's cool," Bobby said lightheartedly. "We have been best friends longer than anyone I know. I guess we've been lucky that way." Sam's thoughts and feelings were always clear and direct, but tonight, she was a jumble of the ambiguous. "Like I said, I like you too. You're the only girl I know who gets my geeky-ness."

"Bobby," she said, getting more frustrated. What did she need to do to get him to understand? She decided to hold nothing back. "That's not what I mean. Have you never noticed how I blush when you look at me? Even your touch makes me blush. I like you so much... much more than just a friend. I'd do anything for you, Bobby." She looked down in embarrassment.

"Uh... sure. I mean... We have always had a special connection. It goes deeper than just being friends."

Sam thought her head would explode. "Listen to me, Bobby. I mean... Oh heck, this is what I mean." She took his face in her hands and kissed him firmly on the lips.

It took a few seconds for Bobby to react to the unexpected kiss from his best friend. The shock of it made his mind go numb. He stepped back from her. At the same time, he pushed her away with a little more force than intended.

"What...," he yelped.

The landmine beneath his foot blew up in both their faces. He hadn't meant to be mean or to reject her. Sam, however, took his reaction the wrong way. It was a heartless rejection. The bold confession, ending with a kiss, hadn't surprised him. It scared him. Now, nothing kept him from sensing Sam's true feelings. He had crushed her. It had hurt her something awful. Her pain became his pain... and with a true vengeance.

"Sam, I am so sorry," he said. "I didn't..." The moment's emotion caught in his throat, and his eyes filled with the threat of tears.

Sam covered her face with both hands and burst into tears. Sobbing, she turned and ran toward the parking lot and the safety of her car.

"I'm sorry," he said louder. "Sam! Please come back! Please, Sam!"

Sam stopped and turned to face him - her eyes wet and her face red. "My name is Samantha, you stupid... dork!" She ran away.

Bobby stood stunned. Sam had just called him a dork. Was he being a dork?

Delia and Amy watched the whole horrific scene unfold. As expected, Amy immediately ran after Sam. Delia walked to Bobby. "Well, that went well," she mocked. "What is the matter with you, Bobby? Why did you push her away like that?"

"I didn't mean to. She surprised me. I didn't know..."

"How could anyone be as big of an idiot as you are, Bobby?" Delia said this with plenty of female superiority. "Sam has been in love with you for years. How could you not know that? Even goofy Jeff has figured that one out." She let the tense pressure in her lungs go. "To be fair, she ambushed you with that kiss. You were surprised." She looked at Bobby, more sympathetic this time. "Look, I'll talk to her and try to smooth things over." She then turned and walked away to join her dear friend.

Bobby turned and walked away from the bonfire, the party, and everyone. "I'm sorry," he said only to himself as he walked into the ever-growing darkness.

******

Little Toe's green eyes went big and round, astounded at what he had just witnessed. The two beings were in an intense interaction. They exploded with waves of energy. First, they were happy, then confused, then the one got mad, and then both were sad. These contrasting waves of delicious energies radiated everywhere. The whole experience had left him feeling dizzy. It reminded Toe of how he felt after drinking a liquid made from a fertile clutching vine's fresh, glowing spores. Shadows used this glowing purple concoction to get worked up before a fight. It was not the greatest-tasting drink, but it did give them a fierce boldness. The problem was that the drink brought on overwhelming cravings. You craved more and more until you craved too much. Shadows often went insane with such cravings.

Toe felt intoxicated and hungry. He followed the young male into the dark. It seemed apparent now who was male and female among these creatures, assuming these creatures had anything in common with his kind. A male Shadow always cautiously approached a female; only females made such bold overtures. The energy amassed around the male, who was now alone in the dark, hadn't dissipated even slightly. That urged Toe on.

"If I could only have a little taste," he thought.

******

Bobby walked along the surf. The half-moon cast long, dark shadows across the sand. His regret made the music, the people, and the ocean waves disappear. He felt nothing except for an unforgiving pain in his heart.

He didn't mean to hurt Sam and make her cry. She was the last person in the world he wanted to offend. If she had just stayed and listened, he could have explained that it wasn't the kiss but the surprise of the kiss that caused him to push her away. She hated him now. One thing was for sure: she wouldn't try to kiss him again. For some inexplicable reason, that thought made him feel worse.

How could he fix this? He couldn't think of anything that would take away her hurt expression, now burned into his memory. His heart ached for Sam. The thought of losing his best friend left him empty and alone. Why had he come to this stupid party? He hated parties and Sam's new friend, Andrea from Florida, for causing Sam to change so much.

In a daze, Bobby kept walking, his eyes looking down. Distracted by his bad mood, he saw only his feet on the sand. He didn't see that a shadow was moving. It watched him. It followed him, attracted by the energy of his dark mood. Bobby's sixth sense ability had switched to the off position.

******

This world overflowed with endless forms of energy. The creatures, the lights along the pathways, the vegetation, and even the ocean extending as far as Toe could see pulsed with living energy. Even some non-living objects, the rocks, and the fabricated structures seemed to emit varying amounts of energy. It's probably a residual effect left by the giant sun in the sky. This whole world was nothing short of astounding.

Toe couldn't resist the young male's smell. This world was an energy eater's utopia. It made him ravenous. In this world, he could eat energy until full and then eat more, never running out of sustenance. The complete opposite of Far Edge, where creatures starved every day. That place only offered darkness, fear, and death.

Fighting had become the most common energy source, but only the winner reaped the spoils. The hungry winner took all, sometimes even the life and body of the loser—a depraved practice in a place populated by desperate Shadows.

Good fortune had befallen Toe when the rupture had appeared in his cave wall. It led him to this new world with fabulous wonders to explore and devourer. He smiled and stepped in front of the unaware male.

"Time to sample the local cuisine," he thought.

******

Knocked back on his butt after walking into someone or something, Bobby looked up in surprise and anger. He would say something like, "Hey, what was that for? You jerk, why don't you watch where you're going?" It was his fault, but he was in no mood to take the blame for anything else tonight. His eyes tried to focus on the dark thing before him, but he couldn't make sense of it. The large body stood on its hind legs, but its shape and long arms were not that of a person. Then Bobby saw those two round, rather disturbingly green eyeballs. It smiled a big, phosphorescent, slobbery grin. Without further thought, Bobby opened his mouth and let out a shrill scream. The thing bounded atop him, and Bobby's world went black.

Chapter 8

STRANGE DREAM

Bobby sat atop the giant playground slide in the park across the street from Sam's house. Confused, he looked around. How had he gotten here? Not only that, but everything was wrong. First, the playground jungle gym wasn't the colorfully painted steel and formed plastic set the city installed eight years ago. It was the old wood and steel pipe set that existed in the park when they moved to El Palmar. Second, his arms, legs, hands, and feet were small, like a little kid. This dream brought an old memory into his sleep.

Bobby had always been small for his age. Although he was five at the time of this particular memory, he only looked four years old. His less-than-average size encouraged the other kids to tease him. They kept calling him Baby-Bobby, which made him cry in front of everyone. Thus, the nickname stuck for a long time.

One day, while trying to make him feel better, his mother told him, "The day will come when you will like looking younger than everyone else." He had no idea why she thought that would somehow make it better. What he needed was a growth spurt, and he needed it as soon as possible.

A covered platform on the third level of the old jungle gym was the launching point for the long, steep`, and slick metal slide. It ended a foot above the soft playground sand. Heights made Bobby anxious enough, but this slide had an unnerving wavy bump halfway down. According to the other kids, the bump added an extra thrill to the sliding experience. The older kids liked to ride a little red wagon down the slide. The wagon's wheels fit just inside the side rails. They called it a roller coaster. Bobby called it sheer madness.

It had been an early summer evening when little Bobby had decided to climb to the top of the jungle gym to take the slide back down. Like any dutiful father, his dad stood at the bottom of the slide, encouraging him to let go. The other kids in the neighborhood taunted him. Over and over, they said, "Go, baby Bobby, go." Everyone but him had braved the giant slide down. Now was his time.

"I'll be right here at the bottom to catch you," Bobby's dad said with a hint of annoyance. His dad lacked patience for what Bobby thought of as simple common sense. Bobby trusted his dad and could sense that he intended to catch him at the bottom. Yet, his sixth sense also told him there was a danger. Yes, his dad would attempt to be there for him, but even at five, Bobby had figured out that the best intentions of adults, even moms and dads, didn't always match his expectations. Sam told him he tended to over analyze things, but even Sam had slid down the giant slide alone.

Sam? There was something important about her, but he couldn't remember. He needed to fix something, but what? They had been best friends because she liked bugs, dinosaurs, robots, and spaceships as much as he did. Sam had always been one of the guys - or was it Samantha?

Bobby stalled for as long as he could, but time was up. It was now or never. He looked down at the long slide. "I just need to trust Daddy and let go," he told himself. "If you can't trust your daddy, who can you trust?" Holding his breath, he let go.

Everything happened so fast because now he was sitting, not on the slide, but inside that crazy, little red wagon. Between the sensations of outright terror that made him want to cry and the tickle in his tummy that made him want to laugh, his mind shut down. In his panic, he remembered a TV cartoon he had watched earlier in the day - *Coyote and the Roadrunner*. No matter how hard the coyote tried. No matter what he did to catch the roadrunner. The coyote always ended up getting hurt.

"I am the coyote," Bobby concluded, "not the roadrunner."

His dad looked up at him with a proud smile, then disappeared. Something big, fuzzy, and black had taken his dad's place. Another wave of fear swept over him as the red wagon rolled at full speed toward a dark face with green eyes and a big, slimy grin. Paralyzed with fear, Bobby screamed.

He awoke startled. Instead of the red wagon, he was in a bed. Bright sunlight came from a window, causing him to blink and turn his head away. He saw his mom reading a book in a chair beside the bed.

"Mom," he croaked out of a dry mouth.

She closed the book and hopped up to the bedside. "Bobby! Welcome back, kiddo."

"I'm thirsty." She poured water into a cup and gave it to him. "Where am I?"

"You're in the hospital. You gave us a real scare."

"Oh... uh... sorry. Why am I in the hospital?"

"Well, the police believe someone assaulted you, but we don't know for sure what happened."

Bobby sat up and took a quick inventory of his body parts. Nothing seemed amiss. He was stiff but not in pain.

"We were hoping you could tell us what happened when you awoke. Do you remember anything from Friday night?"

"Well, Sam and I went to the party... then we..." He remembered the kiss and the fight. "Anyway, I ended up walking on the beach alone. Then something hit me. I guess I blacked out after that."

"Sam and her friends found you lying on the beach. They said they heard a scream. Not a goofing off scream, but a serious 'I need help' scream. They ran toward it and found you unconscious and in a real mess."

The memory of his scream flashed back into Bobby's mind. "Sam found me?" His mom nodded. He felt the deep regret again. He looked away.

"You've been unconscious since the attack," she added. "I don't mind telling you, your condition scared us. How are you feeling now, honey?" She ran her soft hands over his forehead and cheeks.

"I feel fine. You say I've been out since last night?"

"Honey, it's Sunday afternoon. You've been out for two days." Her face showed concern.

"Two days," he blurted out. "Why? I don't feel hurt. I'm thirsty, but otherwise..."

"That's the weird thing. When we first saw you in the emergency room, you looked a real fright. Your clothes torn, partly ripped away, and covered from head to toe with sand and this thick slime."

"Slime! What the heck?"

"Your dad said you looked like a shoe chewed on by a hound." She made a face. "His quaint way of saying you looked horrible. I'm afraid you did look awful. You smelled awful, too. In the end, the doctors determined you had sustained no serious injuries. Still, you couldn't wake up as though something had sucked every ounce of energy out of you. We were so worried. No matter what the doctors tried, you didn't wake up. It scared me. Anyway, you're awake now, thank heaven."

Bobby's mind spun. He flopped back on the bed. A nurse came into the room and took his temperature and blood pressure. She made notes on his chart. "Good to see you awake, Bobby," she said, smiling. "You look better today. I'll call your doctor and let him know you're awake. He might send you home soon, maybe even tomorrow." She left the room.

"Sorry I made you worry, Mom."

"Don't be silly. That's what mothers do. We worry a lot."

"You said Sam found me?"

"Uh-huh. She kept crying and said she was sorry, quite beside herself." His mom stopped and thought. "Did something happen between you and Sam?" Bobby's face flushed. He dropped his eyes and said nothing, which meant the answer was yes. She decided not to pursue the matter.

Chapter 9

TIARNAS

THE MAGISTRATE

Magistrate Fire Claws stomped through the narrow and crowded roadway that traversed the residential district of Far Edge. His destination is the cave of an insignificant creature known as Little Toe. The Magistrate's menacing presence forced everyone to dodge out of his way. The Shadows of Far Edge feared Fire Claws for several good reasons. First of all, he was a lot bigger than most Shadows. Second, his angry red eyes flashed like fire. And third, his ill-tempered disposition made him downright dangerous. But what everyone feared the most were Fire Claws' long, clawed fingers extending from both hands. The sharp, segmented, armored fingers measured as long as his forearm. This physical trait puts Fire Claws at the top of the food chain. Even the Shadow Lords cautiously approached the brute, so they appointed him to Regional Magistrate for Law Enforcement - a position traded for his continued loyalty. Of course, Fire Claws had little respect for the rule of law. As the leader of the most notorious criminal organization in the Shadow Empire, he used his position to enforce his will on others.

As Claws pushed through the crowded street, he deliberately dragged the clawed fingers across the stone road, spreading fiery spark explosions with every step. The ability to create fire with his claws, which he used to significant effect, had become a symbol that fueled his insatiable desire for power. This ability had something to do with the composition of the claws and that of the mineral-rich surface of Tiarnas. Once, an over-educated Shadow from the capital tried to explain the phenomenon to him, but the big ideas, coupled with the long explanation, only made Claws angry. Losing patience, he made the self-obsessed brainiac stop talking by slicing off his face. He didn't care why he could cause fire. It only mattered that he could. Hunching forward, he allowed his claws to scrape the ground. Then, he slashed at the rocky cliffs above the occasional cave opening for an extra punch of drama, sending lowly onlookers fleeing back into their dark holes. It amused him to see others cower in his presence.

Far Edge had a rustic terrain. A place where the poor and the weak could carve out a meager existence. Wizards and witches cleared and reshaped the landscape in places frequented by the wealthy and powerful. Eye-pleasing structures and gardens spread across such cities and villages, glorifying the homes of the most powerful wizards and witches on Tiarnas. Magic created dwellings and places of business that were clean and spacious, but Far Edge meandered through several deep black canyons - each residence nothing more than a depressing hole.

Two of Fire Claws' lieutenants followed close behind. The massive, yellow-eyed Spine Back was taller and broader than his boss. Claws kept this Shadow around because of his size and strength. Spine Back had a limited mental capacity and didn't excel at much else. Besides his size, his distinguishing feature was the frill of long, sharp quills wrapped around the back and neck. Whenever Spine Back faced a fight, he flared the luminous, red, and orange quills to enhance his size and intimidate his opponent.

The green-eyed Spike was the smallest of the three Shadows. Spike had a single blade-like horn protruding from his forehead. This long, razor-sharp horn was half as long as Spike was tall. It curled upward at the end and tapered into a pointed tip. The lethal-looking horn made up for what Spike lacked in size. He used it to skewer, disembowel, and decapitate. Far Edge residents gave all three thugs plenty of space to pass.

The three black shadowy bodies shuddered and churned with each stomp of their feet. The only undisturbed body parts were Fire Claws' red eyes and long clawed fingers, still sending sparks everywhere, Spine Back's yellow eyes and flared quills, and Spike's green eyes and horned head. Such dominant features identified every Shadow's individuality.

A fourth gang member, Broken Fang, waited at Little Toe's cave entrance. The name given to him at birth had been Long Fangs. Then, one day, after a fierce fight, Fang lost part of his left-side tusk, leaving it two inches shorter with a razor-sharp jagged edge. He adopted the new nickname with malicious pride. More intelligent than most, Broken Fang had earned his place as Fire Claws' number one enforcer. Claws gave him this place of honor for two crucial reasons: first, because Fang was ruthless, and second, because you always kept potential enemies close. Fang was a dangerous rival and the only creature in the empire who posed a threat to Fire Claws' position as Magistrate.

As Fire Claws approached, he could see the unnatural glow of light coming from deep inside the cave. "Grunt, sniff," Claws vocalized. Then he thought, mind to mind, "Have you found Little Toe yet?"

"Bruff... Not yet," Fang thought. He glanced back into the cave. "He may have gone through the rupture."

"Useless little imp." Claws growled. "Show me."

The cave entrance was big enough for Little Toe, but these four had to hunch over and squeeze through. For obvious reasons, Spike went in first. After passing through two smaller chambers, they reached the larger rear chamber and the light source. Half of the back wall and part of the adjacent side wall had gone missing. The short tunnel created by the rupture gave a good view into the other world. This remarkable phenomenon made Claws grin with greed.

Fire Claws growled again. "He reported this to no one?"

"No one."

"The little imp tried to hide this from me. Did Little Toe think he could keep this a secret?"

Fang thought, "I suspect the piece of dust thought he was about to be rich. I do not understand why he didn't head straight to the capital and make a claim. That is what I would have done."

"Gruff." Claws glared at Fang. "Are you sure he did not do that?"

"I checked. He made no claim."

Claws' grin returned. "Good. I will take care of that for my little friend. Too bad Little Toe died. Gruff-um-frit-frit," he snickered. "As his guardian, I will take his cave and worldly possessions. The rupture belongs to me now."

"Gruff, snort, gruff," laughed Spine Back and Spike.

Claws turned to Spike. "We will leave immediately for the capital city for an ownership claim. I need several enforcers to travel with me. I do not want anyone thinking they can take this from me."

"Sure thing, boss," Spike thought. "Snort." He turned and left.

Spine Back inched closer to the rupture and sniffed it. His quills relaxed. He closed his eyes in bliss and purred, "The rupture thing smells good."

"Yes," Fang noted. "I noticed that too. I suspect that enticed Little Toe to go to the other side. The little imp would be unable to resist an opportunity to explore."

Claws' eyes narrowed. "Stupid fool. Post guards. If Little Toe returns, kill him. I just declared the little imp dead. I want him to stay dead."

"He might not come back," Fang added. "Maybe someone should follow him and find out what he is up to."

"Gruff." Claws thought, "By someone, you mean you?" Fang smiled. "You might get stuck over there."

"Worth the risk. This rupture is worth a fortune. Little Toe could make trouble for us. I will go after him and make sure he never comes back."

Claws nodded and grunted.

Chapter 10

THE POLICE

The hospital released Bobby. That afternoon, two police officers came to the Williams' home. One of the officers started by saying, "Tell us everything you remember about the night of the assault."

Bobby's bizarre memories of that night made no sense, so how could he describe the horrible event in a way that might be useful to the police? His imagination had kicked into nightmare overdrive while lying unconscious in that hospital bed. Somehow, he needed to separate the nightmares from reality. But what was the reality?

"I don't remember much of anything," Bobby told them.

"Okay then," the officer said. "Let's try reconstructing the evening's events. Did anything unusual happen earlier in the day?"

"Other than me agreeing to go to that stupid school party? No."

"You don't like school parties?"

"I don't know. Maybe. I guess parties are okay. But after what happened, I plan to avoid them like the plague. Otherwise, I'd say it was a fairly normal Friday afternoon."

"Did you go to the party by yourself or with friends?"

"With a friend."

"Who was that?"

"My friend Sam."

"Why did you leave the main party and go off by yourself," the officer asked.

With his mom sitting next to him, Bobby didn't want to divulge too many details of that horrible night. "It was stupid of me to go off alone like that."

"Don't worry about that. Just tell us why you walked away from the party."

"Well... I needed some alone time to deal with a personal issue and think."

"Think about what? What kind of personal issue?"

"You know... teenage drama stuff?"

The second officer, who had a couple of teenage boys, asked, "Did you get in a fight with someone at the party?"

"No... uh... not exactly," he replied.

"Then what, exactly?"

Bobby thought, it's bad enough that Sam was mad at me, but if Mom found out. "Look, I had a little misunderstanding with my friend Sam, that's all." He glanced at his mom. She had her poker face on.

"This Sam fella," the officer probed. "Did you two get physical?"

Bobby's face flushed. His mom intervened. "Let me explain." "Sam is Samantha, Samantha Thomas. She lives in the house right behind us, facing the next street. Bobby and Sam have been friends since they were little." She looked at Bobby with an intense stare.

"That misunderstanding between you and Samantha. Did it involve another boy? Did you get in a fight over her?"

"Jeez, no."

"What happened, honey? What did you do to Sam?"

"Why do you assume I did something to her? Maybe she did something to me. The look on his mom's face indicated that she doubted that possibility. Bobby looked down at the floor, dejected. "Honest, Mom. I didn't do anything wrong." He sighed. "But... I guess I didn't do anything right either."

Bill Williams stifled a laugh. When it came to the woman in his life, what he didn't say or do got him in the most trouble. He smiled at Bobby, but his wife did not.

The officer flipped through his notebook. "Wasn't she one of the students that found you on the beach?"

"That's what Mom told me. I don't remember that part."

"So you were walking alone."

"Yeah."

"Did your attacker come from behind?"

"No. That's right. Now I remember. I walked into the guy while looking down at the sand."

"That's good. Can you remember anything? Any distinguishing features?"

What Bobby remembered made little sense. "A big guy, a lot bigger than me. He knocked me back. I fell on my butt. Then I looked up. He was dark."

"Dark skinned?"

"No, dark... and fuzzy." Bobby shook his head. "Maybe he wore a dark coat or something like that. Sorry, I'm not making any sense."

"You are doing fine. You are sure the attacker was male," the officer asked.

"Yeah, I guess so," Bobby answered. "Or a super strong girl. All I know is that a big, dark figure appeared before me. He, she, or it knocked me to the sand. I blacked out after that."

"It?"

"I just remember something else weird. It had animal-like eyes that glowed green in the dark," Bobby said. His mom gasped. But that can't be right. That's too weird. Right?" The two officers looked at each other, and Bobby's parents did the same.

The officer made a note in his notebook. "Witnesses said they heard a scream. Did you see anyone else on the beach with you? A woman, perhaps? We are hoping someone who saw you attacked will step forward."

It embarrassed Bobby that he had screamed so loud and shrill. He considered telling them he hadn't heard a scream to save the embarrassment. But he did remember the scream, better than anything else. Who knew his vocal cords were even capable of such a screech?

"Well, to be honest, officers. I think that was me."

It was the officer's turn to laugh. "That's okay, young man. Most people don't realize how loud they can scream under extreme stress. Just be glad you are okay."

They stood to leave. "Mr. and Mrs. Williams," one officer said, pulling them to the side. "You need to know that your son is not the only victim. Since Friday night, there have been three more attacks. These new attacks were similar. Passersby found each victim unconscious and covered in the same unknown substance we found on Bobby. Also, like your son, each victim remained unconscious for several hours afterward."

Mrs. Williams looked to her husband with more significant concern. Something unusual had attacked their son and was still attacking others, and she worried about what it might be. Returning to Bobby's side, she brushed his hair off his face.

"Mom." Bobby pulled back from her. "You're messing up my hair."

She smiled for the first time since the officers had arrived. "Are the others going to be alright?"

"Yes. That last victim woke up an hour ago. He told us that, other than feeling groggy, he felt fine. Unfortunately, Bobby was the only one who saw the attacker." The officer turned to Bobby and smiled. "If you remember anything, no matter how trivial or weird, let us know immediately. Will you do that for us?"

"Yes, sir."

Chapter 11

TOE'S SCIENTIFIC SAMPLING

Thus far, the buffet of exquisite flavors had been incredible. Nothing back home tasted as good as these creatures. Toe chose each sample because they generated large amounts of this world's exotic energy. No doubt, the subjects' emotions at the time of tasting created an unusual release of energy.

Before starting this taste test, Toe decided on a few sensible rules. Without clear safety rules, he might cause harm. A random sampling of exotic energies had inherent dangers. Powerful energies could cause a Shadow to get lost in the ecstasy of feeding. A feeding frenzy could quickly overwhelm his good intentions. The desire to consume part or all of the subject was a genuine concern. He would do no lasting harm by only feeding on the energy the creatures emitted. Although he needed to eat to survive, he saw no need to harm or destroy. An old and often-forgotten Shadow proverb said, *"That which can grow and continue to give should continue to live."*

Toe shuttered at that thought of losing control, having almost lost control during the first subject. If the male's scream hadn't brought others, he might have caused severe damage. Such stupid and reckless behavior had ruined his world; it could destroy this world. Little Toe liked it here. Abundant life filled this environment with so much beauty. Then he remembered the unattended rupture still open in his cave. It would be bad if more Shadows followed him here. Few Shadows shared his regard for life and beauty.

With the rules in mind, Toe's second sampling was far more successful. Earlier in the evening, he had observed three males talking to a young female. She must have liked what the males said to her because she became distracted. She was happy as she walked alone along the beach. Toe waited for the right moment before grabbing her from behind. She fell unconscious immediately. As he licked the female's soft skin, he noted how fragile she was. Toe loved her delicious, sweet flavor. That reminded him of the urgent need for self-control.

"When she wakes up," he thought, "she will feel tired and slimy but unharmed."

The third sample, another male, emitted high-energy waves of cheerful intoxication. He was celebrating with other males, none of whom could walk straight - not an unfamiliar sight. Shadows got intoxicated on fermented liquids all the time. The male's companions left him alone, so Toe moved closer. He found the subject asleep on a bench... Toe dragged him into the nearby bushes. The unusual flavor was a combination of sweet and sour, or maybe tangy and salty. Whichever, it left him feeling lightheaded.

The following day, Toe found another male running in a nearby park. Distracted by his aggressive activity, this male paid little attention to his surroundings. The creature was tall and muscular. Maybe he thought of himself as the alpha male of this part of the world. Even though Toe stood at least a foot taller, he wondered if this sample might be too dangerous to confront. Putting that concern aside, he followed the male. The fireball in the morning sky had not yet risen. Toe tackled the male from behind, slamming him to the ground hard. It concerned Toe that he may have hit the runner too hard. Toe relaxed his hand to allow it go misty and gently laid his hand over the male's nose and mouth. Breath caused dark particles to drift away from his hand. Toe sighed with relief and then satisfied his hunger. Aggression was a hot energy, not necessarily fire hot, but spice hot.

Toe stayed in hiding for the rest of the day. After dark, a new search began. He soon found a lone female who appeared to be nervous and fearful. That made her far more aware of her surroundings and more challenging to follow. She kept looking around as though she expected something to jump at her around every corner. This behavior gave Toe reason to pause. What kind of threat worried her so much? Should he be worry too? He sniffed for a sense of danger in the air but found nothing.

Toe knew the taste of fear. It tasted like bitter acid, and everything in Far Edge tasted like bitter acid. Because of this new sample's agitation, he considered leaving her alone. Yet, all he needed was a little taste. He would not bother her for long. Then, the female surprised Toe. After rounding the next corner, she started to run. Toe picked up his pace as well. The female made another turn onto a pathway between two buildings.

He thought, "Something has made her run."

Before she could get away from him, he broke into a full gallop, using his long arms to stabilize the forward thrust of his legs.

******

The twenty-nine-year-old Kathy Stewart had just ended a tragic and violent marriage to the once love of her life, Brian Stewart. She had been on edge all day. Brian was a mean and brutal man with an explosive temper. The court order delivered earlier may have angered him to the breaking point. While walking home after a late shift at work, she got a bad feeling that someone was following her. Fear had dominated her emotions as of late.

She couldn't see who followed her, but if not Brian, then who else? Brian had always done what he wanted. No court restraining order would stop him, so she had good reason to fear retaliation. This time, he won't just put me in the hospital, she thought, trembling. He will kill me for sure! Because he kept harassing her day and night, she had thrown her cell phone away. There hadn't been the time or the money to buy another. Her only hope was to get to the safety of her new apartment. There, she could call for help on her landline phone.

Like a frightened rabbit, she ran. Her heart pounded with ever-growing fear. "Almost there," she said, struggling for breath. Just around this next corner, up one flight of stairs, I will be safe."

She reached into her purse and fumbled for the keys. They needed to be in her hands by the time she reached the apartment door. She pulled the keys out at the bottom of the stairwell to her apartment. In spite of her eyes blurred by tears and her shaking hands, she found the right key. Then, just before reaching the first stair landing, she tripped, dropping her keys. They fell through the space between the steps to the concrete pad below.

"Somebody, please help me," she tried to say, but she was too out of breath. Turning, she ran back down to retrieve the keys. That was when she saw the monster that pursued her. She gazed in confusion at the black figure crouched in front of her. "You aren't Brian," she said. She backed into a corner, never taking her eyes off the strange animal. Her mind reviewed a list of animals that might have come down from the hills or escaped the local zoo. Nothing made sense. A gorilla, maybe?

The creature moved closer. Kathy's mind filled with the memory of the last time she had been with Brian, right before the police arrived and arrested him. It must be Brian, her confused mind concluded. Trembling with paralyzing fear, she couldn't even let go of a scream. Sliding down the wall into a sitting position, she pulled her legs tight to her chest.

"No, stay away," she said through the trembles. "Please... don't hurt me." Finally, she got a voice and screamed out, "Leave me alone, Brian. Don't kill me. I don't want to die."

******

Toe saw the fear in her eyes. It surprised Toe that he had frightened her. She misunderstood his intentions. He meant no harm, yet she had crouched, shaking and afraid, in the corner of the stairwell. The others didn't react like this. Then he remembered. Except for the first male, none of the others saw him coming. The earlier encounters were surprise attacks. Would they have been as terrified of him as this female?

Then he saw the powerful images forming in the female's mind. One of her kind, a male, stalked her, cornered her, and beat her until she lay bloody and motionless. Toe shook his head to stop the horrible vision.

"I will not do that to you. It is okay. I will not hurt you," Toe tried to tell the woman, but she didn't understand. Then, the terrible truth flooded into his mind and soul. But you don't know that, do you?"

How many times had the Far Edge bullies cornered him like this? He stopped his approach. For the first time in his poor and pathetic life, a life of beatings and fear of beatings, Little Toe had become the bully! This revelation made him sick. - so sick it hurt. His green eyes filled with fluid as he backed away from the frightened female. With remorse, he turned and ran away into the night, hoping to hide his shame.

Chapter 12

MAKING UP IS HARD TO DO

"I'm fine," Bobby told his mother. "I've rested enough. At least I'll have something to do at school."

"I want you to stay home and rest," she countered. "You just got out of the hospital, for heaven's sake."

But after several more hours of annoying complaints, his mother relented. The next morning Bobby got out of bed, dressed, and left for school. There was some concern. He did not want anyone to pity him. He wouldn't act like a victim. But when he entered the school's front doors, he remembered the other victim from Friday night. Sam would sit at the desk in front of him during the first hour. Now, he regretted the decision to go to school so soon.

Bobby found Jeff waiting at his locker. "I suppose you heard about what happened."

Jeff nodded. "Sorry, dude. The word has spread."

"What should I do?" He knew how foolish it was to ask Jeff for advice, but at the moment, he had no one else.

"Look. I am sorry you got hurt," Jeff said. "I am sorry for your troubles with Sam. I am. But didn't I warn you about going to that party? Nothing good ever comes from attending all school functions. They make people crazy. Now you have to deal with the consequences."

"Well, if you had come with me like I asked you to, none of that crazy crap would have happened. Besides, a very creepy person or thing assaulted me." He remembered those weird green eyes. It was more than just getting hurt.

"No. If I had come, I would have walked away from the party with you. Then your nut job attacker would have put me in the hospital as well."

"It happened because I wandered off by myself. That made me an easy target. If you had been there, Sam wouldn't have kissed me. I wouldn't have felt the need to go off alone."

"I don't think so, dude. Sam has wanted to kiss you for a long time."

"How do you know that?"

"Everybody knows that... except you."

Bobby sighed. "Delia called me an idiot."

"Drama... drah mah," Jeff mocked. "I hate drama. That's why I don't go to school parties. It always ends in drama. You are on your own with this one, my friend."

"Oh, thanks for your support... best friend."

Jeff just laughed and walked away with a wave. "Drah mah," he said over his shoulder.

Bobby waited outside the classroom door. What should I say to Sam, Samantha, he thought? Should I keep quiet and let her speak first? What if she says nothing? Then what?

The bell rang. He sucked it up. Looking at the floor, he walked into the room and sat at his desk. When he looked up, he saw Delia, not Sam, sitting before him.

Delia turned around. "Bobby, we didn't expect you back so soon. How are you feeling?" She glanced quickly at Sam, who stood next to what had been Delia's desk. Bobby followed Delia's gaze. He and Sam made eye contact for a second, then Sam turned away and sat. His heart sank. She hated him.

"Ugh," Delia groaned. "You two..." She cut that thought short as the teacher entered.

The rest of the day didn't go any better. Sam avoided him. She wouldn't even look at him for more than a second, which distressed him even more.

Making it worse, Jeff started stalking him. "Drah mah," he kept saying. Bobby did his best to ignore him.

Still, some way, somehow, he had to talk to Sam, Samantha. He needed to explain and apologize. This was more than a stupid boy thing. This was his life. Sam hated him, and he couldn't live with that thought. She had to forgive him before the stress made him go crazy. He sighed. How could he live without Sam?

The last opportunity to talk to Sam would come after the day's final bell when Art class was over. Bobby intended to stop her from leaving the room. Waiting in intense anticipation, he jumped at the sound of the bell. He stood and headed straight for Sam. But she moved faster and darted out the door. The entire day went by without saying a single word to her. He raced to her locker, but instead of finding Sam, he found Delia and Amy.

"I figured this would be your next move," Delia said. Amy had a sheepish grin on her face. She stayed behind Delia and let her handle it. "If you expect to intercept Sam, you'll be waiting a long time She isn't planning to return to her locker tonight." Bobby looked at the floor, defeated.

"Honestly, you two are the biggest..."

"Is she that mad at me," Bobby asked. "What does she want me to do?"

"I don't think she knows what she wants. I don't think she's still mad at you, either. She is more embarrassed than anything else." Delia couldn't hold back a giggle. "Although, I applaud the daring move. To just outright kiss you. That was daring and risky." She smiled at Bobby. "Don't worry. I talked to her and explained that it had been unfair to ambush you like that. But we all agreed that you overreacted."

Bobby assumed that by "we," she meant all girls in the whole world, including his mom.

"You hurt her, Bobby. If you weren't so clueless, you would have known how much she liked you. You're as much to blame for this as Sam, maybe even more."

"Yeah, but..."

"No buts, Bobby. Quit being such a wuss. Find a way to talk to her. Get her to listen."

"How can I? She keeps avoiding me."

"Find a way or..." She knew that Sam and Bobby were perfect for each other. They were the cutest couple of geeks, but both were clueless about ordinary boy-and-girl relationships. This state of affairs had kept their relationship neutral for far too long. She made a fist right in Bobby's face. "Bobby, make this right with her, or I will personally put you back in the hospital. Got it?"

"Alright... I will," he agreed.

"Promise me you will do it tonight." He gave her a sheepish smile. Delia's tough girl talk amused him. "I'll try again tonight."

"Nerd." Having accomplished her mission, she turned to walk away. Then she stopped and looked back to Bobby, "At least you're a cute nerd."

Bobby smiled big. "That makes three girls that think I'm cute."

"Is that right? You've got Sam and me. So, who is the third?"

"My mom," he replied.

"You are the biggest nerd in the world, aren't you?" Delia said, and Amy giggled.

Bobby looked hopeful toward Amy. "Would there be a fourth girl who thinks I'm cute?" Amy giggled and hurried away, following Delia.

******

Bobby walked home, considering his options. He imagined going around to Sam, Samantha's house tonight after dinner. He would knock and wait for someone to come to the door. He imagined Sam or rather Samantha opened the door. Seeing him, she slammed the door in his face. He thought again. Sam wouldn't slam the door in my face, but she might look through one of the six small panes of glass at the top of the front door. Upon seeing me, she might run to her room and leave her mom, dad, or little brother, Kevin, to answer the door.

Okay then, he thought. What if Sam's mom answers the door? "Bobby," she would say. "Come on in. I'll tell Samantha you are here." She would then go to Sam's room and knock on the door. "Samantha, honey. Bobby is here to see you." A long silence followed by a muffled sound came from Sam or Samantha's room. Her mom would then return to make an excuse. "Sorry, Bobby, but Samantha can't come to the door now, but I'm sure she will see you tomorrow." He would walk away even more sad.

Her dad might be home. He would insist she come to the door and be polite. Then Bobby remembered how her dad always called Sam "My little girl." What if his little girl had told him how Bobby had hurt his *little girl's* feelings and that she never wanted to see that mean boy again? Bobby's heart fell.

He imagined Mr. Thomas opening the door. Frowning, Mr. Thomas would say, "What do you want, dork?"

"Is Sam at home," Bobby would ask, trying to ignore the gross insult.

"Not for you. And my little girl's name is Samantha! DORK!" The door slammed in Bobby's face again.

Maybe Kevin would answer the door. Ten-year-old Kevin was a cool enough kid. They got along. Once again, he imagined knocking on the door. Kevin opened the door and stared at Bobby. Then he hollered, "Mom, Samantha said never to let Bobby in the house again, but he's here. What should I do?"

It took two more days of Delia's threats and Jeff's mockery to summon the courage to bring this misunderstanding to an end. On Friday after school, Bobby ran home. At first, he planned to wait in Sam's or Samantha's front yard, but this needed to be a private conversation. Instead, he stayed on the street corner at the end of her block.

"I will keep her from passing me by," Bobby proclaimed. Even if he had to jump in front of her car, I'll make her listen to me."

Bobby paced back and forth for the next hour, wondering if she had taken a different route home. Finally, he saw her car coming up the street. "What if I step out into the middle of the road and force her to stop?" He thought again, "It might be best to wait until she isn't mad at me. I'll just stand on the corner and make sure she sees I am serious."

Sam slowed down as she got closer. Their eyes met. This time, she didn't look away. She pulled over to the curb and lowered the passenger side window. "Delia said I might see you tonight."

"Can we please talk," he pleaded.

She nodded. "Get in. Let's go to the park." She then drove around the corner and parked in front of her house. Sam's mom, Anne Thomas, was weeding in the flower garden. She looked up just as they got out of the car. She wore a big, floppy straw hat and pink garden gloves.

"Oh, hi, Bobby," Mrs. Thomas said. "I haven't seen you in a while."

"Hi, Mrs. Thomas."

"We're going to the park for a while," Sam told her mom. She grabbed Bobby's hand and led him across the street to the park. Three kids played and climbed on the jungle gym. At the far corner of the park, two old men sat at a picnic table playing a game of chess. Bobby and Sam headed for the unoccupied swings and sat side by side in the strap-seated swings. The swings in the park had always been their conference room, strategy center, and think tank. Over the years, whenever they needed to discuss a problem, this was the location of choice. Swinging always created a soothing and comforting feeling. It helped them to think. Both started to swing without a word. Then, at the same time, they both said, "I'm sorry."

Bobby continued, "I'm sorry, Sam, Samantha. I mean, I'm sorry for the way I acted at the beach party. I didn't mean to hurt your feelings. I feel terrible. I was..."

"No, I'm the one who should apologize," she interrupted. "I ambushed you. It's such a dumb thing to do. I didn't know how to say what I wanted to say. So, I did that thing."

"Well, you have always been a girl of action," Bobby tried joking. To his relief, Sam laughed. Then she slugged him in the arm.

"And then I ran off and left you alone, and you got hurt and ended up in the hospital. It's all my fault!"

"I'm the one who went off into the dark to sulk. It's not your fault I am that stupid."

"You're not stupid. Well, maybe just a little." She gave him a sideways smile.

"I got the message, Sam... I mean Samantha. About that. Can I please just call you Sam? I've been calling you Sam since I could talk!"

Sam laughed. "Yes, it's okay to call me Sam."

"I get it. You are a girl who wants me to treat you like a girl. That's fair."

"I'm so embarrassed. I can't believe I kissed you without asking permission, without warning."

"Well, it did the trick." He smiled. "I can't stop thinking of you as anything but a girl."

Mortified, Sam covered her face with both her hands. "I'm so sorry."

"Look, the kiss wasn't a bad thing, just unexpected. You know how clueless I am. You had something important on your mind, but clueless me didn't give you a chance. I guess you needed to make me shut up and listen. Can we start over? Please. But slower this time?" She nodded. "Still friends then?"

"Still friends, but…" She couldn't just leave it at that. He wasn't getting off that easy. "Bobby, I didn't kiss you just to make you shut up. I kissed you because I wanted to kiss you. I have wanted to kiss you for a long time. You need to understand how much I like you. I want you to feel the same way about me." She looked away, embarrassed but determined to confess her feelings. "Can you be my friend knowing I want more than that? If not now, then someday. I need you to be honest. Tell me how you feel about us." Her fists clenched the swing's chains tight. "Because if you don't take me seriously, you will break my heart. It would be better to go back to the way it was before the kiss than to hope for something that will never happen."

There, she had said it. Now, she waited for Bobby's reply. She sat still in the swing, waiting for him to say something. She needed him to make her feel safer and less vulnerable.

Deep in thought, Bobby continued swinging. Sam's friendship was precious to him. He had seen how romance messed up friendships before. He needed to think. Sam was the most incredible girl he knew. In many ways, she was the girl version of him. He didn't want to lose her friendship. Until now, he hadn't thought about Sam romantically.

"I guess," he said. "I need time to think about it. But yes, I can be your friend, knowing how you feel. Can you still be my friend, knowing I need time? Time to figure out how I feel."

Sam smiled. "Yes," she said. I agree to your terms." She extended her hand to him, and they shook hands as best friends. Far in the west, the sun cast long shadows across the park. The kids and the old men had left. Bobby walked Sam back to her front door.

"I'll see you tomorrow then?"

"Absolutely," Sam said with a cheerfulness Bobby hadn't seen in days. He was happy that she was happy again.

******

Toe watched this teenage pairing ritual with fascination from the protection of the tree limbs. A powerful bond existed between these two beings. There was more to these two creatures than emotional energy. He saw real, tangible power. Some kind of magic flowed between them. The last few days Toe had followed the scent of his first victim. That word made him choke with guilt, but victim was the right word. He had taken something from the male and the others that didn't belong to him. He stole their energy. It hurt to think that he had been so selfish. That he had acted as mean as any other Shadow.

Toe didn't understand why but felt compelled to find this young male. Maybe he was looking for forgiveness - a rare principle in his world. Yet, the more he thought about it, the more he knew it was true. What a great relief forgiveness would bring. That idea had become more important to him than his safety and his life. It was risky to contact this male again, especially if he had magic. But after watching the young male and female tonight, he sensed they were kind, understanding creatures. Fate had made their paths cross. Toe felt compelled to find out why.

Toe darted over the rooftops to see where the male went after leaving the female. He watched him enter the structure right behind the female's home.

"How perfect," he thought.

Toe spent the night under the tall flowering bushes that separated the two backyards. The colossal blue, white, and purple hydrangea bushes were more beautiful than anything he had ever seen. The flowers had a magical aura around them. He noticed that the colorful bushes formed a simple magic circle with an outer ring of bushes with a triangular open space in the center. The perfect circle spanned the width of the two backyards. Here, he would hide. The flowers would give him needed shade and shelter during the day. The magical energy would provide nourishment. Toe would wait for the right time to make contact.

Chapter 13

THE SECOND SHADOW

Dr. Miles looked over the latest report—finally, some good news. The rift, now called the Eugene Miles Rift, hadn't moved or grown in the last forty-eight hours. It had finally come to rest four meters from the outside wall of the main building. Its present size was about three meters tall and one and three-quarter meters wide, an opening large enough to allow an astronaut wearing an EVA suit to step through. The frigid air around the rift, hovering at minus ten degrees Celsius, made it uncomfortable for anyone nearby. The uncomfortable temperature forced the guards to wear winter coats underneath their white protective clothing. The frost clouded the air and frosted over their face shields.

The Miles Rift had already given a wealth of new information about interdimensional rifts. Yet the opening remained a mysterious dark void. It refused to give up any visible detail of what might lay beyond. Lasers, sonar, and other sensing devices failed to penetrate the void. With an extending pole, the team tried to insert a small sensor device into the center of the void. It took some effort to push it through. The signal lasted only a few seconds and then went dead. When they retrieved the pole, the device was gone. They needed specialized equipment if they wished to penetrate into the other side. The pressure inside the rift environment was too dangerous for a human explorer to enter, so they ruled that option out.

General Bates provided a solution. Bates pulled a few strings and got permission to use a NASA drone engineered to explore hazardous and unknown environments. NASA called it the *Harsh Environment Surveillance and Analysis Drone*, or HESAD.

NASA's HESAD team arrived two days later and set up beside the rift. The control pod looked like a virtual reality game booth at an arcade. The pilot sat inside, monitoring the drone's many functions and controlling its flight path. This particular HESAD had traveled to the bottom of Earth's deepest ocean locations. A similar device was now on its way to Jupiter, where it would attempt to dive into the gas giant's atmosphere.

The drone had a sixty-centimeter sphere suspended in the center of a solid, saturnine ring. The ring contained the drone's maneuvering controls. The sphere housed specialized cameras, electronics, and various sensors that would gather the needed data.

After a complete system check, the HESAD came to life and lifted off the floor. It glided to the rift and hovered briefly as the pilot waited for the order to enter. Over the communication system, they heard the pilot say, "Do I have a go for the mission?"

General Bates nodded to the HESAD team leader. The team leader, who had just completed a second check of the system, replied, "You have a go."

The drone entered the void but soon slowed to a complete stop. The pilot increased the forward thrust, causing the drone to tilt forward. It penetrated deeper into the rift, then disappeared. Everyone watched the video feed with great interest. At first, the drone's lights and cameras picked up nothing but a black void. Then, the other side came into view. The drone's bright light reflected off a faceted rocky surface. It looked like volcanic obsidian found on Earth. The HESAD performed a three-hundred-and-sixty-degree horizontal pan, revealing a cave-like chamber. Sensors gathered data. It was much warmer inside the rift. The external pressure was significant. It strained at the drone's spherical structure.

The HESAD reported a surprisingly similar atmosphere to Earth composed of nitrogen, oxygen, and argon, with trace amounts of carbon dioxide and methane.

Miles smiled ear to ear. "I hope you all realize the significance of this." The group nodded, gasped, and wowed. We," he said so everyone could hear, "are the first humans to get a view into another universe, and, believe it or not, it has substance. Astounding."

The pilot's voice broke in over the speakers. "I hope your view is as good as mine," he said. We can see what appears to be a cave. I assume it is natural, although the rock walls look like it may have been shaped with tools. An expert would know what it is. What do you think?"

Miles said, "Exploration at its best. Here, we are sitting in the comfort of our lab. It makes me believe anything is possible."

The pilot broke in again. "What the... Did anyone else see that?"

The monitors all went dark as the drone went offline. This historic moment in exploratory science had lasted only a disappointing four minutes and thirty-seven seconds. The HESAD pilot, whose view had been in high-resolution clarity, came out of the control unit looking shaken. His face was white. He had seen something frightening.

"What happened," the General asked over the comm.

The pilot said, "There was an amber flash. Not sure what it was. It crippled our drone."

"A discharge of energy," the HESAD team leader said after a quick look at the data.

The pilot thought carefully before saying anything more. After the other side had come into view, the atmosphere around the drone had turned smoky. Then, just before the drone's cameras went out, two non-human, amber eyes looked back at him. He knew better than to say anything until he verified by the video recording. This gig with NASA was essential to his future, and he wanted to keep it that way.

"Are you telling me you lost the HESAD drone," Bates bellowed.

"We don't know, sir," said the NASA team leader. "We are attempting to get it back online.

The drone pilot spoke up. "I need to take a closer look at the captured images."

Approximately five minutes later, the HESAD rocketed out of the rift scaring anyone who had the misfortune to be standing nearby. The device hit the far wall with enough force to chip the concrete. The drone ricocheted back onto the floor, tumbling to a stop. The billion-dollar HESAD now looked like a deflated medicine ball inside a broken Frisbee. Later, when the pilot and team leader examined the recorded images, they only found what looked like a lens flare. The pilot decided to say nothing more about it.

The drone incident changed everything. The DOD containment team posted extra guards and maintained a 24-hour security barrier around the center.

******

Broken Fang had watched the creatures on the other side of the rupture. He could see them well, but soon, it became apparent they couldn't see him, which gave him an advantage. He spied on the creatures' movements and patterns of activity for several days. His primary goal was to find an opportunity to slip through unseen. The creatures remained close to the opening at all times.

Then, one day, a strange object floated through the rupture. The object hovered in the air in front of him. He had no idea what it was, so he stepped closer. Reaching out, Fang grabbed it out of the air and gave it a cursory examination. He sniffed it, licked it, and bit it. He banged it against the cave wall. Getting impatient, Fang threw it to the ground and stomped on it. Finally, he picked it up and threw it back through the rupture as hard as possible. Few things ever amused Fang, but the other creatures' reaction to this made him laugh.

After that, everything changed on the other side. Fewer creatures stayed close to the rupture, which was a good thing. But those who remained around the rupture wore armor-like uniforms and carried what looked like weapons. Just as Fang guarded his side of the rupture, armed enforcers guarded the other side.

If that was true, his mission just became more dangerous. Fang regretted throwing the strange object back through the rupture. Breaking it and leaving it on the cave floor would have been smarter.

After a while, the other side established a rotating pattern of activity. Only the enforcers remained on duty during the periods of lowest activity. Fang soon found his chance to slip, though unnoticed. With the next lull in activity, he snuck through the rupture unseen. Growing as Little Toe had done, Fang felt the same unpleasant disorientation.

Fang gazed around the area for armed enforcers. None lingered nearby. He needed a way out of the enclosure. A green light hung on the far wall. Hurrying toward the light, he found an opening to the outside. Fang stepped back out of sight. Two enforcers stood with their backs toward him. To Fang's surprise, these enforcers were much smaller than him. Fang had expected giants. He marveled at the change in perspective from one side of the rupture to the other. Although he saw no other enforcers, he could hear noises from different parts of the structure. Time was short, and this was the obvious way out. Moving fast, Fang wrapped his large hands around the two creatures' heads and slammed them together with a crunch. Their bodies went limp. Dragging them back into the darkened building, he turned and exited out into the open air.

In the distance, a single fiery torch sat atop a pole. Beyond, Fang saw nothing but dark shadows with many hiding places. He bolted for the darkness. The bright light on the pole blinded Fang and he ran full force into a chain-link fence, making a loud bang. Part of his misty body flew through the open chain links. His head bounced back onto the ground as his body flowed back into shape. That blunder had taken too much time and had made too much noise. Fang looked up at the top of the fence. Sharp, coiled thorns hung across the top. It was up and over, or get caught.

Two guards rounded the corner of the building. They expected to see students or reporters trying to climb the fence. The upped security had attracted unwanted attention, but what they found staring back at them was a large shadowy figure. In their confusion, they lost precious seconds. The guards reacted and fired a burst at Fang.

Fang anticipated the hostile attack and dodged out of the line of fire. In a blur of movement, he overtook the first guard. Fang's hardened black fist knocked the man unconscious. The second enforcer raised his weapon, but too late. Fang quickly knocked it away. He grabbed the man, opened his mouth wide, and sank his two long fangs through the guard's upper body. With one violent shake, the limp body fell in two. The taste of the human's blood energy quickly clouded Fang's mind. He grabbed the first enforcer off the ground and took another large bite. The powerful craving caused him to stagger backward. Oblivious to the danger, Fang began lapping up the gushing blood.

More gunfire brought Fang back to reality. Several rounds hit vital parts of his body causing intense pain. Enforcers kept firing as he bounded over the fence and disappeared into the night.

Chapter 14

A NORMAL WEEKEND

Life for the gang of three returned to normal. The weekend started Friday night at Jeff's house for a *Double D Dragons II* marathon. The plot revolved around the typical harem comedy (slash) sci-fi adventure. Jeff loved this vivacious anime. An *Anime News Central* fan poll gave this anime a 96.9% approval rating with 20,349 likes and 629 dislikes. Of course, 19,000 of those fans were girl-hungry male geeks.

After a somewhat contentious discussion about too many boob and panties references in the dialogue, Jeff said, "It's just a goofy fantasy, Sam."

"To be specific, a goofy male fantasy," she countered.

"Can we change the subject," Bobby pleaded. "I'm not comfortable talking about boobs or any part of a girl's anatomy."

Sam gave Bobby an embarrassed smile. "The point is, if a girl wants to show off her boobs but hide her panties, a longer skirt would work."

"I'll give you that one," Jeff said.

"Bobby, would you like me to wear a dress too short on both ends?"

"I have no opinion," Bobby wisely replied. Besides, you never even wore a dress until this year."

Jeff smirked. "I bet you would like it now that Sam is your girlfriend."

"We're just friends," Bobby and Sam yelped with too much protest.

Bobby had reached his limit on this particular discussion. "It's getting late," he asserted. "So anyway… games tomorrow afternoon at my place."

"I will be there at 3:00," Jeff replied.

"Yeah, I do get your point, Sam," Jeff looked down. "Look. I know the dragon girls are far from realistic. Think about it, what do I know about girls? I've never even had a girlfriend, not a real one. Anyway, if I had a real girlfriend, she wouldn't be like the dragon girls. I want a nice, normal girl." He took a deep breath. "Now, if only a nice, normal girl would like me back."

Jeff usually kept such revealing thoughts to himself. Watching fantasy shows like *Double D Dragons* helped him avoid what he believed to be a dull existence. His cousins in Japan were so athletic and cool. But what was he? The bravado act covered up his Insecurities that had dominated his life since puberty.

Sam said, "Thank you, Jeffrey. That gives me hope for you. You just haven't found yourself yet." Sam picked up her bag, ready to leave. "But please, for all our sakes, keep looking."

Jeff responded, "What do you mean by that?"

Bobby walked Sam all the way home. The sun had already set on a beautiful day.

"Let's swing in the park for a little while," Sam suggested. She wore a sweater, and the nights were getting colder. She shivered. "It's chilly, but I'm not ready to go inside yet."

Bobby removed his zippered hoodie and said, "Here, take this."

"But won't you be cold?"

"I'll be fine. I would like some alone time with you. If that means suffering the chilly air, then so be it."

Sam draped the hoodie over her head and shoulders as they walked across the street to the park. They sat on the swings and began swinging in unison for several quiet minutes. The peaceful night sky was bright with stars. That had to be one of the best things about El Palmar. Most nights, you could see the stars. Bobby thought the night sky was magical.

"Sorry about tonight," Bobby said, breaking the silence.

"Sorry about what?"

"Jeff can be rude."

"Oh, that. Jeffrey is who he is. That's all we can expect. He'll grow up someday."

"You're sure about that?"

She laughed. "I got a little touchy, didn't I?"

After a thoughtful pause, Bobby said, "The rude things Jeff says about girls, I don't think about girls... you... like that."

"Oh really? Then what do you think about me," she teased.

That reply made him wonder if he had said something wrong. "I mean... I respect you. I don't ever want to offend you again."

"Thank you," she said. "You're a real nice guy, you know that? Several of my friends have even said so."

"Which ones?"

"Sorry... secret."

"Do any of them think I'm cute?"

"What?"

"I've been keeping score."

"You're such a nerd-head."

"I know." They continued to swing for a while longer. "I like this little park at night. I have always liked how the streetlamp cast shadows on the trees, the bushes, and the playground equipment. It's so..."

Bobby's sixth sense alarm went off. The shadows looked off. They didn't match up. A big, lumpy shadow that shouldn't be there lay on the grass about twenty feet away. He threw his feet to the sand and brought the swing to an abrupt stop. The memory of the night at the beach flashed in his mind.

Sam noticed the change and stopped swinging, too. "What's wrong?"

"We're not alone. Something is watching us."

"You said something—not someone or somebody." Unnerved, she looked around the park. "What?"

Bobby pointed toward the large, odd-shaped shadow. It moved. Sam grabbed Bobby's arm and pulled her swing right next to his. It moved again, but this time, it looked up. Two green eyes appeared.

Sam gasped, "What is that?"

"That," Bobby replied, "is what attacked me on the beach."

"Oh, no! Bobby, what do we do?"

Little Toe sensed that the two subjects of his appeal were afraid. The last thing he wanted was for them to run away or turn and fight. The female had power. She might attack to protect the male. Pushing himself further into the grass, he prostrated as low as he could. He kept his head down and his arms crossed in front of him. He scooted along the ground from that position, moving closer to the young couple.

"What's it doing," Sam whispered.

Bobby considered the creature's behavior - so different from his first encounter. "It reminds me of how animals act around the dominant male or female. Maybe it's trying to be submissive."

"So, you're saying that the thing that attacked you and put you in the hospital for two days now thinks you are the alpha male?"

"Or that you are the dominant female. It wants to show us it's not a threat. Look how it's moving." Bobby stood and walked a few steps toward Toe.

"What are you doing," Sam hissed.

"Let's see if it means it."

"Isn't that the oldest trick in the book?" She followed right behind Bobby. "Pretend to be all friendly, then slash, bite."

Bobby took a few more steps toward Toe. Toe didn't move, but he looked up just long enough to see their reaction, then buried his face in the grass again, and scooted further. Bobby and Sam took a few more cautious steps, then waited for Toe's response. Again, Toe did the same. Bobby took a few more steps until he was about three feet from the oddity. Bobby spoke, "What are you; what do you want?"

Toe looked at Bobby and let him see his whole face, ensuring his expression remained calm. He gazed up into the young couple's eyes and pleaded in thought, "Please, help me."

Stunned, Bobby and Sam reacted. "Did you hear that," Bobby said.

"Yes," Sam replied. "I didn't exactly hear it, but I felt it and understood."

They looked at each other in shock and then back at Little Toe. Little Toe's large, sad, puppy-dog eyes melted Sam's heart. She couldn't help feeling compassion for the poor thing. Letting go of Bobby's arm, she stepped forward, knelt, and extended the back of her hand like you would to a strange dog - a huge strange dog.

Toe recognized Sam's gesture as goodwill, so he stuck out his tongue and licked her fingers. A wave of pure pleasure flooded his mind. Not prepared for the extra dose of euphoria from the female, an unintended thought slipped out. "You taste good!"

Sensing a strange vibe, Sam pulled her hand back. Toe remembered the other female he had cornered in the stairwell. The smell of fear on her was so strong it sickened him. That moment of revelation had left such a sadness in his heart. Once again, emotion overwhelmed him, and liquid dripped from his big eyes.

Chapter 15

A LEVEL "ET" EMERGENCY

"I'm home," Bobby yelled to anyone listening. He closed the front door and headed for the stairs.

"Got any homework," Sarah Williams asked.

He hesitated before answering. Not wanting his mom to come checking on him at a time like this, he said, "I got most of it done this afternoon. I still have a couple of things to do. Don't worry."

"Okay, hurry and finish; you don't want to be up too late," she replied.

"It's Friday night, Mom. No school tomorrow."

"Well, anyway, don't stay up too late. Oh, and Bobby?"

"Yes, Mom."

"Have you been picking the hydrangeas in the backyard?"

"No. Why would I do that?"

"Well, the flowers in the backyard have been disappearing. Those flowers are important to me."

"Don't have a clue, Mom." She said nothing more, so Bobby hurried up the stairs to his room. After closing the door, he locked it. He darted across the room to the sash window notched into the sloping ceiling and the sidewall. It opened onto the side roof. Opening the window, he stuck his head through and whispered, "Sam."

The trees and bushes on this side of the house kept the side yard well secluded. A sturdy old garden trellis provided a safe ladder to climb the roof. Over the years, when his comings and goings required covert action, the trellis and window had been his room's secret entrance and exit.

"I'm here," she whispered, climbing over the roof's edge. She turned back and looked down. She beckoned to their strange new friend below. "Come on. Don't be afraid, you're safe here."

Toe climbed the trellis onto the roof in one quick, fluid motion. When Sam climbed through the window, he followed right behind her. It was a tight squeeze. As a Shadow made chiefly of black particles, Toe would normally compress his body to fit the smaller size of the window. Not only was this world making him more solid, it was making him fat. He almost didn't make it through the window. No doubt, this resulted from feasting on this world's rich energies. Toe felt guilty all over again. Judging from the woman's reaction in the stairwell, these new friends seemed unlikely to give him permission to lick their body energy. For now, he would rely on the delicious flowers in the backyard. He looked longingly at Sam, remembering how good her hand had tasted. He licked his dark lips.

Sam sat down on the edge of the bed next to Bobby. They watched as Little Toe investigated his new surroundings. Sam broke the silence with, "What do we do now?" Bobby picked up his phone to make a call. Sam looked at him, questioning.

"Calling for reinforcements," he said. "Jeff... Yeah, I know, but we've got a level three emergency going on here."

"More like level ET," Sam added.

"Yeah, good one, Sam. No, we're not kidding. I need you over here right now. Yeah, she's already here. Okay, get here as fast as you can. Oh, and use the trellis. We don't want any parental guidance on this one! I'll explain when you get here." He ended the call and tossed the phone on the bed. "Three heads are better than two, right?"

Jeff decided that his math homework could wait. He assumed Sam was joking about the whole ET thing. Still, that had to be one weird phone call. His parents had already gone to bed, so he turned out his light and snuck out the back door. At top speed on his bike, it only took five minutes to get to Bobby's house. On arrival, he parked the bike behind a bush in the Williams' front yard and then made his way into the side yard and up the trellis. Remembering that Sam was already inside, he paused. A lot happened between his two best friends in the last two weeks, so he announced his arrival before entering. "Can I come in," he whispered.

"Yes, get in here before someone sees you," Bobby hissed back.

Jeff climbed through his legs first. He turned to find himself face-to-face with a startled black creature. The menacing green-eyed stare made Jeff's face turn white. He froze.

Sam hopped up to reassure Toe. "It's okay," she said in a calm voice. "He's a friend." Toe seemed to understand and backed away. Toe sat back down, taking up considerable floor space at the end of Bobby's bed.

For Jeff, the strange creature's retreat didn't relieve his the shock in the slightest. Those green eyes were still staring at him. Jeff stayed by the window just in case he needed to run away. "I guess you weren't kidding," Jeff said in a controlled whisper, trying to not make any sudden moves. "What is that?"

"We don't know," Bobby replied.

"Where did it come from?"

"We don't know that either," Bobby added. "The only thing I can tell you for sure is this is what attacked me on the beach the other night."

Jeff's eyes and mouth opened wide. "Are you kidding me? You're sure?" Bobby nodded. "Then why is it in your house?"

"Sam and I were in the park swinging." Jeff was well acquainted with Bobby and Sam's swinging therapy sessions. He had taken part in several of them.

"Then whatever it is came to us all repentant-like," Sam said. "We think it wants our help."

Jeff forgot about the ET in the room and became fixated on Bobby and Sam sitting together on the bed. "So you guys were swinging, huh?" He had that annoying, weird grin on his face. "You two love birds having fun without me?"

Bobby and Sam scooted away from each other. "Would you stay on task, Jeff," Bobby barked a little louder than he intended. He looked to the door, fearing his parents might have heard. "This is serious," he said in a harsh whisper. "We need to decide what to do."

Jeff sat in the chair beside Bobby's desk and scratched his head. "It's funny, isn't it? I mean, something like this doesn't happen every day. It seems odd that we can accept this so easily. Do you suppose our lines between reality and fantasy have gotten too blurred? He leaned forward toward Toe. "Hey, big fella, where did you come from?"

Jeff's vivid imagination kicked into high gear. First, he imagined Toe riding in a spaceship as the copilot of a roguish human hero. Toe tried to read the new male's mind, but all he saw were odd images. Toe Thought, "Why is this male looking at me like that?"

"Is it a boy or a girl," Jeff asked.

Sam replied, "If there is a male or a female of whatever it is, I'd guess a male."

Jeff tried to imagine the female version of the creature. Toe became a space pirate with a bodacious companion. Since Jeff's knowledge of anatomy was human-based, his imagination created a rather voluptuous version of their new friend. This alien female pirate wore a light blue spandex outfit. She sashayed up behind the new and improved Little Toe, who now wore shiny battle armor with skull and crossbones on the chest and a red leather cape down his back. The female kissed him with her juicy red lips.

Astonished, Toe blinked. "This male cannot be a normal member of this species."

Toe couldn't make sense of the boy's confusing mental images, but that last vivid image left no doubt. This male was insane. If he believed Shadow females looked and acted like that, he had lost his brains somewhere. For the first time in ages, Toe laughed.

"Bruff-bruff-bruff." Then he shook. "Squee-flit- huff, bruff, bruff."

The laughing continued as drool dripped and splattered from his mouth. He fell back onto his back and continued to shake. The three teens watched in fascination.

"What's he doing," Jeff asked.

Sam smiled. "He's laughing."

"At what?"

"Well, he was looking at you," Bobby replied. Sam and Bobby laughed. Jeff blinked in surprise, and then he laughed, too.

"Shush," Bobby said, trying to suppress his laughter. He pointed downstairs, where he hoped his parents had gone to bed. Trying to stifle the laughter only made the situation seem that much funnier. After the giggles had stopped, they sat contemplating this strange predicament.

"We still don't know what to do," Sam sighed. "Should we tell somebody?"

Bobby shook his head. "Who could we tell? Who could we trust with something like this?"

"Our parents," Sam suggested.

"I don't know about that."

"My Grandpa Maeda," Jeff said with confidence.

"Your grandpa," Sam said.

"Why," Bobby asked.

"Back in Japan, Grandpa grew up as the youngest son of a shrine priest. That was before he came to the States decades ago. He knows all about weird stuff like this."

"But why would he have any knowledge about alien creatures?"

"Think about it," Jeff continued. "I doubt this is an alien from outer space."

"You think he is a native animal… of this planet," Sam asked. "Because if that is true, he must be an unknown species. Like bigfoot or something."

"Maybe someone's science experiment gone wrong," Bobby suggested.

"That's way too Hollywood," Sam mocked. "Too weird."

"Too weird," Jeff asked. He couldn't let that go without stating the obvious. "A strange, black creature with green eyes and slime dripping from its mouth is sitting in the middle of your boyfriend's bedroom floor."

"We're just friends," both Sam and Bobby replied.

"Whatever," Jeff continued. "It's fair to say we cannot exaggerate the weirdness factor of this situation. All I am saying is our friend here might be more supernatural than an alien. We need help from someone who knows about the supernatural. That would be my grandpa. Besides, he is the only adult I would trust with something like this. Grandpa won't freak out."

"Will he help us," Bobby said.

"Oh sure, he's a great old dude. Like I said, he knows everything about the supernatural."

"Okay then, that will be our next step," Bobby said.

Sam looked over at Toe who sat contented. His tongue hung out the side of his grinning mouth. "We need to give him a name."

Jeff spoke up immediately. "He kind of reminds me of a pet dog I had. His name was Cooper. We had to put the poor old guy down four years ago."

"Cooper," Sam snickered.

"Yeah, I know, but it seems to fit. Don't you think?"

They all looked at Toe again. "Cooper, it is," Bobby proclaimed.

Chapter 16

THREAT ASSESSMENT

Special agents in dark suits and earbuds entered the Center for Interdimensional Physics. They told Miles' people to step away from their stations and escorted everyone to other rooms for questioning. The agents took control of the entire facility.

"What is going on, General," Miles asked.

"I talked to the Secretary of Defence this morning," Bates told Miles. "This incident is a clear threat to national security. Because of the classified nature of your research, the Secretary agreed that the Department of Defense should conduct the investigation."

An agent approached the General. "General Bates," he said, extending his hand. "I am Agent Bob Solinger, the lead investigator.

"Welcome, Agent Solinger," Bates replied. "This is Dr. Eugene Miles. You will want Dr. Miles' help. He and his people know the science issues better than anyone. We need to resolve this matter as soon as possible. I would appreciate daily progress reports."

"Of course, General," Solinger said. "The Secretary labeled everything that has happened or may happen as Top Secret. We need to conduct this investigation with great care. The fewer people that know why we are here the better."

"Understood."

"I would like to see the bodies, General."

Bates led the agent through the tunnel to the HGC building, where they stored the bodies. The VIP group entered the containment building. Agent Solinger stopped to make sense of the open rift before him.

"Is that it," Solinger asked.

"Yes," Miles responded. "Impressed?"

"Indeed. Mind-boggling for sure."

The bodies lay in a row on the floor. The General stooped and lifted the tarp covering the first body. "From the looks of these guys, an animal attack sounds more likely than anything else."

"Could this be the work of a foreign agent, made to look like an animal attack," Miles asked.

Solinger replied, "At the moment, we aren't ruling anything out."

The agents interviewed everyone on duty the night of the attack. Of course, only a few had seen the alleged assailant.

"I saw a large dark figure, hunched over like an animal," one witness said.

"The whole thing was over in seconds, sir," said another. "I can't be sure of what I saw."

"It looked like it might have been an ape or something. Damn weird."

"If it was an animal, it was the weirdest-looking animal I have ever seen."

"Honest to God... I've never seen anything like it," the last witness told them. "We shot at it, but it just kept going as though the bullets went right through it."

By now, the itch in the back of Dr. Miles's head had become a pounding headache. When the interviews with the guards concluded, the agents shifted their focus to the center's personnel. Dr. Miles and his team met together first, then as individuals. In an interview with one of Miles' people, Solinger learned that about two weeks before this incident, there were four, maybe five, unexplained assaults on locals.

"It was all over the news," the technician had said. "But none of those victims died. I have a friend who's a local cop. He told me the first victim may have gotten a brief view of his attacker. A possible fifth victim claims to have escaped an animal attack. The woman described it as a large primate. It had stalked her as she walked home from work. It ran away when she screamed. My cop friend thought her story was pretty kooky."

"Maybe it wasn't that kooky," Solinger said.

Solinger sent two agents to investigate this new lead. Although he had difficulty believing there was a giant ape somewhere, he decided to discuss it with Miles.

"Dr. Miles," he said. "We may need to consider the possibility that what killed the four guards was an animal. All descriptions of the assailant point to that. Have any thoughts about what this creature might be?"

"Afraid not," Miles said. "TV news and newspapers would have caught the story if something had escaped from the zoo. Considering the damage to those guards, it would have to be one crazed animal. I don't think even a gorilla would be that violent. Still, I have a growing concern. I have no logical reason to believe a direct connection exists between the Miles Rift and the attacks, but It bothers me that those earlier attacks coincide with the day the rift opened. What if the animal came through the Miles Rift?"

"You think the animal may not be from this world?"

"Just a thought. I will have my technicians search every pixel of the images caught on camera that night. I'll have them start from the beginning." The notion, now plaguing Miles, chilled him to the bone.

After two days of eye-numbing searching, the technicians discovered the two separate anomalies. What they found appeared as nothing more than fleeting shadows. In each instance, the shadowy shapes appeared to exit from the rift. The first anomaly appeared after the rift had opened. The second anomaly appeared minutes before the attack on the guards. *Shadows* best described the misty, formless shapes the cameras captured. One noticeable difference between the two anomalies was that the second Shadow was much larger than the first. Two separate individuals had come through the rift. Both were alive and dangerous.

The exterior security cameras had caught the second Shadow and its deadly attack. The creature moved fast and knocked the guards to the ground. Whatever killed the four guards had to be solid, yet the vague shapes caught by the cameras looked like ghosts. How could a ghost cause so much damage?

After showing the files to Agent Solinger and General Bates, Solinger gave a stern command to everyone. "An invasion of non-terrestrial origin has occurred. The National Security Act is now in full force. Each of you will need to sign a NDA. Breathe a word of this to the outside world, even to your wife or significant other, and you will spend the rest of your life in a federal prison cell. Do I make myself clear?"

Some nodded, others said yes.

******

The underground maintenance and utility tunnels between the university campus buildings gave Broken Fang a place to hide. The tunnels were dark and secluded. He could stay out of sight while his body healed. Fang had guessed right; the enforcers carried weapons. Although most of the projectiles passed through his body with no harm, a few had hit vital parts. He bled. Fortunately, he would heal quickly. All he needed now was time.

Fang felt tired and hungry. He remembered the exquisite taste of the blood. The euphoric effect of the blood energy had overpowered his common sense and had almost got him killed. When darkness returned to the outside, his mouth slimed with eager anticipation of a feast. Over the next two days, three students and one campus maintenance worker went missing.

Chapter 17

THE INFAMOUS GRANDPA MAEDA

Late the following evening, the three friends and Little Toe, a.k.a. Cooper, met in the park. The plan was simple. Show up unannounced at Jeff's grandpa's house and introduce their mysterious new friend. They hoped Grandpa Maeda could tell them something about the creature. Jeff had charted a path to avoid as many lights and people as possible. Since this quiet bedroom community tended to go dead after 9:00 pm, Jeff felt confident they could get to Grandpa Maeda's house safely and unseen. Jeff led the way, followed by Bobby, Sam, and Little Toe, whose big hand wrapped tight around Sam's right hand. The orange-colored street lamps only lit up the intersections. The foursome skirted the light, taking advantage of every shadow.

Bobby wondered out loud, "What would happen if someone saw Cooper?"

"Probably scream and run," Sam replied.

Jeff said, "I don't know. After a double-take or two, they might just decide they were seeing things and return to bed."

"Maybe. No one would expect to see something like Cooper," Bobby conceded.

"He's pretty good at hiding," Sam added. "So, I doubt he would allow anyone to see him."

Bobby asked Jeff, "Are you sure it's okay to drop in on your grandpa like this?"

"He won't mind. Besides, how do we explain this to him any other way? I thought showing Cooper to Grandpa and seeing what he thinks would be easier."

"Jeffrey," Sam said, "I don't know if introducing Cooper to an old man is a good idea. How old is your grandpa?"

"He's eighty-three."

"Eighty-three," she gasped. "Look at Cooper. He scared me the first time I saw him. He might scare your old grandpa to death."

"My grandpa," Jeff scoffed. "Nothing scares him. Just wait until you meet him. You'll see. He's one tough old geezer."

Toe maintained a firm grip on Sam's hand as though he was afraid to let go. Earlier, she had tried to extricate her hand, but it upset him. So, she let him have his way. "This is like having a three-hundred-pound toddler in tow," she complained. "My hand is going numb." with her free hand, she patted Toe on the arm. Black dust puffed up and out from under her hand gently. "He's not even that solid. How does he squeeze so tight?"

"He trusts you," Bobby said.

"Well, I wish he would trust me a little less tight." Once more, Sam tried to get Toe to let go, or at least to loosen his grip. She looked him straight into his big green eyes and pleaded. "Listen, Cooper... honey, I am not going anywhere. I'll stay right by you. You can even hold my hand, but could you not hold it so tight? You're hurting me." Toe reacted to her request. He saw a mental image of Sam in pain because of her hand. He understood and, to her relief, softened his grip. She smiled and said, "Thank you." Toe smiled back. He licked her hand and then licked his lips.

Grandpa Maeda's house was only about a thirty-minute walk under normal circumstances. It took them over an hour to get there by Jeff's roundabout route. Like every other older house near the university, the house was an Arts and Crafts bungalow. Over the years, Grandpa Maeda had added many traditional Japanese elements to the home and garden making it unique to the neighborhood. The three young adults snuck up to the house and sat on the front steps next to the window. The porch light was out, Grandpa Maeda had drawn curtains for the night, and the television was blaring.

"Okay, this is what we will do," Jeff whispered in the dark. "I'll knock on the door and talk to Grandpa first." Jeff peered through the window. Grandpa Maeda sat in his favorite living room chair, watching a British comedy show. A woman's voice spoke in a broad Scottish accent.

"Your back from the doctor already?"

A man's voice replied, "Ai, but it was a complete waste ah time."

"Whatever do yah mean? What did he do?"

"The man is barking mad, I tell ya."

Bobby couldn't resist. "Your Japanese grandpa is watching BBC America?"

"Oh yeah," Jeff replied, smiling. "He loves Brit-coms. Especially the golden oldies like this one. I forget the name of the show." He leaned toward Bobby, "Like I said, I will go in first and tell Grandpa I want to introduce my friends."

There was lots of loud canned laughter from the TV. Something funny happened, and Grandpa let out a hearty, "Oh... ha-ha!!"

Bobby realized this BBC comic skit was a bit off-color. "Go knock on the door. Let's get this over with."

Grandpa, delighted with the next set of jokes, laughed enthusiastically. "Ah ha-ha-he-ho-ho," he hooted and clapped. Another low-brow joke brought on even greater laughter from Grandpa Maeda.

Covering his mouth to stifle the noise, Jeff shook with suppressed laughter. "I love my grandpa's laugh, and I love that grandpa thinks old British comedies are funny."

Sam rolled her eyes. "Jeff, from the TV-Mature dialogue I'm hearing, you and your grandpa have a lot in common."

Sam's hand remained Toe's personal property. Toe kept looking at her with great admiration. He licked her hand again. She glanced at the creature's big smile. Toe licked his lips.

"Why does he keep doing that," Sam whispered.

"What," Bobby asked.

"Every time I look at Cooper, he licks his lips. He keeps licking my hand, too. It's gross and creepy."

Jeff answered as he stood, "Isn't it obvious? He has a crush on you." He stepped up to the front door.

"Knock on the door, you idiot." She looked back at Toe. He licked his lips again.

Grandpa heard noises coming from the porch and muted the TV. The old man got up as Jeff knocked. "Who's out there," Grandpa barked.

"It's just me, Grandpa," Jeff replied, still trying to stifle a laugh.

"Me who?"

"It's Jeffrey, Grandpa!"

"Oh, well then, what are you standing outside for," Grandpa hollered.

Jeffrey tried the door and found it unlocked. "Grandpa, what have Mom and Dad told you about keeping your doors locked at night? Someone might break into the house."

"Oh, nonsense. I've lived here for over sixty years and have had no problems. Besides, I can take care of myself, you know." He took a wobbly martial art pose. "So, why are you here? It's kind of late for you to be out."

"It's okay, Grandpa. Besides, I can take care of myself, you know." He copied his grandpa's pose, only making exaggerated moves.

Grandpa Maeda laughed. Then, with a mock frown, he glared at his grandson. "You little *baka*. Watch your mouth, or I'll roundhouse-kick you to next Sunday."

"No, no, no... Forgive me, honored one," said Jeff with an overdone bow at the waist.

"At your age, I had to fight off an army of attacking ninjas. I killed twenty-three evil monsters single-handedly and saved my family from sure death."

"That number gets bigger every time you tell that story, Grandpa. Last week, it was only eighteen monsters."

"*Baka*," Grandpa said, putting his arm around his favorite grandson and drawing him toward the sofa. "What do you know? The only danger you have ever faced is in one of those computer games."

Jeff laughed. "I'm afraid that's true." Jeff gave a deep bow. "I humble myself before your superior experience."

"Darn right you do," Grandpa said, shaking his finger at Jeff. They both laughed and hugged.

Bobby peaked through the front window. Grandpa Maeda was a jolly old man. The old man's eyes seemed to twinkle with sprite-like mischievous intent. Mischief seemed to fuel his demeanor. The only flaw in his cheerful face was a long scar that started just above his right eye and ended at the jawline.

"So, this is where Jeff gets his craziness from," Bobby told Sam. She nodded in agreement. Bobby stepped into the open front door. "Ah, Jeff. I don't want to interrupt this familial reunion, but did you forget about us?"

"Who the heck are you," Grandpa barked.

"Oh yeah," Jeff remembered. "I want to introduce my friends. Come on in, guys." Sam joined Bobby in the open door, her right hand out of sight. "This is Bobby and Sam. Her name is Samantha, but we call her Sam."

His grandpa smiled. "She's pretty. Is she your girlfriend, Jeffrey?" He gave Jeff an elbow jab to the ribs.

"Nah," he replied. "Sam is Bobby's girlfriend."

"We're just friends," the couple chimed. Bobby stepped into the room, but Sam remained outside the door.

"Anyway," Jeff continued. "We," Jeff gestured toward Sam standing in the doorway, "have a problem that requires expert advice. That's you, Grandpa."

"I see," Grandpa said.

Jeff chuckled, "I suppose the problem is more Sam's now.

"Oh dear," Grandpa said with a frown. He tapped the side of his nose with his finger. "She's pregnant then?"

"What," Sam squealed.

Grandpa put his hands near his stomach as if holding a basketball-sized abdomen. He laughed.

"No," Sam bleated in protest. Jeff and his grandpa huddled together, laughing. She let out a frustrated, "Ugh! Is your whole family like you, Jeffrey?"

"No, just us two." They let out a loud laugh once again.

"Jeff, please," Bobby begged. "Please, sir. We found, or he found us, a strange creature, and Jeff thought it might be of supernatural origin."

"You found something supernatural," Grandpa asked with a strong hint of disbelief.

"Maybe," Jeff replied. "Since you know about such things, maybe you could tell us what it is."

Sam turned to the unseen Toe. "Come on," she said. "It's okay." She backed through the door, pulling him in after her. Toe's large body went fuzzy as he squeezed sideways through the front door.

"This is our new friend," Jeff announced. Sam closed the door behind them.

Grandpa Maeda's smile vanished. He couldn't believe what these kids had brought into his living room. The last time he had seen something like this, he was fifteen and fighting for his life. The monster war was why he had left Japan, his family, and the shrines his family loved and protected. In the blink of an eye, the old man's face and body transformed from Grandpa, the clown, into Grandpa, the warrior priest. He pushed Jeff behind him with unexpected strength and shouted, "Get away from that thing. Now!"

With his right hand, he formed the sign. The index and middle fingers extended close together, the other two fingers bent into the palm, and his thumb pointed back toward his chest. He made five horizontal lines in the air, then slashed four vertical lines, crossing the first five. This action disturbed the air with magic. Chanting, Grandpa Maeda called out a nine-syllable mantra, *"Rin, pyo, to, sha, kai, jin, retsu, zai, zen!"* Grandpa changed the hand sign to a flat hand bent upward, palm forward. With firm emphasis, he shouted, *"Kage oni* must die." He dropped his wrist pushing the hand downward. Little Toe immediately fell face forward to the floor.

Grampa made the first sign again and repeated the chant: "Rin, pyo, to..." Toe looked up at Grandpa, his eyes wide with surprise. Then he closed his eyes as if the old man's chanting had given him a massive headache. Toe shook his head violently and arched his back. Then he fell unconscious.

Sam screamed, "What are you doing to him?" She threw herself over the fallen Toe's head.

"Sha, kai, jin..."

"Grandpa, no," Jeff shouted.

"Grandpa, Grandpa!" Jeff stepped in front of his grandpa.

"Get out of my way." Grandpa shoved the boy aside, causing Jeff to trip and fall. "... *Retsu zai zen!* Die demon." He took another quick breath and continued. *"Rin, pyo, to..."*

Jeff jumped to his feet and clasped both of his hands over the fierce old man's hands. "Stop, Grandpa! You have this all wrong."

The old man stopped chanting and looked at his grandson, first in surprise, then in anger. He barked, "What is this, Jeffrey? What have you three been up to? And how... how dare you bring that thing to my home?" Jeff had never seen this side of his grandpa.

"I'm sorry, Grandpa. Let me explain. Cooper came to Bobby for help."

"Cooper? You gave it the name of your harmless dog?"

"Please... please," Sam sobbed, her eyes full of tears. "Cooper is not what you think. He's sweet. Please, don't hurt him!"

Grandpa glared at Sam. "Young lady, do you know what you are protecting?"

"No, I don't," she yelled back. "But obviously, you do. That's why we came to you - for your help. Help us. Help Cooper."

The old man stepped back aghast. Now, he had seen and heard everything. "Sweet, you say," he asked, returning to his old self. The crying Sam nodded. Toe awakened, his big, round green eyes blinking with confusion from under Sam's arms and upper body. She protected his head even though behind her, Toe's butt stuck up like a big mound of black coal.

"Well, I'll be," Grandpa said with a chuckle. "Would you look at that, Jeffrey? He's actually kind of cute."

Chapter 18

SMELL OF MAGIC

Fang's upper back bristled into an angry hump. "Someone," he thought, "just created a powerful spell. That little imp must have stirred up trouble. Only a witch or a sorcerer made such spells."

Curiosity always led to trouble. Shadows did not fear danger, but Little Toe's actions made no sense. The imp had taken the appearance of a rupture in his cave wall as an invitation to explore a new world. Fang thought, "Why do something so foolish?" Few Shadows were what one might call inquisitive. Of course, this was Little Toe he was thinking about.

In ancient times, Shadows explored other worlds, but not anymore. Shadows these days live for exploitation, not exploration. With the knowledge to open ruptures to other worlds forgotten, Tiarnas' time for conquest ended long ago. The exploitation of their world had replaced conquest. The only knowledge necessary for a Shadow these days was to know your enemies well.

Fang's desire to kill Little Toe began on the day they met. The little creature's intelligence threatened him. Magistrate Fire Claws thought of Little Toe as an object of amusement. The Magistrate was a fool for not seeing the danger that little imp posed. Shadows like Fire Claws and Broken Fang lived by a simple wisdom that revolved around needs and threats. The average Shadow's brain was an instinct-focused organ. If Fang needed shelter, he found shelter. If he needed to fight, he fought with ferociousness. If hungry, he ate. If the food tasted good, he ate more of it, whether it was a plant or another creature. He planned to eat Little Toe after he killed him. That was the way it should be.

Little Toe's intelligence was dangerous because Little Toe had developed a sense of right and wrong. Such ideals guided the little imp's choices. Morality didn't exist in Fang's world. What if many generations of Little Toes existed? All running around teaching others nonsense about what is right and what is wrong? If the Little Toe's intelligence propagated, new generations of Little Toes would threaten the empire's existence. Shadows like Fang and Fire Claws would become extinct.

"I have a future," Fang thought. "I won't let Little Toe take it away from me. The little Shadow doesn't belong in my world."

Fang bolted at full speed through the tunnels toward the beach exit. The metal gate banged open as his powerful body rushed out into the night air. He needed to get a fix on the magic before the waves of its power dissipated. He rose high on his legs, sniffing in every direction.

"There it is," Fang thought. "The magic still smells strong." Fang charged off toward the magic.

Chapter 19

MONSTERS AND DEMONS

The three young adults sat on the sofa, and Little Toe sat on the floor next to Sam. Grandpa Maeda sat in his favorite chair and described a bizarre world where monsters and monster slayers existed. As Grandpa talked, he watched the creature who had once again taken hold of Sam's slender fingers. This creature had intelligence. It listened to their conversation, looking back and forth as each person spoke. That attentiveness made the old man wonder how much the beast understood.

Intense emotions created more explicit mental images for Little Toe to draw upon for understanding. Because of the earlier confrontation, everyone in the room radiated plenty of emotion to tap into. Toe soaked up as much information about this world as possible.

Jeff said, "Grandpa, you called Cooper a demon. Do you mean like the devil?"

"No, not the devil," Grandpa replied. "That Lucifer fellow is a different kind of creature altogether. The devil and all his kind are fallen angels, you see. True, people also refer to Lucifer's fallen angels as demons, but they are not the same as your Cooper. He is what I call a *Kage oni,* or Shadow demon. *Oni, Akuma,* and *yokai* are Japanese terms for creatures like demons, monsters, fiends, and so many other nightmares. Nowadays, most people don't believe such things. Most things depicted in modern-day horror movies are pure nonsense. Hollywood inventions. But I tell you, no, I warn you. Monsters are quite real."

"Where do these Shadow demons come from?"

"They come from otherworldly realms."

Bobby's eyes widened. "Are you saying Cooper is an alien?"

"Well, not in the way you're thinking," Grandpa continued. There are many kinds of demons and monsters, too. That includes the ones often mistaken for aliens—those creepy little gray guys. People often mistake demons for fairies, goblins, and devils." Grandpa shrugged. But what is essential to understand is that these things don't belong in our world."

"Don't belong," Bobby asked.

Grandpa pointed an old finger at Little Toe. "Your Shadow demon friend... his presence in this world is not good for us or him."

Sam jumped in, "How could anything about Cooper be bad?"

Grandpa looked at Bobby. "You are Jeffrey's friend—the one who ended up in the hospital."

"Yeah. I mean, yes, sir," Bobby replied.

"Was it this fellow that attacked you?" Bobby was reluctant to admit it, but he nodded, confirming it.

"To be fair, some demons and monsters are neither good nor evil. Are tigers or great white shark's evil? No, they exist in nature and can be dangerous to humans. Although, if one wanted to have you for lunch, you would not consider it a benevolent act. A couple of months ago, a cougar had attacked a bike on an urban trail. Animal control had to shoot it. This woman on TV said that a beautiful animal like the cougar had done nothing wrong. That is true. But then she said, 'A person should consider it a great honor that this beautiful creature chose them for its next meal.' I very much disagree with that notion."

"But how did Cooper get here," Bobby asked. "He acts intelligent to some degree, but I can't see him flying a spaceship."

"When I say he came from another worldly realm, I didn't mean from someplace like Mars, Venus, or Alpha Centauri. Your Cooper comes from a different space than ours." The three listeners looked confused. "Sometimes, when the fabric of our space gets stretched too far," the old man continued. "Things like this fellow squeeze through from their space into ours."

"Oh, I get it," Sam said. "Like from another dimension?"

"Or universe," Bobby added.

"Multi-verses," Jeff added, snapping his fingers for emphasis. "So that's where demons come from?"

"Monster is the best word for the myriads of creatures in other spaces. As far as dimensions and universes go, you know more than me."

"Not really," Bobby said. "I don't think anyone fully understands stuff like that."

After another minute of awed silence, Jeff asked, "Grandpa, you said there are many kinds of demons... monsters. What do you mean?"

The old man thought back. "They came decades ago, back in Japan." Absentmindedly, he touched the scar on his face, rubbing it just below the eye. "It started after the end of World War II. Japan was still in the grips of recovery when the openings began to appear. Then, as if hell had opened its doors, everything unimaginable, horrific, and monstrous came into our world."

"Did you know I started training when I was only five? The training included the martial arts, the katana, the staff, archery, and priestly arts of exorcism and spell casting. Under the tutelage of my grandfather, the head of the Maeda Clan at the time, I grew strong and confident. All the young men and women in the Maeda Clan became exorcists and monster slayers." Grandpa's face darkened. "The training was exciting, especially for a young man full of self-importance like I was. I thought it was cool, awesome, or whatever slang you use today. I felt invincible. But then the monsters came. That war ripped all my romantic notions to pieces, replacing it with a bloody, terrifying reality. Many died before we could drive the monsters out. My grandfather and my father, both of whom I thought were invincible, died in that war. Both were honorable men. I miss them terribly."

"Such creatures come in all sizes and shapes," the old man continued. His words became more somber along with his mood. The scar on his face flushed red as he talked. "There are creatures that are nothing more than dangerous animals, much like wild animals you find in this world, but there are also creatures with a degree of intelligence... like Cooper here. I don't know, maybe he is not as intelligent as us, but he is clever and cunning. Most of the monsters I have encountered are aggressive and dangerous..."

Sam started to protest, "But..."

"But Cooper is a true anomaly. But do not assume all Shadow demons will act like this fellow. In my experience, they are killers by nature." Grandpa said, "There are creatures so far above us in power and intelligence that they appear to be gods, but don't be fooled. They are not gods. Some have great civilizations. Some of those civilizations are peaceful, even helpful to humans, but be wary. They can also be capricious and vengeful. Some creatures are beautiful, and others are monstrous and ugly. My father lost his life because he mistook beauty for goodness." The old man sighed. "In the future, the wisest thing for you three to do is to stay away from such things. Such creatures tend to give us little time to decide whether they are friendly."

"But Cooper is already here and needs our help," Sam said. "What should we do?"

"You need to get him back where he belongs as soon as possible."

"But how?"

"There is a hole somewhere that allowed him into this world. It must be near El Palmar since this is where he appeared. You need to find that hole and shove him back through it into his world."

"That's a tall order," Bobby pointed out. "I can't even guess where it might be."

Sam was becoming increasingly anxious. "What will happen to Cooper if he has to stay in our world?"

"He will die, dear girl." Sam put her hand to her mouth. Little Toe reacted as well. "I am sorry. I see no happy ending for Cooper. He doesn't belong here. Sooner or later, one way or another, his presence in this world will lead to his death."

Sam looked into Toe's eyes. "Don't worry, Cooper," she said. "We will do everything possible to get you back home." Toe smiled. At the same time, he let his tongue take an extra-long lick across that wide, lippy smile. "There," Sam blurted out. "Did you see that? He did it again."

"What is that," Grandpa asked.

Jeff explained. "She's freaked out because every time she looks at Cooper, he licks his lips."

"Oh well, that's obvious," the old man said. "He likes you. In fact," the old man studied Toe's expression closer, "I would say he wants to make lovey-dovey with you." Both he and Jeff roared with laughter.

Shocked, Sam pulled her hand away from the amorous creature. Toe's smile faded. He didn't understand, but he sensed that she was angry - no, something else - repulsed. Sadness washed over him. Why had her affection changed so fast?

"Oh, look," Jeff said, mocking her. "Now you've hurt his feelings."

Sam could see that Toe did indeed look hurt. Once again, her heart melted. "Okay then," she said, extending her hand. Toe grabbed her hand and squeezed. "Owe," she snapped at him. "And no funny business, you hear me?"

Toe gently licked her hand. It tasted so wonderful.

"Like that," she added, looking somewhat cross.

Toe didn't understand, so he gave her a sheepish smile and softened his grip.

******

The effects of the magic had gone cold, but Fang knew he had gotten close. He sensed the morning coming. There wouldn't be time to go back to his tunnels. He needed to find a new hiding place to continue his search with the next nightfall. Although the trees and bushes flourished in this residential section of the city, such vegetation could only provide limited shelter during the night. Fang needed to stay out of sight through the day.

Most of the residents in the neighborhood had gone to bed. All the lights were out except for the house at the end of the block. Fang moved closer. The occupants, an elderly couple, were up late. The male sat in one room, captivated by a lighted box hanging on a wall, and the female occupied another part of the dwelling. Seeing no sign of others, Fang climbed over a fence into the backyard. These two individuals would be easy prey. Licking the drool from his fangs, he thought, "And I am hungry."

Chapter 20

THE SLAUGHTERHOUSE

Two days later, a niece checked on her elderly Aunt Edith and Uncle Norman. They hadn't answered her phone calls, and that concerned her. Upon entering the home, she found a slaughterhouse. The niece's scream alerted the neighbors, who called 911. The scene inside the home defied description. The killings were violent to the extreme.

Agent Solinger took immediate jurisdiction over the crime scene. Agents searched the neighborhood but found no other victims. Neighbors up and down the block told the agents that the Pritchetts were the nicest, kindest people they knew. No one could conceive why anyone would want to harm them. As Solinger and Miles surveyed the remains of the two bodies, they wondered which parts belonged to Norman and which to Edith.

The cover story released to the press asserted that a wild animal had attacked the couple. Close to the truth. These wild animals came from another world, and the Eugene Miles Rift had unwittingly brought them here. Not that Miles felt responsible. Freak accidents happen. Besides, no one could have predicted this particular outcome. However, judging from the horrific scene at the Pritchett home, Miles realized they needed to find the two shadowy creatures before the creatures could killed again.

The next day, police found another family slaughtered in their home only half a mile away from the first. A neighbor had heard a lot of loud noises coming from the house the night before. Later the next day, the neighbor got worried. That morning, he hadn't seen any of the usual family routines around the house. It was quiet, too quiet, so he checked on them. The perpetrators had gained entry through a sliding glass door at the rear of the home. The killers had ripped the door frame out of the wall.

This time, a miracle had occurred. The family's youngest child, a seven-year-old boy, survived the ordeal by hiding in a storage closet. The police took the boy to the hospital for evaluation.

Chapter 21

THE AWAKENING

A deep bond had always existed between the Williams and the Thomas families. Over the years, the adults of the two families set aside at least one Friday night a month as a special night. On these nights, they did grown-up stuff like go out to a nice restaurant, have a game night, attend a concert, or play at the university. They even tried bowling for a while, a fun game in an old-school way.

Sam and Bobby didn't mind staying home on these nights. When younger, they stayed with a babysitter at one home or the other while the parents did their thing. Although they no longer needed a babysitter, Sam's little brother still required supervision. So, once Sam reached the appropriate age, she became Kevin's designated babysitter. Of course, now that she was in high school, Friday night activities damaged adult date night plans, except when their parents called a family council meeting. These parents-only meetings always took precedence over school activities. Bobby's sixth sense told him that their parents talked about far more serious matters on those occasions. He was curious, but not enough to make him want to sit through a boring family council with his mom and dad.

Tonight, was one of those nights. The recent animal attacks in town had caused concern. The deadly attacks had everyone in El Palmar on edge.

Because tonight's meeting came at short notice, Bobby and Sam volunteered to babysit Kevin.

"I don't need a babysitter," Kevin argued. "Why can't I stay at home alone."

"No," was all his mom said.

"No? How about this? I could go to a friend's house instead?"

"No?"

"Why not?"

"Because I am the mom, and you are the kid."

"But..."

Mrs. Thomas opened her eyes wide and said, "No." That told Kevin he had pushed it too far.

"Fine," Kevin grumbled.

Sam, who had remained out of the conversation until now, said, "We will have fun, Kevin. You will see."

A defiant Kevin told Sam, "You can't boss me around. You can watch over the house, but not me."

Sensing trouble ahead, Bobby offered Kevin a face-saving solution. "Kevin," Bobby said, "If you promise to cooperate and listen to your sister, I promise to play computer games with you until bedtime."

Kevin paused to think. "The cooler games that you and Sam play?"

Bobby nodded, "Yup."

"Okay."

Mrs. Thomas shook her head and walked away. Their parents left and headed through the backyard to the Williams home.

Bobby worried that the recent attacks had something to do with Cooper. Not that he thought Cooper capable of such terrible acts of violence, but he sensed a connection nonetheless. Bobby had always been a good judge character and felt no evil in Cooper. This fuzzy, non-human was an innocent, kind creature. Yet, tonight brought a nagging uneasiness. An unidentified evil lurked somewhere, and he felt it getting closer.

At 11:00 pm, a reluctant Kevin went upstairs to his room. Sam checked on him later and found him sound asleep. Toe came out of one of his many hiding places. If Kevin woke up or Sam's parents returned home unexpectedly, Toe would run for cover. He could move with exceptional speed and stealth.

Little Toe watched his two friends play games together. Good fortune had brought him to these two. He felt exceptionally fortunate for his relationship with Sam. She was special. He loved her. Love was an uncommon emotion among his kind. It hurt to think he would have to leave her someday soon, but he had accepted his fate. For now, he would spend what time he had with his friends. Bobby and Sam continued to play games, all the time joking, laughing, and taunting each other. The evening melted away.

Around 1:00 am, Sam went back upstairs to check on Kevin. When she returned to the living room, she found Bobby and Cooper staring out the front window.

"What are you looking at," Sam asked as she entered the room.

Bobby didn't answer, nor did he move. A new heaviness filled the room. Something was wrong. Bobby's face and neck dripped with sweat. Cooper leaned forward on his long arms, his back arched. Although her two companions faced away from her, she could see their reflected faces in the window glass. Their ridged expressions implied considerable tension and fear.

"Bobby, what is it?" she asked, sensing his fear. Again, Bobby said nothing. Sam grabbed him by the shoulder and spun him around. "Bobby!" That broke his fixation on the window. "What's wrong?"

"I... I had a weird feeling. Then everything went dark."

"Dark? Did the lights go out?"

"No, no. Not that. I just couldn't see. I saw darkness - only darkness."

Little Toe felt it, too. Panic washed over him. It felt like Far Edge - like Tiarnas. Only one thing explained the darkness he felt. Something from Far Edge had followed him into this world. Another Shadow was nearby. Toe shuttered. If he sensed another Shadow, then no doubt it could feel him. Toe made a whimpering sound that unnerved his human companions.

"We need to close the curtain and turn out the lights," Bobby yelled.

"But why?"

"Just do it. Maybe it won't find us in the dark."

"What won't find us?"

"Do it, please," he said. Bobby pulled the front curtains closed and locked the front door.

Sam turned out all the lights in the living room, running into the hallway and kitchen to get those lights. Then she returned to the front room. The bright front porch light backlit the closed curtain. Toe crouched next to the window; his whimpering turned into a deep growl.

"Cooper, get back," Bobby said. "Come on, buddy, go protect Sam." That got an immediate reaction.

"Must protect Sam," thought Toe.

Toe scooped Sam into his arms and leaped over the chairs, coffee table, and sofa clustered in the middle of the room. He placed her on the floor behind the couch, then jumped back over in front to guard her position with his body.

Bobby backed away from the window. "It's coming." His voice quivered. "Oh crap, it's coming."

"What's coming?"

"Can't you feel that?"

"Feel what?"

"Sam... oh, Sam." Bobby turned to her in a whisper, "It knows we're in here. I should have turned out the porch light."

The light coming through the curtain went dim as something big blocked the light. The two young humans and Little Toe remained motionless, afraid to breathe.

Sam whispered, "What is that?"

"Something... very... very... bad."

The front window exploded. Glass and wood fragments ripped through the curtain. Bobby dove out of the way. Sam screamed. She watched in horror as the curtain material tore from the wall and draped over Broken Fang's colossal shape. Sam screamed as loud as she could and kept on screaming.

Toe bolted into action and leaped onto the massive curtain-draped figure. He began pounding Fang with his fists as hard as possible, but it had little effect on the adversary. Hoping this attack would scare the Shadow away, Toe kept hammering away at the back of the creature's head.

Broken Fang roared angrily. "Get off me, your worthless little imp," he thought.

"Broken Fang? Shadow dust," Toe thought in utter despair.

Fang's replied with seething hate. "Finally, I get to kill you, and there is no one to stop me."

Highly motivated by his resolve to protect Sam, Toe fought fiercely. He wrapped his arms around the hated enemy's neck. Solidifying his hands and arms, he tightened his grip with all his might. To Fang's surprise, Toe choked him with considerable might. He held onto Fang's neck, refusing to let go. The two Shadows struggled, thrashing around the room and destroying everything. Fang finally grabbed a hold of his smaller opponent and threw him into the adjoining dining room. The dining room furniture shattered into pieces. Yanking the curtain fabric off his head and shoulders, Fang stood in defiance. His shoulders scrunched up into the ceiling, breaking the drywall and joists above him. Debris fell to the floor. A terrifying glottal roar left Fang's open mouth. The room shook. Fang saw Sam crouched behind the upturned sofa. He bared the entire length of his two uneven, dangerous fangs.

Sam screamed again. What else could she do?

Bobby recovered and rushed to help her. Fang intercepted his move and backhanded him aside. To Bobby, it felt like a car hit him at thirty miles an hour. Flying across the room, he hit the wall with enough force to leave a dent in the wallboard. The air left his lungs, and he gasped for air. Blood dripped down his face.

"Bobby," Sam screamed through her sobs.

Fang grinned and moved closer, enjoying the act of terrifying her. "You tiny creatures," he thought. "You taste better when you are afraid."

Sam instinctively scooted back, pushing with her legs to escape the monster, until she found the wall behind her. With nowhere else to go, she closed her eyes and put up her hands, extending her arms in front of her in a desperate attempt to push the attacker away.

"Stop," she screamed. "Go away!"

What happened next lasted only seconds, although the world around her seemed to crawl to a stop. The room fell silent. Sam's body tingled. She felt the sharpness of pins and needles in her hands. It hurt. Both hands got warm, then hot, and then burning hot. So hot that Sam feared the room had caught on fire. When she screamed with pain, a loud crack of thunder and a brilliant flash of lightning filled the room. Even though she had closed her eyelids tight, the bright light still dazzled her. Then, all went dark and silent.

Shaken, Sam slowly opened her eyes. The awful creature was gone. She looked to find Bobby. He sat up against the wall to her left, his eyes wide open as he stared at her in shock. She looked in the opposite direction toward Cooper. He also looked at her with big, round eyes.

The back door of the house banged open. Toe vanished out the open front window just as Bobby's and Sam's parents charged into the living room. The lights switched on. The four adults paused, shocked by the aftermath of the attack. The two mothers hurried to their respective children. The two dads took a somber walk through the destruction.

A frightened Sarah Williams looked up from her son, tears in her eyes. "It's happening again. Isn't it, Bill?"

"This seems to confirm what we feared. Still, let's not jump to any conclusions just yet."

Anne Thomas snapped. "Look at this place. A human didn't do this. Something awful attacked our children." She looked at her husband. "Why? We were safe here."

Rich Thomas crouched next to his wife. "Try to keep calm, honey." He spoke to Sam, "How's my little girl? Are you hurt, sweetie?"

"It was so big and scary, Daddy."

"I felt it coming," Bobby exclaimed. There was something outside. I could sense the dark mind. I could feel the anger. I don't know why, but I knew it had come for us. I could feel it."

His mother hugged him hard. "I'm so sorry we didn't get here sooner, Bobby. I'm so sorry."

"Wait," Bobby pushed back from his mother. "What did you mean... *it's happening again?* What is happening again? Has this happened before?"

"Not right now, son," his dad said. Sirens whined in the distance, getting closer. "Someone must have called 911. We don't have much time. What else happened, Bobby?"

Bobby got excited. "Sam... You should have seen her. First everything went slow motion and hazy, then fire shot right out her hands!"

The Thomas's examined Sam's hands. Sure enough, they found the telltale signs of scorching but no actual burns.

"It's too soon for this to happen," Anne said, her voice full of apprehension.

"She is further along than we thought," her husband replied.

Bill said, "It must have been the attack, Rich. Fear is a pretty powerful trigger. Maybe fear awakened her abilities. Bobby's abilities manifested long ago, but this is the first sign from Samantha."

Rich nodded in agreement. "But why was that monster here in the first place? Was it targeting our kids, or was this just bad luck?" He looked at Sam and then Bobby. "What were you two doing tonight?"

"Playing games," Bobby said. "That's all."

"I'm sorry about the house, Mama," Sam cried. It was so big and strong—much bigger than Cooper. Cooper and Bobby tried to stop it, but it was too big and strong."

"Cooper," her mom asked. "Who is Cooper?"

"Cooper feared that monster as much as we did, but he jumped onto its back and fought hard. He tried to protect me."

Then Sam's dad said, "Who is Cooper, Sam? Or is that the wrong question? Maybe I should ask what is Cooper?"

Bill turned to Bobby. "Tell us everything, son."

"Ah... well... Cooper. He is a friendly creature. According to Jeff's grandpa, he's a *kage oni* or a Shadow demon. Anyway, Cooper came to us for help. Honest, I don't know why. We have been helping him until he finds his way back to his world."

The sirens were getting closer. The four dumbfounded adults didn't know what to say.

"Before the police and fire department arrive," Bill Williams said, giving everyone last-minute instructions. "Say nothing of demons or monsters to anyone. Our story is this. Vandals broke into the house and made this mess." He pointed to Bobby and Sam. "Do you two understand? Say nothing about your Cooper until we can be alone as a family." The tone of his voice was clear and sharp.

A sleepy, ten-year-old voice broke through the tension. "What happened to the living room," Kevin asked.

Chapter 22

MORE QUESTIONS THAN ANSWERS

The El Palmar Police Department investigating officers accepted the home invasion story, but the federal agents who arrived later did not. The evening went from the Thomases giving statements to the police about a local crime to relentless interrogations by federal agents. Their identifying badges indicated they came from the Department of Defense. The new interrogators made them start over from the beginning. The feds treated the Thomases like the perpetrators of the attack instead of the victims. The Williams family, who had only come to the police station because Bobby was a witness, quickly became part of the investigation.

The agents kept both families in isolation through the night and into the following day. At one point, they interrogated Bobby and Sam separately, without their parents present. An illegal procedure, but no demanding rights under the law made any difference. These guys worked by a different set of rules. The scariest part of the whole ordeal, the agents didn't say why. Why would the Department of Defense get involved with a home invasion case?

"We were playing games," they told the agents. "Noises outside in the front yard scared us."

Sam told the interviewers, "Bobby got the idea to turn out the lights, hoping the intruders would disappear, but it didn't work."

Bobby told them, "Then somebody crashed through the front window."

Sam added a touch of sentiment. "I was so glad Kevin was upstairs in bed asleep when it happened."

"Could you see any of the intruders," an agent asked.

"All we saw and heard were dark shadows and loud noises," Sam told them. "The intruders broke everything and scared us to death."

"Did the intruders say anything? Did you recognize any voices?"

Bobby explained, "The intruder, or intruders, kept growling like a wild animal, all crazy."

Dr. Miles watched all the interviews from behind glass, trying to understand who these people were. When both Bobby Williams' and Samantha Thomas' names came up in connection with the earlier assaults, he knew this was more than a coincidence. The two separate events, in some way or another, were connected.

"These folks are lying," Miles told the Solinger.

"You think so?"

"Yes. Perhaps they are afraid of sounding crazy."

Miles vowed to get the truth out of those two kids. At this stage of the investigation, he had more questions than answers. Sooner or later, the full truth would emerge.

******

Bobby confessed to Sam, "The whole interrogation was intense but kind of thrilling at the same time."

"Thrilling," Sam replied. "Are you nuts? The whole thing terrified me."

"It's just that bending the truth like we did was easier than I thought. What does that say about my character?"

"I always thought you had a little bad boy in you," Sam said. "This proves it." She laughed.

"You may be right."

"I wouldn't worry too much. I'm sure your honor remains intact."

"I have been wondering about something, Sam."

"Like what?"

"Our parents' initial reaction to the attack the other night makes me wonder if our parents are pros at keeping secrets."

"Did you notice how fast they reached the right conclusion about what happened?"

"I know what you mean. I expected them to be bewildered, but they were amazingly calm for some reason. Why was that?"

"What are they not telling us," Sam said.

Chapter 23

FAMILY SECRETS

The evening of the William and Thomas family's conference arrived. Because the Thomas family was still homeless, they met at the Williams' house for dinner. Kevin happily stayed with a friend for the weekend. The evening's discussion would expose facts he didn't need to know. The two families were unique. They had remained hidden from the outside world for fifteen years, but Bobby and Sam had stumbled on something that threatened their anonymity.

Rich, the group's engineer, had maintained privacy inside both homes. He installed devices to protect any conversation that needed to remain private. They had used this technology many times, especially on those adult-only nights. The devices didn't just jam unwanted surveillance. Jamming their conversation would only raise further suspicion. Instead, the technology used complex algorithms to create a false discussion out of the real one. Any unwanted listeners would get bored with the innocuous conversation spun by the algorithms and go home.

The evening started with a light conversation about work, questions about school, etc. Rich and Anne discussed the remodeling and how they longed for everything to return to normal. Everyone talked about anything and everything except for what concerned them.

"Why are they acting like this," Sam whispered into Bobby's ear. "I thought tonight was about getting answers."

"I don't know, but they are still avoiding the main topic."

"Well, it's weird... and annoying. Should we try to change the subject?"

"I want answers just as bad as you, but I sense an underlying current of frustration, maybe even anger. Let's wait and see where this goes. Besides, don't be in too much of a hurry. I'm pretty sure we are about to get blamed for everything."

"That isn't fair. No one has given us a chance to tell our story yet."

"I know."

"I don't understand it. I suppose it is our fault to some degree, but if we had known, our parents knew about demons. That was a pretty big omission in their parental guidance. That makes this as much their fault as it is ours."

After dinner, everyone helped clear the table. Then Sarah said, "Let's go downstairs to the family room. The kids can play games while we visit."

Rich said, "Bill, you won the last pool game. It's time for a rematch."

"Anytime you're ready."

They followed Sarah downstairs, joking, laughing, and acting as normal as possible. Bobby thought they were acting too normal. It was downright creepy. This conversational tone continued as Bill removed a picture exposing the wall safe. Bobby knew the safe existed. One hid behind a picture in Sam's basement as well. Bill keyed in the code and opened the safe, exposing an LED touch screen. Bill keyed in a second code on the touch screen. He then turned back to the group.

"Okay, we can talk freely now, but even with the blinds closed, use your best poker faces tonight. There are lots of ways to watch us, even through concrete walls. Bobby, grab a board game from the closet and set it on the table. Ladies, you have a seat on the sofa. Rich and I will pretend to play pool."

"I'm not interested in playing games, Dad," Bobby said.

"Bobby," his mother scolded. "Do exactly what your father asks you! We don't have time to explain."

"Well, what game should I get?"

"It doesn't matter, Bobby," his dad barked. "You're just pretending to play while we discuss our present predicament." Bobby's face flushed. He didn't like his dad being so mad all the time.

"Jeez, what's with you guys," he mumbled.

Sarah crossed to Bobby and ran her fingers through his hair. "Just relax and act natural," she reassured him.

Bobby's dad added, "We need you to tell us about the past few weeks and leave nothing out." Then he said, "Our lives may depend on what you say. I'm sorry if that sounds dramatic, but you must understand how serious we are." Bobby nodded and did as told.

"Same for you, Samantha," Rich added while racking the pool balls.

She helped Bobby set up the game *Sorry* on the game table behind the sofa. The irony of picking that particular game would later become clear. The adults took their positions as though a well-rehearsed play was about to begin. The two dads were at the pool table, and the two moms sat next to each other on the sofa. Bobby and Sam sat at the game table. Then, the interrogation began in earnest.

"Do any of your friends know what you've been up to," Bill asked while striking the cue ball.

Bobby didn't relish telling them this. "Jeff has been helping us."

"And his Grandpa Maeda," Sam added.

"Why on earth would you involve Jeff's grandpa?" Bill struck a ball that went off course.

"Jeff told us his grandpa knew more about monsters than anyone else," Bobby replied. "So we went to him for help. At the time, we didn't know our parents could help. And by the way, why do you know about such things?"

"Not now, Bobby," his dad replied. "Why did Jeff think his grandpa could help?"

Sam replied, "When his grandpa was our age, he trained to be an exorcist, slash, monster slayer. That was back when he lived in Japan. Jeff figured he could help us with Cooper."

"Did he know about monsters?"

"No kidding," Bobby answered. "He knew what Cooper was."

"But he nearly killed poor Cooper with a magic spell or something. Jeff stopped him just in time," Sam added. "It was like real magic."

Bill turned to Rich and said, "It appears we need to look into Mr. Maeda and the Maeda family. Now," he said, turning back to Bobby, "tell us about this Cooper."

Bobby and Sam gave them the details of their recent activities, each adding to what the other had forgotten. They started at the beginning, the night of Bobby's attack on the beach, and ended with the monster's attack.

Anne Thomas shook her head in disbelief at the whole crazy tale. "I have a hard time believing this Cooper creature is as friendly as you say, considering the earlier attacks."

"And what about the recent deaths," Sarah asked.

"That wasn't Cooper," Sam defended.

"As far as my assault and the other earlier attacks," Bobby noted, "that was Cooper, but he felt so sorry for what he did. Don't forget, none of us were seriously hurt."

"How do you know he felt sorry?"

"I just sensed it."

"Cooper isn't evil," Sam said.

"How can you know," Sarah asked.

"Because Bobby says so," Sam answered. "Besides, he is so gentle. Except when I was asleep or at school, he was seldom out of my sight. Sometimes, he sleeps on my floor, in the attic, or outside in the backyard."

Her mom exploded. "That thing sleeps in my house and you said nothing to me?" She turned to Sarah angrily. "How did they even pull this off without us knowing?"

"I'm sorry I didn't tell you, mama, but Cooper, he's like a great big puppy-dog."

"Demons are not pets. They are monsters," Sam's mom snapped, losing her temper again.

Rich moved behind his wife and put his hand on her shoulder. "Keep calm. Let's just get at the truth."

She smiled and said, "Sam, I have never been so..." That unfinished statement and the forced smile were disturbing. Sam looked away from her mom's angry stare.

"Why are you so mad," Sam said, trying to hold back the tears. "We just wanted to help Cooper. He needed our help, so we helped him."

"Cooper attached himself to Sam," Bobby added in Sam's defense. "We don't know why. He's always calmer when Sam is around. Grandpa Maeda said he thought Cooper had a crush on her," he added nervously.

"Bobby," Sam whispered. "TMI."

"What," Anne exploded again. "That alone sounds dangerous, Sam! Don't you understand? Creatures like your Cooper are dangerous. He could have killed you!"

"No, he wouldn't," Bobby said, raising his voice. "I don't know how I know, but I do. I don't know why he came to find me after first attacking me, but he did. Cooper came to us because he needed help. I believe he even wanted my forgiveness." Bobby sensed the skepticism in the room. "Yes, forgiveness." Bobby barked as the adrenaline flowed into his bloodstream. "I know Cooper is not capable of being evil. As sure as I knew something terrifying and monstrous hid in the darkness outside the front window at the Thomas' house. I could feel that big monster's presence. With Cooper, I sense no darkness at all."

Bill looked at Rich. These two had been friends and colleagues for a long time, and in that time, they had seen the impossible become possible.

"It seems the boy's sixth sense is getting more refined," Bill said.

"Now both of their abilities have awoken," Rich added.

"What abilities," Sam yelled. "What are you talking about?"

"Where is this Cooper now," Bill asked, ignoring Sam's question.

"We don't know," Bobby replied. "After the attack, when you guys showed up, he vanished. We haven't seen him since."

"How about Jeffrey? Would Cooper have gone to him?"

"Jeff would have said something by now," Bobby answered.

"You said you showed Cooper to Mr. Maeda. What did he tell you?"

"He called Cooper a Shadow demon," Bobby answered. "It was funny. When we introduced Cooper to Grandpa Maeda, he became alarmed."

Sam said, "But when he realized Cooper wasn't a threat, he thought Cooper was cute. Which he is, by the way."

"He told us that not all demons and monsters are evil, that friendly monsters exist somewhere."

"Then he said that Cooper didn't belong here and that we need to get him back to his world right away or... he will die." Emotion flowed over Sam for a brief moment.

"The question is, where does Cooper belong," Rich asked. "How did he get into this world in the first place?"

"It doesn't belong anywhere," Anne said. "Monsters like this killed my family."

After contemplating, Bill said, "Something tells me that these two Shadow demons, or whatever they are, are why the Department of Defence got involved. I bet they know how the monsters got into our world."

"What about the second monster," Rich asked the kids.

"We know nothing about it," Bobby said.

"They probably came to this world the same way," Bill replied. Either separately or together. The real question is why." He turned his back to the kids and took another pool shot. "So, you believe Cooper came to you for help... to return to his home world?"

"Cooper seems afraid of this world," Bobby said.

"But he was nowhere near as afraid as he was of that other monster," Sam added. "It had to be more than twice his size. Remember, Cooper risked his life to protect us."

"Then Sam did that thing," Bobby said, looking at Sam. "How did you do that, Sam?"

"I'm intrigued by Mr. Maeda," Rich said while he took a shot at the pool balls. "My study of this world's history had given me the impression that monster activity was rare. Most of the stories I read were cultural myths - nothing of substance. Perhaps I was wrong about that. We should talk to Mr. Maeda as soon as possible."

"At your service," came a voice from the stairs. Startled, they turned to see an elderly Japanese man standing beside Jeffrey. "Sorry to just drop in unannounced, but from what my grandson has told me, you need me here tonight."

"Honest," an embarrassed Jeff said. "We knocked first."

Chapter 24

THE LONELY HIDING PLACE

Little Toe found his way to the unpopulated coastal hills east of town. The heavily wooded area provided lots of places for him to hide. He chose a small cave embedded in a rock cliff. The opening was big enough for him to squeeze through, which meant the larger Broken Fang couldn't get to him. The cave opened up further inside. That gave him some maneuvering room and a little more comfort. Settling down against the back wall, Toe faced the opening. Here, he would wait.

Even though several days had passed since the unfortunate encounter with Fang, Toe still shuddered from the experience. Of all the Shadows who could have followed him into this world, why did it have to be Fang? The meanest monster Tiarnas had ever spawned—a bully who had an unnatural hatred of Toe. Of course, the feeling was mutual. Toe couldn't think of anything he had done to inspire such hatred. Once that monster Fang decided to torment you, it never ended. Fang never tired of beating Toe to near death. Back in Tiarnas, Fire Claws had protected Toe, but here in this world, Toe would have to defend himself.

"Fang must have discovered my rupture." That worried Toe. "If Fang discovered it, did he tell anyone else? Did he come here alone, or did Magistrate Fire Claws send him?" After the surprise attack, Toe had no doubt that Fang had come to this world to kill him.

"Even if I survive Fang," Toe thought, "I still am a dead Shadow. When I go home, I will face harsh punishment for not telling Fire Claws about the rupture in my cave - a death sentence for sure. Now, my new friends are in grave danger as well."

Toe remembered almost losing control when he first tasted human energy. Fang saw no need for control. The brute would kill without hesitation. He had no conscience. It was his nature.

"This mess is my fault."

Only one solution remained. Toe had to kill Broken Fang. There was no other outcome that ensured his friends' safety. His friends had shown so much bravery during the attack. Sam, his favorite, turned out to be a witch with enough power to protect herself. Although she seemed as surprised by her power as he was, maybe she didn't know how to use her magic. Still, it gave him some hope she would be okay.

Toe thought with much regret, "I was weak." He looked at his hands. "I was just too weak."

A strong bond had grown between Little Toe and Sam. This new relationship had become more important to him than life itself.

"From this day forward," he vowed. "I will do all I can to serve Sam - my special little witch. I may die trying, but my honor ordains it."

Chapter 25

MR. MAEDA'S WISDOM

They offered Mr. Maeda a place to sit, but he wasn't interested in sitting yet. Instead, he walked up to each adult in the room. The old man looked into each of their eyes, then took their hands and examined their palms and fingertips. He even raised his hands to his nose and sniffed.

"Grandpa, what are you doing," Jeff squawked.

When he got to Bill, he said, "Who are you people? Where do you come from?"

This peculiar old fellow had Bill at a loss for words. "I am Bill Williams, Bobby's dad. Sitting on the sofa is his mother and Sam's mother…"

"That's not what I meant," Mr. Maeda said, cutting him off. "You are not from this world. I cannot be sure you are even human."

"Grandpa! What the heck," Jeff scolded.

"What is your grandpa talking about, Jeff," Bobby said.

"I have no idea," Jeff said with a shrug. "Grandpa, don't be so rude."

Mr. Maeda ignored his grandson and waved Jeff away irritated with the interruption. He continued, "So please, tell me. Where are you from."

They all exchanged bewildered glances. "I assure you," Bill replied. "We are just ordinary people."

"That is not true." The old man pointed his finger at Bill's face. "Ordinary isn't a word I would use to describe any of you people."

"Grandpa, please," Jeff protested. "This is weird, even by my standards."

"Two Shadow demons have appeared in this world. That is a terrible development. It has put your kids in grave danger more than once already."

"We are aware of the danger, Mr. Maeda," Bill replied.

"Are you; are these two aware?" He pointed at Bobby and Sam. "They don't seem to understand the danger. If we can't stop it, that Shadow demon will attack again. Yet, as far as I can tell, your son and daughter are unprepared. They both have hidden powers, yet they know nothing of them. Why is that? Why have you left them so defenseless?"

"We are well prepared to protect them from any danger. We called this family meeting tonight to discuss just that."

"If I am to help you and your kids, and believe me, you will need my help, then you need to trust me. So, please, tell me everything, starting with who you are."

Rich looked over at Bill and shrugged. "Whatever you think, Bill."

Telling their secret to anyone risked exposure. Still, after a short pause, Bill decided to do just that.

"To look at us, you would think we were just like any other average member of the human race. Considering where we come from, we are remarkably similar. We are humanoid, but we are not Homosapien."

Three young adults responded with varying degrees of shock.

"What?"

"Dad?"

"You're kidding me."

Bobby and Sam's faces froze in disbelief. Jeff smiled as though he had just won the lottery. Mr. Maeda got so excited he hopped from one foot to the other, they had just which confirmed what he suspected. He knew they were different from when he first met Sam and Bobby.

"What world do you come from then?"

"Technically, asking which universe we come from is more accurate. Our world parallels yours along with countless other worlds. Our two worlds are similar in many ways, yet different in ways I can't describe. Parallel worlds tend to be significantly different. Evolution creates considerable variations in plants, animals, and humanoids. Diversity spans from the barely noticeable to the profoundly alien."

"But your world is like Earth."

"Again, I said similar," Bill replied. "Our world, like yours, is the third planet from our sun. It is similar in size, atmosphere, land, water mass, etc. One notable difference is the system's fourth planet. Unlike Mars, our fourth planet is habitable. That gave the incentive to pursue space technology at a faster rate than here on Earth.

Jeff looked puzzled. "Is it true," he asked, that our decisions can create new universes? One I went to college, and the other I didn't. One where I'm a doctor, and in the other, I'm a NEET hiding in my room watching anime. I guess I am asking, is there another me in your world?"

"No."

"Oh. I hoped the other Jeff made a better show of it than me."

Bill Williams smiled as he explained. "Timelines and universes are not changed so easily. I'm afraid our individual decisions just aren't important enough to bring about change in the universe. Such things have little to no impact on the future. Many believe the universe is a place of chaos. World and universe-changing events have to be of a sufficient magnitude to initiate change. A large asteroid hits the Earth with enough power to cause an extinction event that, will result in change. So, on one Earth, the asteroid glances off the atmosphere and goes on its merry way. That world has dinosaurs but no people. In another world, the asteroid hits with devastating results. This world has people but no dinosaurs. Evolution, however, is a wild card. Anything can and will happen. That is why we are not exactly human, and there are not multiple Jeffs out there."

"But why did you come to Earth?" Mr. Maeda moved to the chair offered to him earlier and sat.

Sarah answered, "We were looking for a safe place."

"This world is anything but safe. There must be more interesting worlds than this one."

Rich answered, "While traveling from one universe to another looking for a new home, we discovered your world would best suit our needs. The primary reason for leaving home was to hide and protect Sam and Bobby. Here on the North American continent, in the United States of America, is an excellent place to hide."

"Protect them from what, exactly?"

"A terrible war raging on our world," Bill said. "A war against beings we called the Odan." Mr. Maeda sat up straight in his chair. Bill continued, "The war with these Odan began over seventy-five years ago. None of us were born yet. The Odan conquest had spread from one universe to another. Wherever they found a stable dimensional rift, they used it. They attacked and conquered every unlucky world in their path. Our world was one of those worlds."

"Why Odan," Maeda asked.

"The name comes from our mythology. It refers to the ancient god of misfortune. Not that we believed in our old myths, but we certainly encountered a great misfortune when the Odan conquest landed on our front steps. I suspect the war is still raging somewhere.

"I see," the old man said.

Sarah spoke: "We severed all connections with our former world, including our families. We can't go back—at least, not until our children have grown strong enough to fight."

Anne wiped away tears that began filling her eyes. "We don't even know if our world still exists." She took Sarah's hand and squeezed.

"Fate," Sarah said, "has thrown our two families together. Now, all we have is each other. We now call this world our home."

"We will do everything possible to keep monsters like the Odan from coming to this world," Bill told him.

"These Odan," Grandpa said. "Were they demons, monsters, evil spirits, gods of the underworld? There are many other kinds of evil out there?"

"During an effort to translate the enemy's language," Bill explained. "We discovered the Odan considered themselves a superior race. The literal translation of their true name meant *the gods of man*."

"They were not gods," Anne said. "But they sure acted like they were."

"I will ask the Maeda Clan to investigate this possible threat," Mr. Maeda said. "But for now, these Shadow demons are our immediate concern."

Mr. Maeda got up and crossed to Sam. As he had the adults earlier, he took her hands and looked into her eyes. "It was you who did the magic I felt."

"I... I don't know," Sam said. "This is so confusing."

"Magic," Bobby asked.

"Defensive magic. I felt a short but powerful burst of energy."

"It wasn't against Cooper," Sam added. "It was the other Shadow thing."

"I know, dear girl." He turned to Bobby and examined his hands and eyes. Then, holding Bobby's hand, he reached over and took Sam's hand. "Yes, I feel it now. These two kids have a magical bond - magically coupled in some way. Am I right?" Both Sam and Bobby flushed with embarrassment. Neither understood what he meant, but it sounded way too personal.

"Considering all that has happened, the boy must have the gift of discernment. A discerner can sense the presence of evil and judge between good and evil. That is a wonderful ability, young man - beneficial. That would explain why the first Shadow creature, Cooper, came to you for help. He sensed your ability to understand his true nature."

"The girl is a guardian. She can protect goodness and conquer evil." He lifted Sam's chin. "You seem to have the protective instincts. Again, that must be why Cooper has attached himself to you. You make him feel safe. I suspect someday you will become a great warrior, young lady."

"I don't want to be a warrior, great or otherwise," Sam said. "I just want to be a regular girl."

"I Know. I hope you get to stay young for a long time. I lost my youth much too soon. Life is hard, but you are stronger than you think. Of that, I am sure."

"Where did you learn about these things," Rich asked.

"As a child, I learned spells and the powers needed to defeat monsters and demons. Around five hundred years ago, spiritual creatures of light called kami befriended my ancestors. They gave my clan the ancient knowledge of magic and its many uses. The Maeda Clan swore to defend Japan from all evil. They have done so even to this very day. After World War II, the Clan joined a worldwide effort to combat evil.

"There are others like the Maeda Clan," Rich asked.

"Yes. A few. Not enough, I think. All are as secretive as the Maedas."

"Still, it's a big world."

"Fortunately, for better or worse, technology has made the world a little smaller. Nowadays, we hunt monsters using computers and that *interface* thing."

"It's called the internet, Grandpa," Jeff smirked.

"Whatever," the old man replied. "Nowadays, the Clan's forces and their allies secretly stand ready to defend worldwide. Being a direct Maeda descendant to train with the Clan is also no longer necessary. The world is far too big for such archaic rules. The world, in general, knows little of our mission."

"Then you understand why we must keep our lives secret," Bill said. "If the enemy discovered the existence of our children, the Odan would find us and decimate this world looking for us. Thankfully, we had another planet to flee to. You don't have that option. Let us hope the war stays away from here."

"Maybe too late," Grandpa corrected. "We didn't fight your Odan, but I am a survivor of Earth's first war with such monsters. I was a young man still in my training when the first monsters appeared in Japan. We don't know why the creatures chose my homeland as a place for the invasion. Perhaps the creatures wanted to test the Clan's resolve. We were fortunate to have help from the *kami* and defeated the invading monsters. They retreated, but not before taking the lives of my grandfather and my father. Many good warriors died." Mr. Maeda closed his eyes and sighed. "I trained to fight these creatures from childhood, but how was I supposed to fight something I had only seen as drawings in ancient books? The real monsters were not what I expected. They were smarter, more cunning, and unbelievably bloodthirsty. Those creatures terrified me."

"I am sorry for your losses," Bill said. "I... we have felt that same fear. How were we to fight something we didn't even know existed? The Odan came out of nowhere. Unlike you, we had no drawings in books, no ancient records, and no *kami* to favor us. Even with our superior technology, we couldn't defeat them. Nation after nation fell. Those monsters tore our world apart. Fortunately, no stable rifts ever opened on the second planet in our system. Millions of refugees fled their home planet and took refuge on the second. The monsters didn't follow because they didn't know how, or maybe because they couldn't. I don't know. That gave our scientists and military leaders time to learn how to fight back. The six of us are part of that effort. We traveled to this world to protect Sam and Bobby and the coupling magic they possessed."

"Forgive my arrogance," the old man said. Facing them, he gave a deep bow. Then, standing up straight, he said, "Well then, let us join together to end this new threat before it is too late. First, we find Cooper and send him home. Then we find the second Shadow demon and kill it. We cannot allow it to leave this world alive!"

Chapter 26

IDENTITY CRISIS

Bobby paced back and forth in heated frustration. Sam sat alone, not wanting to look at or talk to anyone. Jeff still had a big smile on his face. It gave him immeasurable delight to know his two best friends were, in fact, aliens. It gave him a whole new perspective on the issue of undocumented immigrants.

"Bobby," his mom said. "Please stop pacing. It's annoying."

"Oh, excuse me," he snapped at his mom with unintended sharpness.

"Don't speak to your mother in that tone," his dad reprimanded.

"I just found out my life has been a lie, so what tone would you like?"

"Your life has not been a lie," his mom said. "Please, sit down so we can discuss this."

"We just found out that we aren't exactly human. Even under everyday circumstances, I have personal identity issues, but this just knocked those issues out of the ballpark. Sorry, I hate sports metaphors. How about this? My identity is a spacecraft that overshot the moon, leaving it lost in space with no chance of recovery. This is an identity crisis on a galactic scale.

"Don't be ridiculous," his dad said.

"When someone asks me, 'So, Bobby, where do you come from?' They expect an answer like California, Arizona, or maybe even

Canada. But what do I say? I come from an alternate universe. Have you ever been there? My parents said it was nice until monsters took over. But what the hell? No place is perfect, right?"

His dad said, "That is the most ridiculous…"

Bobby's mom interrupted. "We are the same people and the same family. This revelation changes nothing."

Sarah approached Bobby. She was about to run her fingers through his hair, but Bobby pulled away.

Sam's mom went to Sam and said, "Everything will be okay, honey."

Bobby replied, "It's bad enough being our school's resident geeks, but Sam and I are now the resident freaks!"

"Don't you think you're a little over dramatic," his dad interjected.

"No, I don't, dad! This is crazy! What else haven't you told us? Sam and I have sat here eating humble pie while you yelled at us for not telling you about Cooper. Well, what about you? You sure withheld some pretty vital information from us - life-changing information. How many other lies have you told us over the last sixteen years?"

"No one has lied to you, Bobby," his dad explained. "Not telling you about our former lives… that was for your protection. Besides, no one at school, except for Jeffrey, knows about this. No one will treat you like a freak."

Bobby scoffed. "Knowing that Jeff is the only one who knows isn't that comforting."

Jeff protested, "Hey, what's that supposed to mean?"

"Jeff thinks this is wicked cool. He would love to shout it from the school's rooftop."

"That would be unfortunate," Grandpa Maeda said, frowning at his grandson. Bill and Rich Thomas exchanged worried glances. "Jeff, you must swear on the honor of your ancestors that you will take this secret to your grave."

"Come on, Bobby," Jeff said. "You know me. I would never betray your trust."

Bobby breathed deeply to calm his emotions, "I know... sorry, Jeff."

Jeff noticed the anxious look between Mr. Williams and Mr. Thomas. "I understand how dangerous this is for you guys. I mean, you won't need to kill me or anything."

Rich laughed, "Now that was over dramatic. We're refugees from another world, Jeffrey, not the Russian mafia."

Jeff smiled sheepishly, "Anyway, all this will take time to get used to."

Anne tried one more time to offer some comforting words. "Listen, you two. We are your parents. We love you both more than anything in this world. Even if we have to give up our lives here, we will protect you. We did it before; we'll do it again."

"I don't want you to have to give up anything for me," Sam said, breaking her long silence. "Things are crazy enough. I couldn't bear being the reason we lost our homes and our lives here in El Palmar."

Her mom replied, "Whatever it takes to keep you safe. Do you understand?"

Sam turned to Bobby and said, "There is that, Bobby. We are loved."

"Yeah, you're right. We are loved."

Chapter 27

BACK TO THE THINK TANK

Bobby's and Sam's parents gave strict orders to refrain from discussing the recent events anywhere except downstairs in an electronic shielded environment. That wasn't just unreasonable; it was impossible. Since their fifth birthday, they had discussed every life crisis, big or small, while swinging together on the swings at the park. This life-changing event was rated the biggest crisis either of them had ever faced. They needed to cope the only way they knew, in the park on the swings.

Sam looked around to ensure no one lurked nearby. Even the black car down the street had left. Sam whispered, "What should we do next?"

Bobby sighed, "I don't know."

"I'm worried about Cooper. I want to look for him and bring him back home."

"Yeah, maybe that should be our next move. Besides, doing anything will be better than sitting at home hiding. You know what I mean?"

"But where do we start?"

"What was it that Grandpa Maeda called me... a discerner?"

"I wonder what he meant by that?"

"Last night, I looked the word up for greater detail on its meaning. To discern means to understand and to differentiate. But I like this phrase: *to identify the true nature of something.*"

"But what does that have to do with..." She lowered her voice. "Magic and magical couplings?"

"Think about it. Haven't I always been able to sense the thoughts and motives of others? That means my sixth sense is a magical gift. Maybe I can use it to find Cooper."

"Okay then, discern away."

"Let's swing on it." They both started swinging.

After a few minutes, Bobby said, "I suppose we need to consider how a Shadow de..." He caught the D-word in his mouth just in time. Nervous, Bobby looked around. He couldn't see anyone. He whispered even quieter, "How would our new pet Shadow react under stress."

"How can we know that?"

"Cooper's actions and emotions have been pretty straightforward so far. I have a better sense of what he likes and needs. Cooper thinks and reasons much like we do."

"I suppose so."

"What would you say Cooper's frame of mind was before he ran away?"

"That big... you know what, sure scared Cooper, but he didn't run from the fight."

"You're right. It didn't run until our parents arrived. Cooper understood the situation as well as we did."

"So, he didn't run because of fear. He only left when it was necessary to get out of sight. Of course, he might worry that the, you know what, will come after him again."

"Or come after us if Cooper does return."

"Yeah."

"What would Cooper consider a safe place to hide? If not back to your bedroom, then where?"

Sam thought for a minute, then whispered an observation. "If it were me and I couldn't go back to the safety of my home, I would look for someplace that reminded me of home. That would make me feel better."

"Except, we don't know what his home looks like."

Sam sighed. "Let's think some more." They pushed back and let the swings go.

Once Bobby was high enough, he leaned back in the swing and closed his eyes, letting the soothing sensation wash over him. He felt the blood rushing out of his head as he swung backward and then rushing back again as he swung forward. This movement caused a temporary, yet euphoric, lightheadedness. It cleared his mind of distractions.

Bobby thought shadow demons were dark creatures, dark shadows on a night. Cooper's natural environment might be a dark place. But where could Cooper find such an environment in El Palmar? Maybe an old abandoned building. Homeless people hide in a place like that. After his first encounters with humans, Cooper avoided any more contact with people except us.

Bobby continued to swing without saying a word. Cooper needs a dark, out-of-sight, and defensible place. If the giant Shadow demon went after him, he would need a place that would not just hide him but hide his scent as well—a place big enough for Cooper but too small for his bigger enemy, a place with only one small entrance. It would need to be away from people, so it would probably be out of town somewhere.

Bobby opened his eyes and dug in his heels to stop his swing. "Sam, are there any caves around here?"

Chapter 28

THE SEARCH FOR COOPER

Bobby's sixth sense came alive. "Wait," he said. They all stopped. "I feel something."

"What," Sam asked.

"I don't know, just something."

Jeff asked, looking around nervously. "Plant, animal, or... Shadow demon?

"Emotion."

"Emotion," Sam said.

"I feel fear... but I also feel a lot of anger."

"Are you talking about an animal, like a mountain lion, or do you mean Cooper?"

"I've never actually felt an animal's emotions before. Maybe it's Cooper. The anger feels dark and malignant. That's probably the other Shadow."

They all looked around nervously.

"Holy Crap," Jeff gasped. "I forgot about that other Shadow creature. Maybe we should get out of here."

The local library kept a collection of topographical trail maps detailing the wooded areas surrounding El Palmar. The maps led them to all the known cave sites frequented by local hikers and high school and college partiers. But they soon realized that none of these sites fit Bobby's established profile. They also discovered that dozens more unmarked small caves must exist for every cave marked on the map. So, every day after school, the three friends drove up the hills and searched until just before dark.

Hiking all over the hillside with that other monster still on the loose represented a clear and present danger, but they tried to ignore that reality. They were on a rescue mission to find Cooper. That belief had pushed away any common sense. No parent had sanctioned this trek through the woods. Asking for permission would have resulted in another order to do nothing, which was unacceptable, so they hadn't asked.

Sam looked around. She never wanted to face the big Shadow again.

"The fear feels more desperate. My best guess. It's Cooper."

"Poor Cooper, he must feel pretty desperate by now," Sam said.

"The anger feels distant, but the fear is somewhere close."

Jeff said, "Are you sure it's not me you're sensing? I'm so scared. I'm about to wet my pants."

Bobby said, "I can feel both yours and Sam's fear. I'm a little scared, too, but this is not you guys. Let's keep going. I need to get closer."

Sam felt a wave of panic. A flashback of the bigger Shadow played out in her mind. Searching the woods for Cooper had initially seemed like such a great idea, but now she wasn't so sure.

"Bobby," she said, "maybe Jeffrey is right. We should call it a day. Sorry, but if the big Shadow is nearby..."

"I know, Sam," Bobby reassured her. "If we can hold on a bit longer, we are close to finding Cooper. I'll follow the fear."

"Are you sure about that," Jeff asked, reluctant to move.

"Would you like to walk toward the malignant anger instead," Bobby quipped. Jeff shook his head hard. "Aren't you supposed to be from a long line of brave samurai warriors?"

"Monks and priests, not samurai," he replied. "Big difference... I think."

With some reluctance, they followed Bobby. Sam grabbed Bobby's shirt and stayed close behind him. The fear he sensed got stronger with every step.

Bobby stopped. "It's strongest here. My heart's beating faster. Instead of continuing on the well-worn trail, Bobby headed straight into the hillside's scrub brush.

"This way," he said, holding onto branches to keep his balance.

"Whoa, dude," Jeff squawked. "Where are you going?"

"Follow me. Watch your step. There's loose gravel under the brush." Bobby climbed up the slope. Sam followed. Jeff shrugged and followed Sam. The landscape leveled out at the top of the hill. After hiking for another half, a mile, they ran into a rocky cliff about thirty feet high.

"What do we do now," Jeff asked, out of breath from the climb.

"Shh," Sam said. "He's thinking."

Bobby closed his eyes and concentrated. "This way," he said again as he turned and continued to the right. The wall of rocks led them to a triangular opening. It was about five feet tall at the upper point and three feet wide at the base. He looked into the dark opening. "This is it. In there."

"I'm not going in there," Jeff protested.

"No, I mean, he's in there."

"Who, Cooper," Sam asked. Bobby nodded.

"No kidding," Jeff exclaimed.

Sam gazed into the cave. "Cooper, this is Sam. Bobby and Jeffrey are here, too." She looked up at Bobby.

"He's in there. I'm sure of it now."

"That was amazing, dude," Jeff said. "That was like a psychic superpower."

"I've always had it, but it has gotten stronger for some reason."

"You've always had it?"

"You know, my sixth sense thing. I use it all the time. That's why I always win when we play games."

"Hey... that's like cheating. And here I thought it was because you were better than me."

"What can I say? My sixth sense makes me unbeatable."

Sam spoke to Little Toe in a soft and calm voice. "You can come out now, honey. We are here to help you." She took a few steps into the opening and extended her hand. "Come out, Cooper."

A dark, fuzzy hand reached out of the darkness and took her hand. She pulled, and Toe gave in to her. He emerged out of the cave. His green eyes looked tired and weak. Sam put her arms around the Shadow's head and held him tight. "Thank you," she said. "Thank you for trying to protect me."

"He looks kinda sick," Jeff observed.

"I doubt he has eaten much," Bobby said. "Come to think of it, what does he eat?"

"Oh yeah, I have a theory about that," Sam said. He licks our skin. Remember what happened to you? You ended up covered in his gooey drool. He licks my hands all the time. It's gross, but it always makes him feel better."

Bobby said, "True, he must have licked every inch of me. I still don't see how that gives him nourishment."

"This may sound far out, but could he be feeding on our... living energy? After he attacked you, you slept for two days, right? He must have sucked the energy right out of you. That would explain why you couldn't wake up."

"Maybe..."

Sam took off her jacket and extended her bare arms. "Cooper, lick my hands and arms." Toe looked at her. He recognized her gesture of kindness. Starting at her fingertips, he licked her arms and shoulders. Now, your turn, boys." Both boys did the same. When Toe finished, he looked a little better but still not his usual self. "He needs more," she said. Both of you take off your shirts."

"What? Why me," asked Jeff.

"Because I can't take mine off in front of boys, dummy. Will you just do it?"

"This is going to be so weird," Jeff said. Bobby agreed, but they did as Sam requested. When Toe finished, he looked much better.

"He needs more," Bobby said. "Turn around, Sam. Jeff and I will take off our pants."

"Oh, man," Jeff groaned. "No peeking, Sam." Sam flushed and turned around quickly.

When Little Toe finished, he looked so much better. The boys dressed.

"I feel so gross," Jeff whined.

Bobby said, "Let's go home before we lose the light."

The foursome made their way back to the main trail, headed toward the trailhead, where they parked the car. Toe stopped along the way to pick wildflowers to eat. Wildflowers had been his only source of nourishment for days.

"It sure is quiet today," Jeff observed, Considering it's Saturday and all. There are usually more people around."

"I'm glad it was a quiet day," Sam replied with a big smile. "It's a perfect day for a rescue mission."

Bobby walked into the open parking lot at the trailhead to see if the coast was clear. The others stayed hidden, so he retreated.

"Something doesn't feel right," Bobby whispered.

"Should we wait until it's dark," Sam asked.

"No."

"Do you think it's the other Shadow demon," Jeff asked.

"Maybe."

Sam shuddered. The cold fall air had crept into the shaded woods.

"How do we get Cooper in the car," Jeff asked. "Will he even fit?

"Put down the back seats and let him squeeze in through the hatchback door. He'll fit," Sam insisted. It's amazing what he can do when he goes all misty."

"But where will we sit," Jeff protested.

Bobby suggested, "Sam, take Cooper to your house. Jeff and I can walk home."

Jeff didn't like the idea of walking all the way home. "Come back and pick us up if you can."

"I'm nervous about taking Cooper by myself. What if he freaks out on me?"

"As long as he is with you, he will be okay."

"Yeah. Just take Cooper and go," Jeff said.

"Come on, Jeff. Let's go open the car doors. The quicker this is over, the better."

Sam passed the keys to Bobby and watched the boys enter the open. At the car, they looked around one more time. Bobby raised the hatchback while Jeff laid down the back seats. They waved to Sam once the car was ready.

Sam pulled Toe toward the open lot. "Come on. It's time to go."

Sam and Cooper hurried out into the open. An unexpected loud crack filled the air. A second crack followed. Sam screamed and jumped. Instinctively, Toe pushed her to the ground and took a defensive position over her, but it was too late. Two large, heavy nets landed with a thud covering them both. A few seconds later, a silent helicopter swooped in and landed nearby. Two agents grabbed Bobby and Jeff from behind and pushed them to the ground. A dozen more agents circled Little Toe and Sam with weapons raised and ready. Dr. Miles stepped out of the helicopter and walked up to the edge of the net.

When Toe looked up to see the arrogant male standing close by, he wanted to lash out and tear the male apart. Something snapped inside Toe. He wasn't afraid anymore, not of this male or his armed warriors. Despite the heavy nets, Toe pushed up and let out a menacing roar like an angry grizzly bear. The sound echoed through the surrounding hills. Toe's eyes blazed with anger, and he lunged at Dr. Miles.

Miles fell back onto the ground. He said, red-faced and gasping for breath, "I don't think the nets will contain this monster for long." Miles hurried to his feet. If this was the smaller of the two Shadows, how would they catch the second and larger one? He shuttered at that thought.

Miles and the agents had been watching and following these kids for days. It amazed Miles how the girl coaxed that beast out of the cave. Although it looked like a monster, it responded to her with gentleness. That thought gave him an idea.

"The girl," he ordered. "Aim your weapons at the girl!" The agents did so.

Even though they had Bobby's face pressed into the dirt, he yelled, "Sam!"

"You guys can't do this," Jeff insisted. "Let us go."

Miles looked the creature in the eyes and said, "Shoot at her if the creature does that again." The agents looked at Miles in disbelief. "You can hit the ground next to her, but it has to believe we will hurt her," he explained. "Point your weapons at her! Threaten the girl."

Toe saw the image in the bad male's mind. "He wants to hurt Sam. Unless... unless I stop fighting." He whirled around as best he could under the heavy nets. Sure enough, all their weapons pointed at Sam. Terror showed in her eyes, making Toe even angrier. Thoughts of escape swirled through his mind, but only one solution made sense. He didn't dare fight back. For Sam's sake, he would surrender. "The bullies of this world," he thought, "are just as ruthless as they are in mine."

Toe turned back, looked Miles straight in the eyes, and sent a vivid message. "Hurt Sam, and I will kill you first!" Then he sat beside Sam, his back straight, his eyes proud and defiant. "I surrender to protect Sam, but this is not over," he thought. "Better to live to fight another day." He fixed his blazing green eyes on the man who just become his newest enemy.

Chapter 29

RESCUE MISSION NUMBER TWO

Rich Thomas, Bill Williams, and Mr. Maeda stood in an alleyway across the street from a mundane concrete and glass office building in downtown San Diego. The sign outside read, *Department of Federal Contracts and Business Affairs.* The men assumed that the Department of Federal Contracts and Business Affairs did far more than the name implied. In this case, somewhere inside this building, DOD agents held at least two of their three missing teenagers in custody.

When the two families fled their home world, they brought advanced knowledge and technology that didn't exist in this world. Magi-tech fussed with magic and technology to make weapons to counter the power of enemy magic. Such things had ensured their survival for many years. As refugees, they also knew that any overt use of magi-tech might draw unwanted attention. Long ago they had adopted rules of conduct regarding their situation. Rule number one was never to call undue attention to yourself or your family. Rich and Bill were about to call attention to themselves, but they couldn't avoid it. Today was a rescue mission.

They planned on breaking two other vital rules: act according to this world's definition of normal and never propagate unearthly technologies. They had made these rules for a wise purpose, but someone had allowed two monsters to cross into this world. Those creatures had wreaked havoc in El Palmar. When the DOD abducted their children, they realized rules were just rules. But family was everything.

Mr. Maeda listened as Rich explained how the magi-tech worked. He asked, "Do we disappear?"

"No, not disappear," Rich replied. "More like unseen."

"What is the difference?"

"As far as I know, no mortal being can become invisible. We can, however, become unseen. with this device." Rich held up a large wristwatch the size of a cell phone strapped to his lower left arm. "People will see us, but with this device, they will forget they saw us instantly."

"I see. It's a Jedi mind trick." The old man chuckled.

Rich continued adjusting the settings on his large wristwatch. "Jedi? Is that Japanese? What does it mean?"

"It's from *Star Wars*. You know, the Jedi knights and the force."

"Oh, I think I've heard of that. Isn't Star Wars an old movie? The kids said something about it. *'To boldly go where no one has gone before.'*"

Mr. Maeda sighed. "Never mind. I guess it was before your time."

"Sorry. Little time to watch movies."

"Does the device require a spell?"

"Yes and no. Primarily, it's just good old-fashioned technology. Magi-tech has magic embedded inside. Magic tends to make everything work better, but I don't have to cast the spell. The technology does that for me."

"I don't know that much about technology. I don't even have a computer. I do, however, know a thing or two about spells."

Rich handed Mr. Maeda a wristband. "Here, put this on, and don't lose it."

Mr. Maeda put the band on his wrist, and it tightened in place. "What purpose does the wristband serve?"

Rich showed Mr. Maeda the screen on his device. "We want others to forget they saw us, but we want to see each other. The green dots on the screen are the three of us. My device, yours, and Bill's wristbands will keep us connected."

"Oh, I see. What are the two red dots?"

"That is Sam and Bobby inside the building."

"I hope we find Jeffrey with them."

Bill said, "If Bobby and Sam are there, so is Jeffrey."

"Okay," Rich said. "Let's see if we can get them out of this place."

Rich touched his screen, and the air around the three men trembled. They stepped out onto the main sidewalk. Mr. Maeda found himself in the direct path of a young couple. Mesmerized by the magical cloaking technology, the unaware couple almost walked straight into Mr. Maeda. Bill caught Maeda by the arm and moved him out of the way.

"Oh, excuse me," Mr. Maeda said politely.

"What," said the young man.

"What's that," said the young woman.

"I'm sorry," the man said back.

"Why," she asked playfully.

"I..." He laughed. "I can't remember."

"Now you sound guilty. What are you up to?"

"Honest. Nothing." They laughed. Then, they shrugged off a strange feeling and walked away without further comment.

Bill whispered to Mr. Maeda, "Stay close and avoid contact with others. They can't walk around you if they can't see you."

"I understand."

The directory inside the building listed several other offices. The United States Department of Federal Contracts and Business Affairs occupied the first and second floors, but another listing read: U.S. *Federal Offices, Basement Level 2.*

Rich said, "I am guessing we go down. Secret rooms are always in the basement."

Bill said. "They like hiding in a hole in the ground."

"I can't wait to say *we come in peace. Take us to your leader,*" Rich said with a broad grin. Mr. Maeda gave a hearty laugh. "So, you know an old science fiction reference like that, but you've never heard of the Jedi and the force. Remarkable."

Chapter 30

KIDS IN CAPTIVITY

Dr. Miles opened the door and entered the room. He sat down at the table across from the three bedraggled teenagers. "I am Dr. Eugene Miles from the Center for Interdimensional Physics. I would like to have a little chat with you three. But first, would you like something to drink?"

Jeff answered, "That would be great. I'm starving, too. Can we get something to eat?"

"That's right, you must be hungry after sleeping on the floor. After answering a few questions, I will ensure you get something to eat." Miles hoped sleep deprivation and empty stomachs would entice the teens to cooperate. Miles got up and opened the door a crack. "Get some drinks for these kids," he told the guards.

"Yes, sir."

The feds had brought them to this location blindfolded. They had no idea where they had ended up. It was in a city. They could hear the traffic noises along the way. The interrogation room had no windows. So, there was no way to get their bearings. The last time they saw Cooper, the agents had forced him inside a big black armored truck and hauled him away to who knows where.

"Please, sir," Bobby said, trying not to make things worse. "We just want to go home,"

"I will take you home when I am satisfied you have told me everything you know about the two creatures."

"What about our parents?" Sam protested. You can't question us without our parents' consent."

"Yet, here we are. Look, this will go easier and faster if you cooperate."

Sam barked in defiance. "I want my mom and dad. I'm not saying anything until they're here."

Miles raised his voice. "Isn't that precious? The little princess wants her mommy and daddy."

Shocked and offended, Sam's mouth fell open. No one, except her dad, had ever called her a princess.

"Until I get answers," Miles said, "you won't see anyone but me and the guard outside this door. Whether it takes a day, a week, or a year, that is up to you."

"You can't do that," Bobby said. "There are laws."

"Not for me, young man. I'm not here to read you your rights. You buried yourselves up to your necks in a major national security incident. At present, you have no rights. So, let's get started, shall we?" The three prisoners sat back in their chairs. Miles had sufficiently scared them. "I want to know what you thought you were doing. Why help such dangerous creatures escape capture?"

"You got it all wrong," Bobby said.

"Oh, is that so?"

"We only helped Cooper. Besides, since when is helping a defenseless animal a crime?"

"Cooper?"

"That's what we named him," Jeff said.

Miles raised one eyebrow, "I wouldn't call these creatures defenseless. The death count has risen since the first creature appeared in this world. You, Mr. Williams, were its first victim. If you had told the authorities what you knew, we could have stopped the creature before it went on a killing spree. Those deaths are on your heads, kiddos. I had to deal with the carnage left in the wake of these creatures' killing spree. What I saw sickened me. Maybe I should force you to look at the bodies or what's left of them? Force you to face the consequences of your actions."

Jeff choked. "We've done nothing wrong." He looked to Bobby. "We haven't... have we?"

"No, we haven't," Bobby replied.

"Cooper killed no one," Sam said. "That was the other Shadow demon, the big one. We almost died the night it attacked us. It ran away, and we've not seen it since." Sam folded her arms and turned away. "So typical. Blaming teenagers for everything. It's so unfair."

"Unfair? How typically adolescent of you."

"Why are you treating us like criminals," Sam yelped. "Bobby and I are the victims here. I couldn't sleep for almost two weeks after that attack. I still have nightmares."

"If Cooper hadn't been there...," Bobby said.

Sam interrupted, "Cooper wouldn't hurt anyone. He's harmless and sweet!"

Miles rubbed his chin in thought. "You called it a Shadow demon. That's an interesting term." Miles relaxed his stern expression. He had gotten them to open up. "The one we captured. That was Cooper?"

"Yes. Cooper."

"You know, your Cooper didn't look harmless to me. I am sure it wanted to kill me."

"That was because you attacked me," Sam exclaimed. "Cooper only wanted to protect me."

"Why would a 'Shadow demon,' as you called it, want to protect you?"

Jeff laughed, "Oh, that's because..." Sam glared at Jeff, so he shut up fast.

"I don't know," Sam said, returning to Miles. "For some reason, he is calm around me—unless someone attacks me." She glared at Dr. Miles.

Miles thought these kids were beyond intriguing. "A minute ago, you said the bigger demon attacked you, and your new demon friend jumped in to save you?"

"That's right," she said.

"So, no vandals. You lied to federal officials when they interviewed you."

"We didn't lie," Sam said. "We told you exactly what happened. We just left out the part about the demon."

Bobby decided it was time to make peace before Sam blew a fuse. "Look, Doctor... uh..."

"Miles."

"Dr. Mile, Sir. That big one is a monster. It terrified Cooper as much as it did us. Still, even knowing how dangerous it was, Cooper jumped into the fight. He risked his own life for us."

Sam teared up. "Please, Dr. Miles. What have you done with Cooper? Please don't hurt him."

Bobby said, "He just wants to go back to his home world, but we don't even know how he got here in the first place. Can you do anything to get him back to where he belongs?"

Dr. Miles remained quiet, marveling at the incorrigible teens. They looked at him with such innocent eyes. The creature they captured remained vital to them for sure. "Why call the creatures Shadow Demons," he asked.

"Because that's what they are," Jeff said.

"And why do you know that?"

"Because my grandpa told me."

Miles laughed out loud. Profoundly amused and amazed, he decided to continue this line of questioning. "Okay, I'll bite. Why does your grandpa know what these things are?"

Jeff knew he had given too much information. "What if these guys go after my grandpa," he mumbled. "I have such a big mouth." He looked to Bobby for help.

Bobby shrugged. "May as well tell him about your grandpa."

"Well, my Grandpa Maeda is, or used to be, a slayer of such supernatural creatures. It was a long time ago, back in Japan."

"Wow, your story keeps getting better," Miles said sarcastically. We've got two demons, and now we have a monster slash demon slayer."

Missing the sarcasm, Jeff continued. Yeah, it's pretty cool stuff. I used to think most of Grandpa's stories were just a game he played to keep me entertained, but then along comes Cooper, a real demon. Turns out, it's true. Grandpa lived and trained at the Maeda Clan training facility on Mount Utatsu in Japan. He was a young man our age when he encountered his first real monster. That war killed half of his family. He doesn't say much about it, though. It's pretty awful stuff."

This kid's kooky story fascinated Miles. The boy believes his grandpa was some kind of protector against the supernatural. "So," Miles continued. "According to your grandpa, this isn't the first time a couple of creatures came to this world to cause trouble."

"A couple?" Jeff mocked. "More like a horde of every monster you can imagine. Like I said, half of his family died fighting in that war. If you must know, it isn't only my Grandpa. Bobby and..." Bobby kicked Jeff under the table to get him to stop talking. "Ow," he hissed at Bobby.

"Look, this is what we have learned so far," Bobby said. "Cooper needs to return to where he came from as soon as possible, or he will die. The other Shadow demon isn't like Cooper. It's pure evil. Jeff's grandpa said we need to kill it. We cannot allow it to leave this world alive."

"The big creature is still out there somewhere," Miles said. "Do you know where it might be?" The three teenagers shook their heads. Dr. Miles' phone chirped.

"Yes," he answered. "I see." He looked at the kids. "I'll be right there." He got up and left the room without explanation.

Jeff jumped up. "Let's get out of here."

"We're not going anywhere," Bobby said.

"He didn't believe us, did he," Sam sighed.

"I guess not," Bobby replied.

"Wow," Jeff said. "We are screwed?"

"No. When our parents find out where we are and why," Bobby said. "Then we will be screwed."

"Miles will call our parents, won't he," Sam said.

Jeff looked worried, too. "What if they don't? What if they have no intention of letting us go? What if they just want us to disappear?"

"Don't go freaky on me," Bobby told him. "I don't care what Dr. Miles says. Real life has rules and laws. We are underage. They have to call our parents. We just need to wait until our folks come and get us."

******

Miles followed the long corridor to the last door, where a guard waited.

"How did they get in here," Miles asked.

"We don't know. I heard voices coming from the room. When I checked, the three just sat there like they owned the place. Then one of them says, 'We come in peace. Take us to your leader.' Can you believe that?"

Miles opened the door to find the three men sitting at a table. "Well, what have we here," he said as he entered a room. "I understand you just walked right in without anyone stopping you. I am astounded."

"I do apologize for the unannounced visit," Bill said.

"I see. I am Dr. Eugene Miles."

"Yes, we know who you are, Dr. Miles," Bill replied.

"In that case, I guess further introductions aren't necessary. I am somewhat acquainted with both of you. So, what brings the Williams and Thomas Clans leaders here today?"

"We are here for my grandson... and their son and daughter," Mr. Maeda barked.

"And who is this old codger?"

"This is Mr. Maeda, Jeffrey Sasaki's grandfather," Bill said.

"Of the Maeda Clan," Mr. Maeda retorted. Rich snickered. This old guy amused him.

Miles eyed the old man. "What makes you think your three missing teenagers are here?"

Rich looked at his wrist gadget. "Sam and Bobby are here for sure. They are in a room at the other end of this hallway."

"We just need confirmation that Jeffrey is with them," Bill said. Miles' expression changed with the rise of an eyebrow, enough to show they had gotten his attention.

Miles nodded. "The boy is here too."

"Thank you," Bill said. "Dr. Miles, we are also here to discuss a matter of utmost urgency. We are already short on time, so if you could hear us out, we would greatly appreciate it."

Miles frowned. "If you make it brief."

"But first, we want to release our kids into our custody."

"In due time. All three are safe and unharmed, but please understand your kids are in considerable trouble."

"I can't conceive why you would say that. Anyway, perhaps we could make a deal."

"A deal?"

"You don't know it yet, but you need our help. Let our kids go. In return, we will help you with your Shadow demon problem."

"Demon problem, huh? Interesting." Miles leaned forward. "Look. Those three kids have answers. I know they do. But instead of straight, honest answers, I got crazy yarns about monsters, demons, and demon slayer grandpas." He looked at Mr. Maeda. "I assume that is you. Their story is quite amusing."

"You didn't believe them," Bill asked.

"Well... I suppose Shadow Demons describes these creatures well. Even I call them Shadows. I would prefer a more scientific term, but until I find something better, Shadow Creatures will do. Your kids believe what they told me is true, but they are just kids. But you, Mr. Williams, are a physicist, a man of science. Are you telling me that you believe in such things?"

"Yes," Bill replied.

"Why?"

"It's a long story. Let's leave it at, I believe."

"Ludicrous. These creatures are mere animals."

"Whales and elephants are animals. Yet, they have complex social structures and the ability to communicate. Wonderful creatures. I assume you have captured the Shadow Demon the kids call Cooper?"

"Yes. Thanks to your kids. They led us right to it."

"I see - so much for listening to parents. I guess it shouldn't surprise us. They are resourceful kids."

Rich join the conversation. "Forgive me, Dr. Miles, but I don't think you understand what you are dealing with here?"

"We are in uncharted territory. I know these creatures are an unknown species and are as dangerous as any wild animal. Well, we have a lot more to learn."

Mr. Maeda couldn't hold back his disdain. "How many more people will die before you know something useful, Dr. Miles? We have come here to warn you. You do not have time to dilly-dally. The killings will not stop just because you captured Cooper. Cooper is not the dangerous one."

"The jury is still out on that."

"The second Shadow is far more dangerous. It is as bloodthirsty a demon as I've ever encountered. You must kill it."

"Dr. Miles, let me get to the point," Bill said. "You have been experimenting with interdimensional rifts - a matter of public record. But something must have gone wrong." Miles stared back, saying nothing. "I know this because you now have two creatures that do not belong here. You made a terrible mistake allowing those demons into this world."

Miles protested again. "Demons. My..."

"Call them what you want, Dr. Miles," Bill said. "It still boils down to the fact that you let them into this world. Correct your mistake before things get any worse."

"To be fair, we had no idea something like this could happen."

"Judging from the mayhem and destruction left in its path, you will not capture the second creature as easily as the first. Close the interdimensional rift those demons came through, and this will end." Miles shifted uncomfortably. "You can close the rift, can't you, Dr. Miles?"

"That is classified information."

Bill looked to Rich, more concerned than ever, "Dr. Miles, if that rift is still open, things are worse than we thought. Close it before it is too late."

"Too late for what?" Miles' frustration showed. "Look, we have always wondered if life existed somewhere other than Earth. Now we know it does. Sorry, Mr. Maeda. Killing these two creatures is not an option. They are far too valuable. We intend to capture and study both."

"That is a dangerous notion, Dr. Miles," Maeda said.

"This discovery will change the world."

"How did you plan to contain a creature you know nothing about," Rich asked.

"Classified."

"Where is Cooper?"

"Classified."

"Miles, you reckless bastard," Rich said. "The second demon nearly killed our kids. It has already killed several more people. How can you in good conscience take such a risk."

"Indeed, how can I?" Miles said. "I have asked myself that question a lot. I believe that all research into the unknown has risks. It is how we learn. We take risks. We must look deep into the darkest places to discover what hides there."

"Yes," Rich barked back, "but you might want to prepare yourself in case something comes out of that dark place and bites your head off."

Miles lost his composure. "I want answers." He slammed his hands hard on the table. "Real scientific, non-supernatural answers. You say you can help. Prove it before I call in the guards and have you arrested. I warn you. I want science facts. Otherwise, the Department of Defence will throw you in jail for the rest of your insane lives."

"Alright then," Bill replied. Here it is." The room had a large, double-paneled dry-erase board. Bill moved to the board, picked up a black marker, and began writing. When he finished, his equations filled both boards and continued onto the adjacent wall.

"This should look familiar," Bill said. "Are you following?" Miles said nothing. "Look closer, Dr. Miles." He circled a specific section of the equation. "This is where I believe you went wrong." Bill stepped aside to let the good doctor think.

Miles went to the board to examine the equation. He followed it, line by line, mumbling to himself as he went. He underlined a section here and there.

"To be fair," Bill said. "Other scientists have stumbled over this same problem. So, at least you made an honest mistake. Unfortunately, your mistake turned deadly. You just opened a rift to an inhabited, hostile world."

"Of course," Miles said. "I see it now." Dumbfounded, he turned to Bill. "How do you know this? Who are you? I should already know you if you know this, but I don't. Why don't I know you?"

"I began studying interdimensional science long ago," Bill replied. "While you are a pioneer in this field, Rich and I have studied under men and women who have worked on this problem longer than you can imagine."

"That is impossible." He looked at the board again. Yet, this man had provided him with an astounding solution. "Where have you been hiding?"

Bill replied, "Sorry, we cannot answer that question. Secrets are secret for a reason."

"If you trust us," Rich said, "we can put your rift program back on track with better safety protocols in place. It's the only way to avoid another invasion."

"I am sorry. I can't accept the idea of monsters and demons."

Bill said. "It doesn't matter if you accept it or not. Allowing those two creatures into this world was a mistake that can never happen again."

"Why come to me now? Why not a year ago or two years ago," Miles asked.

"We have offered our help now. Just take our offer."

"What do you want?"

"We agree to stay as long as needed to help you fix this problem. We only ask that you let our kids go home. They innocently stumbled over your screw-up. They are not your enemy, Doctor, and neither are we."

Chapter 31

THE ESCAPE

Broken Fang had watched in pure frustration as the DoD agents put the object of his mission into a black truck and drove away. Then, a black SUV holding the little witch left soon afterward. That witch had attacked him with powerful magic. He had focused all his attention on Little Toe that night, so he hadn't sensed the witch. That left him unprotected. Fang's mind swelled with insane hatred because the little witch had wounded him. Hatred fueled an ever-growing desire for revenge. This situation forced him to return to Tiarnas empty-handed. Fortunately, the news of this energy-rich world would redeem him. He would then return to this world with reinforcements.

"There is still time to get my revenge," he reminded himself. "I may have lost this opportunity, but another will arise. While the Shadow Empire rapes this world, I will find the witch and get my vengeance."

Late, around midnight, Fang made his move toward the rupture. Quick and silent, he eliminated the surrounding lights. Before anyone could report that something strange had happened, Fang grabbed the guards one by one, sometimes two at a time. Over the next thirty minutes, the guards on patrol disappeared. He scattered their broken bodies in treetops, on rooftops, and in dumpsters in the alleyways behind buildings. No one would realize what happened until he escaped through the rift.

With the threat of the outside guards gone, Fang climbed to the roof of the HGC building. He needed time to think. Not knowing how many guards remained inside, entering through any of the main entrances seemed unwise. He required an alternate place of entry. On the roof, he pulled apart one of several ventilation boxes. The box covered a large opening leading directly inside. The opening proved inadequate for his needs.

Contemplating all tactical options, Fang thought, "If I make the opening larger, it will make too much noise and lose the element of surprise. Then again," he thought further. "I do have the advantage of strength and speed. They won't expect me to come crashing down from above."

Fang smiled as he realized that sudden loud noises and lots of falling debris would confuse the enforcers, catching them off guard. With that thought, Fang jumped into action. In one bold move, he ripped the air vent open wider. The metal moaned and screeched as it bent and scraped. Debris fell to the floor.

"What was that," a security guard yelled, looking up at the ceiling. "It sounds like the whole roof is about to cave in." He waved to a guard near the exit doors. "You, go check it out."

A guard left to investigate. He couldn't see anything from ground level, so he rounded the building and found the roof access ladder. He climbed it.

Fang now had a view of the space below. As expected, more guards patrolled the inside area, but only two stood near the rupture. Fang thought, "I will take those two with me." The Shadow tore away more of the roofing around the air vent. His last move was not elegant. Jumping about fifteen feet straight up, he slammed his extra hardened body into the opening. It gave way with an ear-shattering bang.

The guards below yelled out as debris fell and bounced in all directions. The confused humans fell back, hesitating precious seconds as Fang's enormous figure dropped to the floor and charged at the rift. Fang grabbed the two guards in his path and dove into his world. No one had a chance even to raise a weapon against him.

Back on Tiarnas, Fang got to his feet. Fire Claws and his gang had been busy removing the surrounding rock. Fang turned back for a glimpse of the other world. Then he lifted the two limp human bodies like trophies and gave a roar that every Shadow in Far Edge must have heard.

Chapter 32

FROM BAD TO WORSE

Guards escorted them to a room with cots, blankets, and a change of clothing. The beds gave the detainees at least some level of comfort—not home, but survivable. After a shower and something to eat, everyone felt better. They weren't in a prison, but the guards controlled their every move, making them feel like prisoners.

That night Bobby got the courage to start asking questions. "Will they let us go home? I mean, soon?"

"Soon. Our agreement with Dr. Miles requires you to tell him everything you know about your Shadow demon friend.

"His name is Cooper," Sam insisted.

"Yes, Cooper."

"After they release you three, Mr. Thomas and I will continue to help resolve this situation."

"Mr. Maeda will take you home when that time comes," Rich said.

"But Daddy, what will happen to you," Sam asked.

"Don't worry. We have no reason to doubt Dr. Miles' word. As long as we honor our end of the bargain, I believe he will honor his."

Neither Rich nor Bill wanted to cause any further worry, but Dr. Miles was the least of their concerns. The Department of Defense hadn't agreed to anything yet. With such a wild card in play, anything could happen. They hoped for the best but would be content with the current status quo.

"Let's all get some sleep," Bill suggested. They all settled down for the night in less-than-comfortable conditions.

The following day, after breakfast, two guards led the six detainees to a large meeting room. Dr. Miles and several other individuals waited for them at a large table. Other than Dr. Miles, no familiar faces looked back at them. Miles sat in the first chair on the right side of the table. Six unoccupied chairs spanned the end of the table in front of them. In the other chairs sat five civilians wearing either plain close or suits. Eight more individuals wore military uniforms. One of them had five stars prominently displayed on his collar. Dr. Miles invited the detainees to sit in the vacant chairs.

Bobby's sixth sense surveyed the room. Not a single friend sat at the table besides his family and friends—particularly the one with stars attached to his collar. The General felt exceedingly grumpy. A general animosity weighed heavy in the room. Dr. Miles smiled, but even that wasn't real.

General Bates spoke first. "At the insistence of Dr. Miles, I will not throw you into prison. Not yet, at any rate. You have convinced Miles that he needs your help. I am not convinced. I trust Dr. Miles. No doubt he has his reasons for wanting you here today. So, I will set aside my objections for the time being."

Bobby sensed the lie. "He's lying," he whispered to his dad.

"I know. Keep quiet. I appreciate your concerns, General," Bill said. "I assure you that not only can we help you solve this immediate problem, but we can help Dr. Miles proceed with his rift research without a repeat of this Shadow invasion."

The General grunted. "I feel compelled to doubt your claims. I also doubt your motives. You come here out of nowhere. There are no records connecting either you or Mr. Thomas with rift research. In fact, except for the last few years, the background check revealed nothing about you or your family. I find that quite unusual, gentlemen."

"A fire destroyed our vital records," Bill explained. That was the truth. "Our previous employers insisted on keeping our work secret," That was true enough.

"Then perhaps you could give me the name of that employer."

"Sorry. That information is still highly classified."

"Who do you think you are talking to, Williams? Nothing is above my security clearance. Nothing."

"Well... this is."

"Bull crap. Besides, if your words are true, why are you sharing them with us now?"

"Well, as you know, things have gotten out of hand. Although we are not at liberty to reveal the name of our former employer, the present situation has become too urgent to ignore. I believe this requires a degree of disclosure."

One of the scientists at the table spoke. "I did some checking as well." The man shuffled through a pile of papers. "No one in rift research has ever heard of you. No university records giving degrees to Bill or William Williams. The same for Rich, or Richard Thomas. Everything about you is nothing but smoke and mirrors."

General Bates added, "The same is true for military intelligence and the CIA. You simply popped into existence fifteen years ago. You'd have to be deep black ops spooks to stay that well-hidden."

"As you say," Bill stated. "We're spooks - of some kind."

"All crap," the General said, slamming his fist on the table.

"Now, now," Miles interrupted. "For time's sake, put aside your concerns about where these men came from." Miles picked up a folder from the table in front of him. "By now, you should have read the folder's contents before you. Mr. Williams and Mr. Thomas are here to help us solve our problem, which we haven't solved on our own. I don't know why these men know as much as they do about rift research. They just do. As incredible as it sounds, they may even know more than me."

"As for our motives, General," Bill said. "We want our families safe. In return for our help, we ask for assurances. When the is over, you leave us and our families alone. We do not want or need any further compensation. I understand why you don't trust us, but this crisis threatens this world in ways you cannot conceive. We must trust each other to save this world from what is coming."

"Save the world," someone said. "From what? What is coming?"

"I am telling you, as long as that rift stays open, a bloody confrontation, maybe even war, with these Shadow demons remains a real possibility."

Everyone laughed. A choir of scientists replied, "Demons? Nonsense! Are we in the dark ages? Ludicrous. Maybe you know a couple of witches who can help us fight the monsters." This brought a big laugh.

"You have no idea how much danger this world is in right now, and I sincerely hope you never have to find out. We may sound like *chicken little* doomsayers, but I warn you in the soberest terms that the sky will fall if we do not successfully close that rift." More sarcastic grumblings came from the group.

The General didn't like these men. He couldn't explain it, but his gut told him they hid deep, dark secrets that could prove dangerous to the country. They knew the science and could help Dr. Miles, but at what cost? It had to be more than leaving them alone. Everyone wants something. Sooner or later, these guys would show their true colors. Once he exposed their secrets, he would leave them alone inside a solitary cell at Leavenworth. The General turned to Dr. Miles and nodded.

Then he added, "Fortunately, the immediate problem solved itself."

"What," Miles asked. "Has something happened?"

"The two creatures that came through the rift," the General said confidently. "The one, as you already know, is safely secured. Last night, the second creature escaped back through the rift. It went home. Hallelujah. It isn't my problem anymore. The Department of Defense will take care of the fallout. You guys take care of the rift."

One officer beside him nodded and said, "We have already released the cover story, General."

"The second creature escaped," Miles questioned. "When did this happen?"

"Yes, at 0200 hours this morning," the General replied. "Now get that God-forsaken rift closed and end this." He said this as though he could order the universe to obey his will.

"Grandpa," Jeff said. "Didn't you say we needed to stop the other demon from returning to its world?"

"Yes, I did," the old man replied, shaking his head in disbelief. "This is bad news... terrible news indeed... an apocalyptic kind of bad."

Miles's face darkened. "Mr. Maeda, explain."

"Do you think those two creatures were the only Shadow demons in existence," Mr. Maeda barked. "Are you people that foolish?" Again, more grumbling. "There will be millions more of them. Right now, an enthusiastic demon is telling his friends about our world."

"Superstition and myths," someone said. "Sure, there might be more of these creatures, but they are only animals. They would need a language and a highly developed civilization capable of making weapons and organizing armies to be any threat to us."

"If we can close the rift, it's over," Miles said. "Right?"

"IF... If you can close that rift," the old man said. "Let me ask the General. What exactly happened this morning? How many of your guards died?"

The General said nothing. He looked down to avoid eye contact.

"General? How many?" Miles said, pushing for the answer.

"Twenty-one," the General said. A look of shock spread across every nonmilitary face.

"How many were on duty last night," Miles asked.

"Twenty-five were in or around the HGC building at the time."

"Only four survived?"

Mr. Maeda continued, "That was just one Shadow demon against twenty-five well-trained human soldiers. I am even willing to bet that your men didn't even get a shot at it." The stone-faced General gave no reply.

"It got away without a scratch," Miles asked in shock.

"That monster has learned to defend itself since coming to this world. Now, if you will, consider the mayhem it caused during its brief visit. In addition, it has developed a taste for human blood. Humans may be the best meal he has had in years." He glared at the people sitting at the table. "If we don't close that rift soon, it will return. This time, it will return with a whole army of Shadow demons. How will you fare against hundreds of a thousand, maybe millions of these creatures?"

One military man said, "The day the second creature came through the rift, the guards wounded it. If it bleeds, it can die."

"Yes, you can kill a Shadow," Maeda told them. "Your weapons could make a mess of one individual creature, but this one got smarter. Last night's escape proves that. I would say it got a lot smarter from the number of dead this morning. It will share what it has learned with others."

Another of the uniformed officers added his opinion. "There is just one rift. It is only big enough for one creature at a time. We have a huge tactical advantage even if you say is true. We will slaughter them like cattle."

Maeda laughed, "Didn't I tell you how many creatures will come through the rift?"

Bill added, "We have no hard facts telling us what these Shadow demons can or cannot do."

Mr. Maeda said, "None of those monsters will be afraid to die. Life and death mean nothing to such creatures. They may even worship a glorious death. If the rift stays open long enough, the demons will keep coming until they overwhelm your forces. In the end, with your superior power, you will win - probably. But how many humans will have died by then?"

"We have the other demon... creature," someone said. "It might be prudent to learn more about the creatures' biology... find the best way to kill them."

"No," Sam yelled out. "Cooper is not like the other one. Don't you dare hurt him."

"My daughter has a point," Rich said. "Cooper has been friendly thus far. It may be willing to be our ally. I wouldn't dissect the only individual who can fight his kind."

"He will help us," Sam said. "I know he will."

Miles was fascinated by the girl's feelings toward the creature. "You have a strong connection with the creature," he said.

"Yes, sir. He fought to protect me, and I will fight to protect him." There was laughter around the table.

Rich leaned to her ear and whispered, "Be careful honey, don't reveal too much." Sam said nothing more, but her glare remained fixed on the person who had threatened Cooper. Her hands grew hot and glowed ever so much. She hid them under the table. She whispered to her dad, "My hands. What do I do?"

He looked and saw what was happening. "Breathe slow. Try to calm down."

She nodded. "Right. Think happy thoughts." Closing her eyes, she concentrated on breathing slowly.

Miles saw the girl's hands before she hid then under them under the table. What had he just seen? He watched the girl. She intrigued him. The way she sat up in her chair and spoke with so much conviction. That was more than teen bravado. Another tingle tickled the back of his mind. This girl was special, or maybe unique, was a better word. That rang true of them all. Hidden behind every word were secrets. His hungry mind itched to know more.

Chapter 33

THE CAGE

The next day, Dr. Miles pulled Sam and her dad aside. "I was wondering," he said. "This afternoon, I'm going to the research complex where we are holding Sam's creature. If possible, I would like you two to accompany me."

"No kidding," Sam said, all smiles.

Overhearing, Bobby asked, "Can I come too?"

Jeff caught on. "If you're going to see Cooper, I'm in."

"Just a minute," Sam's father cautioned everyone. Sam started to protest, but he raised his hand to quiet her. "Let's find out what this is about before we agree." He turned to Miles. "Why do you want us to go?"

"Curiosity. That's all. I'm intrigued by the bond between your daughter and the creature. I called Dr. McLeod, the head xeno biologist at the facility, and told him about your daughter. He wants to meet her. We both want to see if the creature will react to her."

"Where is this place," Rich asked. "How long will it take?"

"Daddy, please," Sam insisted. "I need to see Cooper. He needs me."

"Maybe an hour and a half by helicopter," Miles said. "If we left right after lunch, we could return before dinner."

"Please, Daddy."

Rich looked at Sam. "All right, then." Sam jumped with excitement.

"What about Jeff and I," Bobby said.

"Yeah," Jeff said.

"Sorry, son," said Bill Williams. "I can't let you go anywhere without me."

Mr. Maeda added, "I agree with Mr. Williams, Jeffrey."

"But it's important for Bobby to come too," Sam insisted.

"What about me," Jeff said.

"And Jeff, but especially Bobby."

"Why is that," Miles probed.

"I need Bobby's help in understanding how Cooper feels."

"And you can't do that by yourself?"

"We're a coupling. It takes both of us."

Miles chuckled. "What exactly is a coupling?"

Rich covered Sam's indiscretion, "It's just a teenage thing. That's enough about that, Sam."

Sam flushed with embarrassment. "Sorry," she said more to her dad than Dr. Miles. But to her dad's exasperation, she kept on trying to explain. "Uh... It's kind of hard to explain. Bobby and I have always done things together. We think a lot alike. That's what I mean. Besides, Cooper will want to know how we are doing. If both Bobby and Jeff are there, it will cheer Cooper up." She glanced at her dad. He rolled his eyes, which meant he was more annoyed than angry.

They did it again, Miles thought. A coupling? A teenage thing? The awkward explanation and worried glances indicated a much deeper, hidden meaning.

"Okay. If that is what you want, why don't you all come and get away from this boring place? Everyone be ready to go right after lunch, or I leave without you."

******

The helicopter flew over a small Air Force base in the middle of California's nowhere desert. It wasn't an impressive place, just an old airfield with many old buildings. A few hangars, warehouses, and other buildings remained as remnants of its former glory days. If it ever had any glory days. The place showed no signs of recent activity. No base housing or other amenities usually present on an active air base. They saw no other personnel except the two soldiers waiting for them as the helicopter landed.

The guards led Miles and his entourage into a nearby hangar. The hanger was huge and empty.

"Is anybody home," Jeff hollered. His words echoed around the open space. "Guess not."

"Any personnel on this base," Bill asked.

"I understand that from mid-1950 to 1980, this was a busy place," Miles explained. "But then the base became redundant. It has other uses now."

The guards escorted them across the hanger to a tall, roll-up garage door leading to a spacious vestibule and freight elevator. The elevator doors were big enough to drive a truck through. One guard swiped his security card over the card reader beside the elevator. The top half slid up, and the bottom half slid down. The doors revealed a typical large freight elevator with metal and wood side walls and concrete flooring. They entered, and the doors closed behind them.

The guard pushed the B, and the car descended. The ride down seemed much longer than it should have been. Finally, the doors opened to an entirely different world. The massive tunnel went as far as the group could see to the right and the left. "Follow me," the guard said.

The guard led to an area used as a security check station like at airports.

"Please empty your pockets and remove watches, jewelry, and phones. Then remove your shoes." Each party member, including Dr. Miles, underwent the full body scanner. The guard led them to curtained cubicles. "Inside the cubicles, you will find orange jumpsuits sizes small to extra-large. Please remove all outer clothing and put on the jumpsuits. I'll be waiting in the hall when you're ready." When they came out of the cubicles, they looked like prisoners from the county jail on a work detail.

Jeff laughed at Sam. "You look like a little girl playing dress up in your dad's work overalls."

Sam said, "The small jumpers were too small around the chest, and the next size up was too large everywhere. I had to roll up the legs and sleeves."

The guards led them to the final check station with a thick glass wall and a double sliding glass door.

Bobby asked, "Is this bulletproof glass?"

Miles replied, "Yes, it is, and for good reason."

They each had to sign in at the outer desk. The guard pushed a button, and the doors slid open. Another full-body scanner awaited them. After passing that last test, a second set of glass doors opened. Another security station stood just inside, where another guard gave them guest badges on lanyards.

"At least they didn't require us to have full body searches," Bobby whispered. Sam cringed at that thought.

Unlike the deserted hangar above, the area beyond bustled with activity. "Here's the church, and here's the steeple," Jeff whispered.

"Open the door and look at all the people," Bobby finished.

"No kidding. I didn't expect this," Sam said.

"If you will follow me," Miles told them. "And stay close. No wandering allowed. The guys with guns have orders to shoot first and ask questions later." Miles smiled, but no one doubted he meant it. Miles led the group past an open area with civilian and military personnel sitting at computer desks. Through one more set of doors, they found another tunnel almost as big as the first tunnel. Turning to the right, they followed the tunnel past several tall doors on both sides until stopping at their destination. Through the glass windows embedded in this entrance, they saw a massive room that appeared to be close to half the floor size of the hangar above ground. The ceiling was located about fifty to sixty feet above the floor.

Miles pressed a button on the wall comm station. "We are here, Percy."

They heard a tenor voice say, "Eugene. Please, come in."

The doors slid open. "After you," Miles said with a wave of his hand.

Dominating the center of the room sat a large, smooth, light gray cube. It appeared to be about 30 feet by 30 feet by 30 feet. Surrounding the cube were twelve-inch diameter columns - six columns on each side. Across the top, interconnecting metal trusses tied the columns together. Miles waved at a bespectacled young man in a white lab coat. He looked to be in his mid to late twenties. His long, wavy hair made him look even younger. "Good to see you, Percy. How is our subject?"

"It seems a bit depressed at the moment, Eugene," Dr. Percy McLeod said. Dr. McLeod was one of only a few people who addressed Miles by his first name, but it had more to do with the young man's arrogance than friendship. Percy's annoying voice made him sound like the snake from Disney's *Jungle Book*. "I guess that's to be expected... wild animals in captivity can get like that."

Miles said with a grand gesture, "Everyone, let me introduce Dr. Percy McLeod - considered one of the top Xenobiologists in the world."

"I am the top Xenobiologist in the world."

Miles smiled. "He is one of NASA's annoying child geniuses. This guy is always on the lookout for ET. He has searched the skies for aliens for more years than you would think by looking at him."

Jeff whispered, "He looks like an alien-obsessed dude."

"All he needs is a tin foil hat," Sam snickered. "Do you think he has found any ETs yet?"

"What do you think was behind all those other doors we passed," Jeff replied with a smile.

"Well, Percy, have we found you an alien at last," Miles asked.

"Maybe," Percy said, turning to the group. Approaching the three teens, he smiled. It was a creepy, leering smile. "You must be Sam," Percy hissed. "I have longed to meet you ever since I heard how you interacted with our specimen. Fascinating..." She shook his clammy hand and cringed. Then he shook each boy's hand.

"I assume by specimen you are talking about Cooper," Bobby said.

"That's right. You gave it a name," Percy mussed. "Cooper, I see. Fascinating. Why Cooper, may I ask?"

"It just seemed to fit," Jeff replied.

Sam felt impatient. This weirdo's creepy voice got on her nerves. "And he isn't a specimen," she objected. "He's Cooper - a unique, gentle individual with a brain, a heart and feelings."

"He...," Percy asked. "What makes you think it's a male? We know nothing about this species."

Jeff laughed, "If you saw how he latched onto Sam, you'd understand."

"Oh... I don't know," Percy smirked. "There are all kinds of animals... people too."

"No, Cooper is a guy," Jeff insisted.

"Hum, fascinating..." He gave Sam a look that made her uncomfortable.

"Please," she said. "We want to see Cooper. Where is he?"

"He's right here," Percy replied.

She looked around the room. "Where?"

Percy pointed. "Inside the cube."

"You're keeping him imprisoned in a box with no windows?" That thought horrified Sam.

"This is a special box," Miles interjected. "We can create many environments for the specimen, but it can only see what we want it to see."

"That's so cruel," Sam protested.

Rich stepped up and put a hand on her shoulder. "Princess, we don't know what Cooper considers cruel. These people are trying to discover what Cooper likes and dislikes. They are just studying his reactions to things." He gave a side glance at Percy. He hoped he was right about Dr. McLeod's motives.

"That's it exactly," Percy said. "We are trying to see how he reacts to different environmental stimuli."

"Let's see how Cooper is doing for now," Rich told her.

Percy smiled. "Here, let me show you." He crossed to an electronic console and moved a sliding controller to a full-on position.

The walls of the cube became transparent. Cooper sat in the middle of his high-tech cage. His back turned toward them.

Sam ran up to the cube. "Cooper, can he see me," she asked.

"No," Percy answered.

She put both hands on the wall. The surface was smooth and soft, like an unfrozen gel pack. She could feel it pulse with energy. Cooper reacted and turned in her direction.

Percy watched with wonder. "He can't hear you either, and yet..."

Cooper scooted across the floor until he was facing Sam. She left one hand resting on the wall as she watched him. "How are you? I hope you're not too lonely." Cooper raised his hand to the inside wall, mirroring Sam's hand.

Miles moved to Percy's side. "Do you see that?"

"Fascinating," Percy said. "It may look like a wild animal, but it has a high level of intelligence, maybe even telepathic."

"There is something special about that girl," Miles said. Percy nodded in agreement.

Bobby and Jeff joined Sam at the wall. Cooper responded to each of them.

"How are you doing, buddy," Jeff said.

"Sorry we couldn't get you back home," Bobby said. "And I'm sorry they did this to you." He waited a minute before adding. "He's sad, Sam, but our being here makes him feel better."

"I'm glad," she said. "Please don't be afraid, Cooper. We'll find a way to help you. I promise."

"The boy, Bobby, expressed how he thinks the creature feels," Miles said to Percy. "The girl said something about that earlier today. I wonder." Intrigued, he decided to try a little experiment. Walking up to the cube, he put his hands on the adjacent wall as the girl had done.

"Woe, boy," Bobby yelled out.

In one aggressive blur, Cooper darted at Miles. With his teeth bared and his eyes ablaze, he growled with ferocity. The startled doctor instinctively stepped back from the wall.

"He doesn't like you, Eugene," Percy smirked.

"So, I gather. That hurts my feelings."

"He must have been in one of your classes at the University." Percy snickered. "That would drive anyone to mayhem. Interesting though. That was the first noise we heard the creature utter. Sam, sweetie...," Percy said. "Are there any other sounds the creature can make?"

"Yes. When Cooper is mad, he can roar pretty loud.

"When we captured him," Miles said. "He let out a roar that knocked me on my butt."

"I have also heard him laugh, and he sort of purrs when I hold his hand," she continued.

"Laugh? Like in ha-ha laughing?"

"Well, more like a gorilla laughing. It's funny."

"Fascinating... You said he purrs."

"Yes, and hums too."

"You mean hum a tune?"

"That's what it sounds like," she replied. "When contented and comfortable, Cooper hums to himself."

"Yeah," Bobby said. "Heard him do that a couple of times. His voice is lower like a baritone."

"What did you call this thing, Mr. Maeda," Miles asked, turning away from Cooper's glare.

"He is a Shadow demon, unlike any I have seen before. The way he acts with these kids makes him seem almost human. Of course, the way he acts toward you, sir. That's more the nature of such monsters."

Percy eyed the old Japanese man. "Demon, huh? Fascinating. What did you say your name was?"

"Maeda, Ichiro of the Maeda Clan," Grandpa replied with a bow. "Although they don't claim me anymore. Nowadays, I am just Grandpa Maeda."

Percy became animated. "Of course, that explains it."

"Explains what," Miles asked.

"The legend. The members of the Maeda Clan were among the most noted experts in the arts of monster-slaying and demon exorcism," Percy explained.

"We still are experts," Grandpa grumbled.

"Sorry, no offense intended." Percy gave a slight bow of his head. "You are a born and bred member of the Maeda Clan?" Grandpa took a proud stance and nodded in the affirmative. "Why are you here in the States? Shouldn't you be back in Japan fighting demons and monsters?"

Grandpa dropped the pose; his face went sober. "I had enough of blood and death, thank you. I left that behind and came to America, but it seems my past has returned to haunt me."

"Fascinating..."

"Why on earth would you know about this Maeda Clan," Miles asked in shock.

"You know me, Eugene." Percy couldn't hide his excitement and enthusiasm for strange subjects. "I have always liked the weird and strange, the ugly and monstrous. That's why I do what I do. The Maeda Clan is at the top of my list of favorite weird things. The clan's stories and legends span centuries. It's real brave warriors and glorious battle stuff."

"There is no glory in battle, young man," the old man scolded. "There is no glory in killing humans or non-humans. The Maeda Clan trains brave warriors, that is true. They are as dedicated as any other soldier, but let me tell you something about brave men and women. They are ordinary people. They go into battle despite their fears. They push the fear behind them so that honor and love of freedom can sustain them in battle. I doubt any of you have experienced that fear, but I have. I'm a survivor of fear, a survivor of war. No, I tell you. There is no such thing as a glorious battle!"

The entire room fell silent. Grandpa Maeda was a proud man. He was content with his life choices, but as a good man, he had to speak the truth. Far too often, the young waltzed merrily into battle like it would be as easy as a video game.

"Bravery," the old man said, "comes at a high price."

"Are you saying you have fought real monsters yourself," Percy asked. "Are such things real?"

"Of course, they are real. Look at that thing you have in that box. That is a Shadow demon! But this fellow is a puppy compared to the myriads of other monster species."

"Percy looked at the old man in envy. "You must tell me more, Mr. Maeda. You will come back and tell me more, won't you?"

"Perhaps," Mr. Maeda said. "But, I must warn you. In studying this specimen, as you call it, you will learn very little. In the end, you will only prove that you can kill it. Because, in the end, you will kill it."

Sam said softly, "No." She buried her face in her dad's chest.

"Still, you will have learned nothing useful. If an army of demons come to our world, you will certainly wish you had learned more. How will you save the world, Dr. McLeod, when you know so little?" His old heart raced too fast for comfort, so he straightened his back and breathed. "That, of course, is why I am here. I will teach you what I can."

"Splendid," Percy replied.

No one knew what to say after that exchange. Miles broke the silence. "It sounds like we had better get back to work and close our rift." With that declaration, he turned and walked for the door. "It's time to go people."

"What about Cooper," Sam asked. "Please don't hurt him. He will help us if you let him."

"We will see," Miles replied. He turned to see Sam's pleading eyes. "Look," he said in a softer tone. "We have no intention of harming it, but we must study it. We have no other choice, especially if what Mr. Maeda says is true."

Chapter 34

RACE AGAINST TIME

General Bates took immediate action and quarantined the campus area closest to the Center for Interdimensional Physics. At the same time, he requested a hundred National Guard troops to secure the area. By sundown, he had boots on the ground and a security perimeter set up. National Guard troops on a California campus quickly caught the attention of the media and student activists. Local and National news teams from every network and cable news channel arrived to get a handle on the developing story.

The Department of Defence released the following statement to the press. *"Early this morning on the campus of UC El Palmar, an accident caused a radiation leak. Although the radiation poses no immediate health risk to the community, we established a quarantine area around the Center for Interdimensional Physics to ensure public safety. The area will remain in quarantine until cleanup crews can remove all traces of the contamination."*

The President of the University of California System declared with much righteous indignation that the Center for Interdimensional Physics had committed a clear breach of trust. The center had not been fully transparent about the potential hazards to the campus community. Of course, the UC president didn't know the true nature of this particular crisis. For now, the DoD would keep it that way. Miles knew the president well. Her posturing was more about covering her butt than safety. The money pouring into the campus coffers because of the Center's rift research was far more valuable to the president than student safety. Money had a way of persuading bureaucrats to look the other way. Campus politics could be as absurd and as morally corrupt as governmental politics. Miles wondered what the university's president would say if she knew about the Shadow creatures. If everything went as planned, she, or anyone else, would never find out. Someone once said, "*Public ignorance is the government's best friend.*"

To end the crisis as soon as possible, Bill and Rich decided to use their knowledge of advanced science and technology—science that only they understood. Although the risk of exposure grew with each day, this was one of those times when the end result would justify any risk taken. At any rate, time will tell.

"They would have stumbled onto this information eventually," Rich said.

Bill said. "I can live with the decisions we've made."

"I wish Miles and Bates understood the threat. Their lack of concern worries me."

"As long as they trust us, we will do the job."

"Yeah, but how long are they willing to trust us?

Chapter 35

POOR JEFFREY

The word grounded didn't describe the limitations imposed on the three teens after returning home. It was something more akin to martial law. At least Bobby and Sam knew these new measures ensured their safety because the world had become far more dangerous. But Jeff's parents knew nothing of demons, monsters, and rifts to other worlds. After learning their son had been in the custody of federal agents for three days, they became convinced that Jeffrey had taken a sudden turn toward a life of crime and corruption. Next would come the *yakuza* tattoos and swearing allegiance to the Japanese version of the Godfather. Jeff's freaked-out parents instituted an all-encompassing punishment. To keep their secrets hidden, the boy had to keep up a brave front, even though the loss of anime and games threatened to kill his playful soul.

Grandpa Maeda's consulting role in the matter remained a secret. As far as Mr. and Mrs. Sasaki knew, the old man had rescued their son from a fate worse than death. They were grateful for his intervention on Jeff's behalf. This gave Grandpa leverage for negotiating parole. It took an extra amount of bombastic zeal to get the best deal for the boy. Melodrama was, after all, the old man's expertise.

"What Jeffrey needs," Grandpa Maeda insisted, "is discipline. Training in Japanese martial arts should begin immediately. It will build his character, enhance his sense of honor and duty, and reconnect him with his cultural roots. Just the thing the boy needs right now."

They agreed with the added stipulation that Jeffrey's grades not suffer. Studying came first, martial arts second. They suspended all other outside activities indefinitely. Since Jeff couldn't tell his parents the truth, he had to accept this negotiated parole with cheerfulness. From that day forward, he spent two hours after school each day, plus another four hours on Saturdays, in training. Unknown to his mom and dad, Grandpa also taught him the ancient arts of spell casting and exorcism. After discovering the extraordinary truth about his two best friends, Jeff wanted to be ready to help his friends. Besides, this whole situation was way too cool. He didn't want to be left out.

Chapter 36

COUPLING POWERS

"Try again, honey," Anne said to Sam.

Sam took a deep breath and held out both hands with her palms turned up. She had electrodes attached to her head, chest, and back. An ICU monitor showed her heart and respiratory functions, while an EEG monitored her brain waves. Sam concentrated. Soon, both her hands glowed bright. The equipment indicated an immediate reaction. Her heart rate increased, her breath deepened, and her brain waves went crazy. Soon, a ball of energy appeared in her hands. She moved the ball over onto the left hand. A second ball appeared over the right hand.

"Very good, honey. Now, try to make them brighter."

Sam closed her eyes and concentrated. Both balls grew brighter.

Sarah noted the changes to the EEG. Initially, she hoped the readings would isolate the part of the brain that controlled extrasensory abilities. Instead, the EEG indicated that Sam's efforts activated all corners of her brain. It seemed to supercharge her brain during each successive event.

Sarah said, "Try to increase the temperature as well. I want to see how you react." Sarah held out a temperature meter and inserted the pointed tip into one of the fireballs. Once again, Sam closed her eyes and concentrated.

The two mothers had had sixteen years to prepare for when their children's powers would manifest—like it or not, that day had arrived. This difficult chore filled both moms with some hope and a lot of dread. Hope for the safer future that their children might bring about, but fearful of what that future would do to them. How would it change them? Their kids had grown up well, but as mothers, they now regretted the choices made years ago. The reality of that commitment, so courageously made in the beginning, was now hard to bear. Bobby and Sam needed to grow and grow a lot, so helping them get stronger required a renewed commitment to the original goal. Assisting the two teens to use their newly discovered powers provided the best, maybe the only option, for survival.

Bobby sensed a sudden spike of fear coming from Mrs. Thomas. *Why is Sam's mom afraid?* Bobby thought. *Afraid of Sam's power? No. Afraid of Sam? No, of course not. Afraid for Sam. Yes, that's it. Only natural*, he supposed. *After all, Sam's power has an element of danger.* Bobby turned his attention to Sam. The balls of energy flickered. *Perhaps Sam senses her mom's reluctance.* That thought gave Bobby an idea.

"Mrs. Thomas," Bobby said. "The beings that attacked our old world, the Odan. What were they like?"

Anne broke focus on her daughter. "What was that, Bobby?"

"The Odan," Bobby repeated. "What were they like?"

"They were horrible beings," she said.

"In what way?"

"Bloodthirsty... cruel. The Odan destroyed everyone and everything."

"But what did they look like?"

"Ah... well," Anne said, unhappy to broach this subject. "The Odan were the stuff of nightmares."

"Mr. Maeda said there were many different kinds of supernatural creatures. He told us that some even had advanced civilizations."

"That would make sense. We observed a highly developed class structure among the Odan. Experts told us the Odan had a royal class led by a powerful king or Queen. Maybe demigods describe them best.

The leaders of the army were of the royal class as well. The non-royals served as warriors, servants, and slaves. All warriors possessed a relative level of magical power. Most servants and slaves came from several different species. It was hard to know what they were, probably captured prisoners, the spoils of war, that sort of thing. Some appeared to be humanoids physically, but others were disturbingly non-human. We have no idea what the general Odan population looked like. We assumed they looked like those we saw on the battlefield.

Sarah added, "Some slave creatures had wings like a bat. I hope never to see the likes of them again."

"What can I use as a mental picture for comparison?" Anne said, pausing to think. She stood and went into the next room. When she returned, she carried a large book entitled *The Warrior Myth*.

"Before we settled on this world," Anne said. "We began an extensive study of human history and cultures. We wanted to determine if any contact with non-humans had occurred in the past. We found one possible instance connecting with the early cultures in northeastern Europe." She showed an opened page in a book to Bobby. At the top of the page a picture depicting Odin of old Norse mythology, underlined by the heading, *Valhalla*.

"The Odan were Vikings?"

"No... I mean, they looked like the mythical gods the Vikings worshipped." Anne looked at the picture. "At least the royals did. Of course, they were much larger than us."

Bobby said, "If they were part of a game, I would consider them cool characters. Do you suppose the Viking gods were the same creatures that attacked the old world?"

"We considered it, but ultimately, we decided against that notion. No, despite a few obvious comparisons, the possibility seemed unlikely."

Sarah added, "The Odan were powerful warriors. This is an important fact for both of you to understand. Don't underestimate your enemies."

Anne continued, "It was weird. The Odan used medieval weapons and battlefield methods. Our technology should have been superior in every way. Yet, we kept losing battles. The enemy moved with incredible speed and strength. The sheer numbers of the enemy made it difficult, if not impossible, to defeat them. They had tens of millions of soldiers to our two million. They overwhelmed us. It would have ended in total extinction if we hadn't escaped the planet."

Sarah noted the positive change in Sam's vitals as Anne talked with Bobby. The orbs of energy sustained a brighter and hotter light. She watched Bobby as the conversation continued. Her son controlled the conversation, steering it away from Sam's efforts. That, in turn, helped Sam concentrate. Anne, a clinical psychologist, struggled with the changes Sam was going through. But Bobby, using his abilities, manipulated Anne with ease. It's funny how our kids can still surprise us.

Anne continued, "Wherever those monsters engaged our forces, whether on the land, sea, or air, they dominated the battlefield."

"But why," Bobby asked. "It makes no sense."

"The enemy possessed an unknown power that the military strategists and the best scientific minds didn't understand. The Odan had impenetrable protection shields and weapons that defied the laws of physics. Our scientists spent years studying this problem. The tide of war had to change, or our world was lost."

"It was magic," Sam said. "Wasn't it?" She began juggling the fiery orbs like two balloons.

"The discovery of magic shocked everyone. Magic came from children's fairy tales. No one had ever considered the possibility that magic existed. In this world, our defense forces depend solely on science and technology. The Odan used sorcerers and witches who had trained all their lives to draw on unknown powers."

Sarah added, "The Odan were masters of magical warfare."

Sam's fiery orbs of energy flashed with hot flames. The temperature inside the balls rose above five hundred degrees, but Sam showed no signs of distress from the heat.

"No matter how well we built things," Anne said, "our weapon systems remained vulnerable to magical attack. So were the factories that made those weapons. At the same time, our weapons had little effect on magic. No one had the slightest idea of how to fight against magic."

Sarah added, "Many scientists outright refused to accept magic as real. But forward-thinking individuals, like your fathers, took the lead. They formed theories to explain elemental magic."

"Once we perceived magic as another element within science," Anne said, "as a different way of accessing the powers lying dormant in nature, we finally made some progress."

Sam relaxed, making progress of her own. She concentrated and created a variety of shapes in the air, simple geometric shapes like cubes, pyramids, and octahedrons.

Bobby's eyes lit up when he saw what Sam had accomplished. "Try making a sword shape." Sam looked sideways at him. "One of the keys to your ability is your imagination. Visualize a sword in your mind."

"Okay," she said. "I'll try. What kind of sword," Sam asked

"Well, how about a broadsword."

Sam closed her eyes and thought of a sword. Soon, shapes appeared and combined to form a glowing medieval broadsword.

"Now open your eyes," Bobby said.

Sam gasped, "Wow. I did it."

"Take hold of the hilt like you would a real sword." Sam reached out, but her hands passed through the object. "Don't think of it as fire or energy. Think of it as if a solid object, a real sword."

Sam tried again. She reached out and grabbed the sword, gripping it with both hands. She thrust the sword straight out, brandishing it from one side to the other.

"This is so cool," Sam squealed with excitement. "It feels solid like a real sword but with no weight. It's as light as a feather."

"Now. Make the blade more fiery," Bobby said, excited at what they had discovered. The blade burst into flames that seemed to engulf Sam.

"Honey, be careful," Sam's mom shouted. That broke Sam's concentration. The sword flickered and vanished.

"Mom," a frustrated Sam groaned.

"Oh, I'm so sorry. I shouldn't have interrupted you. It's just that...." Anne took a deep breath. "Go ahead and try again. You were doing so well."

Rather than try again, Sam joined the conversation. "What did you do to fight the magic?"

Sarah answered, "We discovered we could disrupt dark magic with light magic. With light magic, we produced many kinds of anti-dark magic weapons."

"But the biggest breakthrough," Anne said, "came when a special-ops team, working deep inside enemy territory, captured an ancient book containing many Odan secrets. We took it from the enemy at a great sacrifice of life. We began unlocking many more magical secrets with this book, known as a magical index or a grimoire."

"No kidding," Bobby said.

"The book gave us much more insight into the nature of magic and its many uses. For instance, we learned that magic worked as well for humans as it did for nonhumans. Any intelligent being could use magic if they had the magic gene."

"A magic gene," Sam said. "Do Bobby and I have the magic gene?"

"Yes. We all do. It is a matter of switching it on. This knowledge led to testing our general population looking for the gene."

"As young couples," Sarah explained. "We volunteered for what our scientists called the Gemini Project. At least one of us had to have the magic gene. I didn't. I was boringly normal. So, they asked me to undergo an experimental gene-splicing procedure. It was risky, but I agreed to it."

"How risky," Sam asked.

"If my body rejected the gene, I would have gotten sick. Quite frankly, I could have died. But it went well. Doctors use our genetic material to create your very special embryos in the laboratory. They then placed the new life in our wombs. That was the beginning of your lives."

"Wow, I'm a test tube baby."

"Artificial insemination was the scientific process used. The grimoire explained how to use magic spells to bless the unborn fetus as he or she developed over the next nine months. The spell process eventually coupled one male fetus with one female fetus. So, when we gave birth to you two, the magic had already bound you together. We expected the gene to remain dormant until three to four years after puberty, between fifteen and eighteen."

"But Mom, you said that my powers had happened too soon," Sam said. "I'm sixteen."

Anne replied with a mournful look. "Too soon for me, honey. Not you."

"Oh... I see."

"But even though both of you are, at least in part, products of a genetic research laboratory, you are our children. We love you as much as any parent could.

Sarah added, "Maybe more, considering what we had to go through to get you."

"All this is hard for me," Anne said. "You are my little girl, Sam. I don't want you to get hurt."

"It's okay, Mom. I understand." Sam smiled at the woman who had given her so much love. "How did you decide I would be a guardian?" Sam played with new energy balls, using her hands to create hoops and hearts.

"We didn't decide anything," Sarah said.

"Then who did?"

"I don't know how it works for sure. I believe it has something to do with you. In some way, your bodies, or maybe your souls, decided the outcome."

Sam frowned. "Are you saying I somehow wanted to be a warrior?"

"I don't know, honey. What I do know is you two need to relax around each other. To become one, you must develop a more profound and unbreakable bond. Coupling magic requires you two to act as one heart and one mind.

Bobby and Sam knew they needed to overcome the awkwardness between them. That meant taking their relationship to the next level of trust. That wouldn't happen as long as they acted like two embarrassed teenagers every time they touched. They needed the willingness and the desire to become one.

Chapter 37

THE SHADOW ARMY

High Overseer Shadow Strong and forty-eight other elite warrior witches arrived at the site of the rupture. Covered in black body armor and a hooded robe, the Overseer's physical image matched her high station among the warrior class. She stood taller than any other witch. Warrior witches wore magical armor made from the hardest mineral found on Tiarnas. It shielded them in battle. Unlike male Shadows, who used their size and brute strength to survive a war, the smaller-bodied witches relied on magic and magical shielding. The interconnecting armor sections covered the head, the chest, and the back. It slid and twisted in liquid smooth transitions as they moved.

The warrior witches' armor, sprouted magical wings, and they flew upward to form a circle high above the rugged mountains, canyons, and towering cliffs of the Far Edge landscape. High Overseer Strong's wings flapped aggressively and quickly took to her place at the center of the circle. With her wings holding her in place, she hovered over Little Toe's cave and the rupture. The other forty-eight witches stood atop mountain peaks and ridges. Some hovered magically in place. Each held a raptor staff. The staff's prominent feature was the head of a raptor that crowned the upper end. The giant raptor, a bird-like demon that nested in the higher elevations of Tiarnas, symbolized a warrior witch's magical strength. Whenever these large raptors appeared in the sky, Shadows ran for the cover of their caves.

Once they completed the mile-wide ring of magic, each witch turned to face the High Overseer at the center. Shadow Strong raised her raptor staff high above her head.

The other witches pointed their staffs toward the High Overseer. Beams of light connected the forty-nine staffs. Three concentric circles appeared within the central circle. Runes also appeared and rotated around the center point.

When the Far Edge residents looked up and saw the raptor staffs glowing bright, they ran for their lives. No one had warned the residents of the clearing spell in progress. It would destroy everything below, wiping the surface of the land clean and any Shadow still in the area.

The High Overseer stretched out her mind and spoke to her sisters. "Warriors chant with me as one,"

The witches chanted. "Clear this circle."

"Clear filth, rocks, and dirt," the High Overseer continued.

"Clear this circle," the witches chanted again.

"Clear mountains and canyons."

"Clear this circle."

"Clear this place for the coming battle."

"Clear this circle."

"As we will, so shall it be."

"Clear this circle."

The black landscape below crumbled away with an explosive roar. The air churned into a violent vortex of power that sucked the black dust and rocks upward. The debris lifted high into the atmosphere, where it would spread across the ethereal void. These black materials would later fall like ash and hail worldwide. When the air cleared, a mile-wide, cylindrical clearing with a flat valley floor had replaced the once mountainous terrain. Little Toe's rupture floated at the center of the open space.

The Shadow Lords, seven powerful sorcerers of the royal family bloodline, had controlled the Shadow Empire for over one thousand years. Shadows Lords coupled their magic with seven senior warrior witches. Each Imperial Witch had risen through the ranks of the empire's warrior class, earning her place of power through heroism and magical skill. Female Shadows had magic from birth, but only a small percentage of females ever desired the grueling life of a witch. Only seven possessed the power to take a place among the imperial witches. Fate decreed that High Overseer Shadow Strong would be the next to move up to this imperial rank. After this conquest ended, she would kill the oldest witch and take her place among the seven.

The current lords and witches who ruled the Shadow Empirehad grown old and weak. The royal family's unquenchable thirst for power had reached a tipping point. If the general population ever discovered their weakness, the temptation to challenge their authority would lead to civil war. To avoid this civil unrest, the royals ruthlessly dominated the Empire through loyal Shadow enforcers while they remained cloistered in the imperial palace. This monolithic tower stood at the capital city's center, continually glowing with imperial magic. Ironically, this self-imposed seclusion only resulted in greater weakness. The royals had lost touch with the natural world crumbling around them. Their grip on power loosened with each new day.

The witches of the warrior class had maintained their ranks, but over time, their status as warriors had slipped away. Tiarnas was an isolated world. That had robbed witches of the opportunity for conquest. The battle arena had become the only place where witches could prove themselves. Nowadays, they lived, fought, and died as gladiators. This brutal form of entertainment had replaced the glorious conquest of long ago. Many witches resented this base role and blamed the royal family. If nothing changed, growing unrest among the warrior witches would sink the final nails deep into the royal families' coffins.

Adding to this gradual downfall, few young sorcerers of the royal bloodlines could take the reins of the empire. Life-sustaining resources had fallen to dangerous lows, causing unrest in the general population. The only thing that kept civil war from ripping the empire apart was fear of the magic of the Shadows Lords and the Imperial Witches. Shadows like Fire Claws and Broken Fang controlled the outer regions of Tiarna's. The royal family needed Shadows like Fire Claws and his gang to keep the poor in the outlying areas under control.

Broken Fang's return from the humanoid world had changed everything. He had given the royal family exactly what they needed to hold onto their power for another millennium. Actual conquest was a real possibility, and Fire Claws and his kind would become brave leaders eager to fight and die in the conquest of this new world. The warrior witches would fall back in line with their status as true warriors restored. The general unrest would die out once newly conquered resources became available. All of creation was a perfect storm of fortunate events.

Magistrate Fire Claws stood at the edge of the staging arena with Broken Fang at his side. Over the next few days, thousands of Shadow warriors would join them. New encampments of eager Shadows already covered the landscape. Filled with eager anticipation, these two Shadows felt the pride of their accomplishment. Soon, the seven Shadows Lords and the seven Imperial Witches would arrive to cast the spell to seal the rupture open. Then, the invasion would begin.

Chapter 38

LOVE MAKES MAGIC

After training, the two students and their moms sat together in the basement. "I miss Cooper," Sam said.

"Me too," said Bobby.

"I think of him every day, but I worry that his imprisonment will cause our memories of him to fade. Or him of us. It's nice our lives have returned to some degree of normal but without Cooper..."

Bobby changed the subject to keep Sam in a positive frame of mind. "So, Mom. You said we were born before we came to this world."

"Yes. It would have been too dangerous to travel while we were pregnant," Sarah replied.

"How did we get here," Sam asked.

"Through an interdimensional rift much like your friend, Cooper, came through," Sarah said.

"Something tells me it was more complicated than that. Cooper came here by accident. We didn't."

"You're right, but I'm afraid that's your dad's field. He will have to explain it to you."

"Oh yeah, I remember what I wanted to ask you. What about my brother," Sam asked. "Is he like me... like us?"

"No, he is just a regular boy," Anne said. "He was born after we got to this world."

"It took you by surprise, as I remember," Sarah said.

"A special surprise," Anne added.

Sam asked, "Surprise?"

"You know, honey." Her mom grinned. "Unplanned, unexpected, a complete shock."

"Didn't you want another child?"

"Don't get the wrong idea, sweetie. You see, I thought I couldn't have any more children."

"Oh," Sam said. "Why?"

Sarah clarified. "When we agreed to be the mothers of couplings, we also agreed to a procedure to prevent another pregnancy."

"Why would you do that," Bobby asked. "I'd like a little brother."

Sarah replied, "And I wish I could give you one, but you and Sam had to come first. Nothing else mattered. Our mission was to take care of you, keep you safe, and prepare you for the future. That level of commitment required single-mindedness. Our future, and the future of all living things, depended on the couplings surviving."

"But then you had another baby."

"Yes. Kevin," Anne said, "was our miracle child. An exciting bonus for us."

"But how did you get pregnant?"

"I think you already know that honey," Anne answered with a grin.

Sam blushed. "Considering the procedure, how could you get pregnant?"

"Sometimes the body heals itself in miraculous ways," her mother said.

Sarah teased, "Especially when you're acting like a couple of newlyweds."

This time, it was Anne's face that flushed. "Were we that obvious?"

Sarah nodded with an even bigger smile. "Oh my gosh, you were so in love."

Anne sighed. "I still am."

Sarah smiled. "The same for Bill and I. I still can't get enough of that man." They both laughed.

"Ah... Mom," Bobby said. "I am sitting right here... on the floor in front of you."

"Oh, sorry, honey," Sarah said. Then, turning back to Anne, she whispered, "I've embarrassed my little boy? We better take our conversation upstairs and let these two talks about things that interest them."

"You mean talking about boys and girls in love," Anne whispered. The laughing continued all the way upstairs. Anne hollered back over her shoulder, "You two behave yourselves."

"Practice your abilities," Sarah called back. The laughter faded.

Sam and Bobby found themselves alone for the first time in weeks. They sat without a word. Then Sam said, "Wow, they're in a good mood today."

"No kidding." They looked at each other and burst out laughing.

"It's nice to know your parents are still in love. We are lucky. Delia's parents got a divorce last year. Her mother took the divorce real hard."

"Love is important."

Sam suddenly felt self-conscious. "Gee, they left us all alone."

"Maybe this is a good time to discuss how we feel about... us."

"What do you mean?" Sam blushed as her heart raced.

"You know... about our training. Stuff like that."

"Oh... of course."

"So, Sam. How do you feel?"

She shrugged, not sure where to start. "You?" Sam knelt on the floor facing Bobby.

"What geek, boy or girl, hasn't fantasized about having a superpower? Right? Yet, I am finding it to be pretty weird. I'm still trying to get my head around it."

Sam added, "Not just that. Since finding out about our mysterious family history, I have felt disconnected."

"Disconnected?"

"From the normal."

Bobby looked down. What she said was true enough.

"Delia said something to me today. I guess I haven't been my usual self. My interest in the usual school activities has waned since all this started. She said she worried about me and wanted to help. I didn't know what to tell her. I wish I could tell her what's going on. All I said was, 'Don't worry.' I just want life back to normal."

"Yeah, it's hard, but I believe things will calm down eventually. We have changed. Even Jeff has become more serious."

"But what are we changing into, Bobby?" Bobby decided not to answer but to let Sam explain. "Last summer," she said, "filled my life with new possibilities. I wanted to make the most out of my high school years. I enjoyed feeling like a girl. Boys noticed me in a new way, and I must admit, I liked it." Bobby felt a flicker of jealousy. "More than anything else, I was glad you noticed the changes and accepted the new me."

"Crashed and burned on that one."

She didn't look at him but grinned. "You recovered nicely."

She reached out and took hold of his hands. He got up on his knees so they could be straight on, face to face. Sam looked into his eyes.

"After learning the truth about who we are, I worried that the new me would get blown away in a storm of other changes. This coupling thing has replaced my perfect dreams with nightmares."

Bobby squeezed her hands. "This coupling thing sucks for me too. I'm constantly afraid of doing something stupid and messing things up between us again. One thing I know for sure: we can't do this if we don't like each other."

"I will never stop liking you."

"This superpower thing is downright puzzling, even for a guy who loves puzzles. This friendship we have is important. The only way to get through this is to get through it together. Like we always have. I may not always be sure of myself, but I am always sure of you."

Bobby had a way of making Sam feel better. Someday soon, life will be good again. The bond between them had grown stronger. That made Sam happy. Neither of them had used the word love yet, but they couldn't deny that something special existed between them. A fresh seed of love, perhaps. They were just waiting to be set free. It would become a beautiful thing if they cared for and cultivated it.

Sam smiled. "We are a coupling," she added.

"Yup, a coupling."

Sam's brow wrinkled in a slight mood reversal. "Controlling my power," she said. "That's a different issue altogether."

"You can control it."

"I'm too inconsistent. It's not like I can let it go full power. I have no idea what would happen if I did. I don't know my limits. That's a serious problem."

"Come on, you're doing great. Besides, It's not like I have any better grasp on mine."

"Better than me."

"No way. Sure, I feel and sense things, but what am I supposed to do with that? It seems kind of useless. At least your power makes sense. You have a weapon. Wow, what you did that night? It blew me away."

"I don't want to be a weapon," she said with more force than expected. "What if I had blown you away?"

Bobby sensed Sam's fear. "Are you afraid to use your power because you might hurt me?"

"Well, yeah. Hurt you or someone else. My ability does frighten me."

"Sure, the ability to create balls of fiery energy is a little scary, but you are not. I know you. You would never attack anyone without a good reason. Someone would have to attack you first."

"That's not the point. Maybe I wouldn't mean to hurt anyone, but accidents happen."

"You focused in on that big Shadow demon without any trouble."

"I had my eye closed," she said, shaking her head. "I wasn't focused at all."

"Even so, you didn't hit me or Cooper. The big Shadow was the only one affected by that energy blast."

"I'm so glad you two weren't hurt."

"Your unfocused attack hit the only thing in the room you feared. Then, bam, the Shadow disappeared. So, even with your eyes closed, you hit the bad guy."

"I was so afraid and didn't want to be that afraid again. If I have to be afraid to make my power work." Sam took a deep breath. "What if I lose control or, worse, fail you when you need me the most?"

"You won't fail. Just believe in yourself."

"Don't you see? I'm not just afraid of using the power. I'm afraid of what this power will do to me." Tears formed and trickled down her cheeks. To Bobby's surprise, Sam threw her arms around his neck. He didn't resist. "What if it changes me too much? What if I turn into the monster that has to be killed?"

Bobby held his arms around her while she let out her pent-up emotions. It felt nice. After saying nothing, he said, "I am the discerner, the judge in this coupling thing. I know you better than anyone except for your mom and dad."

"Even better than them."

"It's your heart I know so well, Sam. I can see how this kind of power could turn someone into a monster, but never you."

She pulled away from him. "But..."

"Never." Then, with sudden excitement, he said, "Wait a minute. That's it."

"What," she asked, drying her eyes.

"The solution for making our powers work. We have been approaching this all wrong."

"How wrong?"

"So far, we have worked on our powers individually," Bobby explained. "As though your powers and mine are two separate things. But they are not separate powers; they are one power—the power of the coupling. As partners, we need to act as one. Oneness will make our magic work as intended."

Bobby continued with newfound conviction, "You and I have always had a unique connection. We have always trusted each other completely. So, consider this. As the discerner, I identify friends or enemies, good or evil. You, as the guardian, need my confirmation before you can act. Then, and only then, can you activate your power. You can't just go off by accident. Trust my sixth sense and trust your power. It is about perfect harmony."

"But that night at the house..."

"Remember, Cooper and I had already identified the danger before that Shadow demon attacked. Your power activated when you needed to release it. It happened, even though you had no idea you had such a power."

"I see. Are you sure about this?"

"We still have a lot to learn, and there are many unknown variables, but..." His voice softened, warm and gentle. "I don't know why, Sam, but I am sure... very sure."

Sam couldn't explain it either, but she knew he had it right this time. She could trust this dear, sweet boy with her life because he was right - right for her.

They smiled at each other and leaned forward, touching forehead to forehead, holding each other's hands. It was a peaceful moment—the right moment. Bobby leaned into her lips and kissed her. Sam had waited so long for this moment. Finally, Bobby Williams kissed her because he wanted to kiss her, and, to her delight, he kept on kissing her. Her heart rate increased, and her hands began to glow. A magical aura spread from their touching lips, engulfing them in a golden warmth.

"Wow," Bobby said as his lips parted hers.

"Wow," Sam said as she kissed him again. Her fears had melted away.

"So… fear isn't the only emotion that activates your power."

Sam giggled and pushed Bobby over onto his back. Then she kissed him with long-anticipated passion.

Chapter 39

MEASURES

Dr. Marshal called for final reports. As each team member said, "Ready," an air of confidence filled the room.

"Are we ready," Bill asked Rich to the side.

"As we can be," he replied. "I'm confident the rift will close."

"Good, the sooner the better."

Marshal announced, "All systems are functioning and ready for rift capture. HGC event number 367.1. Launch in ten, nine, eight, seven, six, five, four, three, two, one, and engage!"

Rich called out, "Engaged." He held his breath as the HGC chamber came to life. The large, ringed sphere floated up into position, and the new, improved gyro rings spun into a blur. After a suspenseful few minutes, a smile spread across Rich's face. "Rift capture is successful. We have control again." The group let out a collective sigh of relief, but no cheers erupted. The rift was still open.

Marshal called for another round of reports. Again, all reported in the affirmative. "All systems are functioning," he said. "Ready for rift closure event in ten, nine, eight, seven, six, five, four, three, two, one, and engage!"

"Engaged," Rich called out once again! The rift responded. "Rift closure at... ten percent, fifteen, twenty percent of closure." He continued calling out the progress until rift closure was at ninety-five percent. He waited in anticipation for the next sequential number to appear. It didn't. "Holding at ninety-five." It held at ninety-five percent for several more nervous minutes.

"What's happening," Miles asked.

Rich shook his head. "Don't know for sure. There is an increase in resistance. The rift is pushing back."

"Okay. Everyone, we need answers," Miles ordered.

"System checks," the Dr. Marshal ordered. Each station reported. Although all systems were optimal, the rift had stopped responding. The numbers oscillated. It changed from ninety-five to ninety-four and back several times.

Rich felt the eyes in the room looking to him for an answer. "We need to push harder," he said. "Perhaps I can do something about that." He went to work sorting out which system functions were essential to the closure phase of the operation and which were now redundant. An hour later he had rerouted power to the current task.

"Okay... Here we go." The gyro rings surged with new power, and the rift immediately responded. Rich called out, "Ninety-six percent... ninety-seven... ninety-eight..." The numbers now oscillated from ninety-eight back to ninety-seven, and so on.

Rich slapped his hand down on the console. "Closure has stopped again. Whatever is causing this continues to increase in strength. I'll try shutting down a couple more functions, but this concerns me. If this counterforce keeps up, we will soon be out of options. We might get stuck at ninety-eight percent."

"What do you think is causing this," Bill asked.

Rich rubbed his tired eyes. "I don't know."

"Natural or magical?" Their eyes met briefly.

Miles moved in closer. "What if we reboot the system? You know... turning it off and then turning it back on again. That works more often than not."

"I'd rather not," Rich said. "The rift should be closing. Yet, something is keeping that from happening."

Miles shook his head. "I agree that *something* is causing this, but can we at least stop worrying about an invasion? The rift is far too small."

"Maybe," Rich replied.

"As long as it remains small," Bill said. "But what happens when we turn off the system? The force pushing from the other side could push the rift back open."

"I don't think so," Miles said. "Since there was no resistance until the rift reached ninety-five percent. It seems unlikely it would push back any further than that."

"An unknown force has caused the counter pressure," Rich said. "If the Shadow creatures are responsible, we need increased strength on our side. To give us some time to close it the rest of the way."

Miles scoffed. "No way those creatures have the capability to combat this technology."

"Who knows what they are capable of," Bill replied.

"In my experience," Rich mumbled, "magical forces are as strong as human technology."

"Magical," Mile scoffed. "It's bad enough that you two, as scientists, believe in monsters and demons. But magic, too?"

"We need to prepare for any eventuality. Dr. Miles, call General Bates. Let him know what's happening."

Alarms sounded, and the HGC chamber suddenly filled with a cloud of thick black dust, causing a camera blackout.

"Miles," Marshal called out. "Something is happening. These readings make no sense."

A team member chimed in, "I am trying to identify the new substance."

"Someone turn off that annoying alarm." The alarm went silent. "Where did the substance come from," Miles asked.

"It came through the rift, sir. Okay. Here we go. It appears to be a granulated material like coarse sand. The charged particles are playing havoc with the electronics inside the chamber."

"Send the information to my station," Rich ordered. He quickly studied the transferred data. Rich looked up from his console. "What do you think, Bill?"

"Magic," Bill said. "This confirms it. Dr. Miles, you'll want to see this. Magic leaves a unique signature. These readings indicate the unknown resistance is produced by magic."

"This is beyond absurd."

"Have you heard of Arthur C. Clarke," Bill asked.

"Of course, I have.".

"Clark said, 'Any sufficiently advanced technology is indistinguishable from magic.' So, call it what you like: magic, voodoo, weird science, superpowers, it really doesn't matter.

"Indistinguishable, maybe. But still science."

"Then let me paraphrase William Shakespeare. 'There are more things in heaven and on earth than are dreamt of in your...' *science,* Doctor. Welcome to a brave new world. Let's hope we can keep Caliban in his place."

Alarms rang out again.

Rich called out. "It's reversing."

"What," barked Miles.

"The rift has opened to ninety-six percent... ninety-five, ninety-four, ninety-three... ninety-two..." Rich let his breath go. "Good, it stopped at ninety-two percent. Let's pray it holds."

"This is insane," Miles protested.

"This is bad," Bill said. "It might be too late to get the rift closed. All priorities need to shift toward stopping the rift from opening any further. Like you said, Dr. Miles. If the rift remains too small."

"So, you're saying that we are now fighting a supernatural power for control of my rift?"

Bill nodded. "Yes."

"And if we can't stop the rift from getting larger?"

"We will have to try more aggressive measures."

Chapter 40

COUNTER MEASURES

The imperial witches encircled the rupture. Each Lord took his place behind a witch, placing his left hand on the witch's left shoulder. All their magical power joined as one, and they chanted mind to mind.

"Seven lords... seven witches..."

"The power of seven times seven." The rupture shuddered.

"Bind those within our circle." The opening undulated and stretched inward.

"Seal it open for all time."

The seven witches raised both arms in front of them, pointing at the rupture.

"As we command... so will it be."

As the spell took hold, the rupture flashed and swirled. It then settled into a soft, even glow. The rupture was theirs to control, or so they thought. Despite the powerful spell, the rupture began to close. Seven witches shifted their positions, pushing their magic forward for a full-power assault.

The cleared arena exploded with magic. The air reacted to the increased heat, causing a dramatic change in air pressure. Hot air inside the arena rose and collided with cold air above. A colossal storm formed. Black dust from the upper atmosphere swirled into the arena and filled the air. Dust vented out through the rupture. As it did this, it obscured the fourteen spell casters. Lightning flashed with several loud claps of thunder. The deafening noise made onlookers shrink back and hide from the power of the event.

Realizing that the imperial witches were in trouble, High Overseer Strong reached out with an order. Forty-eight witches flew forward to aid their older sisters. The ground shook as more witches applied their magic. The shrinking rupture came to a halt just seconds before it could close.

Chapter 41

EUPHORIA AND HORROR

With her head in the clouds, Sam floated through her morning classes. Such an unusual euphoria didn't go unnoticed. Delia pulled Sam aside. "Something happened, so spill it," she demanded. Then her grin widened. "You kissed Bobby again, didn't you?"

"Not exactly," Sam said. "He kissed me." They both squealed.

"Bobby Williams made the first move? Really? That is either a miracle or a sign the world is about to end."

"I'd call it a miracle."

"Wait. How did this even happen? Just yesterday, you complained about having no alone time with Bobby."

"Our moms are best friends," Sam explained. "Usually, they don't leave us alone like that. They were in a perfect mood last night. You know, grownups, they started reminiscing about the good old days. They decided to go upstairs, leaving us alone for the first time in ages."

Delia grinned. "Tell me more. Tell me more?"

"My mom told us to behave ourselves, but we didn't." Sam giggled, remembering the warmth of their two bodies after the kiss activated her power. A euphoric rush caused Sam to blush bright red. Her hands warmed up. Sam hid her hands behind her back and tried to calm down. "Bobby and I talked about our... uh... lives. He was being so thoughtful and sweet. Then, we ended up kneeling face to face. Then he leaned in and kissed me."

"And then?"

"I kissed him back. What do you think? Then he kissed me back, and then..."

"Yeah, okay. A great make-out session ensued."

"Great doesn't cover it. I'm talking freaking fireworks!"

"Hey, did he, you know, try to...."

"No, Bobby has..."

"I'd say he has incredible self-control. Wow, Sam."

"Wow, that's what Bobby said too," Sam replied. "That's what I said too." The look on her face confirmed just how wow it had been. "It may not have been our first kiss, but it was our first real kiss... the perfect kiss... kisses." Sam's face flushed, so she took a deep breath.

"Wow," Delia said again. "Delia fanned a notebook in Sam's face. "Cool down, friend. Ugh. I need a boyfriend."

******

The rift kept growing. The counter force had pushed it back open to sixty percent.

"Why is this happening," Miles shouted. "You said you could close the rift."

"We warned you of this possibility. Let's focus on the problem at hand. The other side is about to gain control of the rift.

"I hate this new world you introduced me to," Miles said. "This is too much."

"Look, Miles. We need a solution," Rich said. "The system has reached its limits. Our technology can't stop this much of a pushback.

Miles replied sarcastically, "Well, I don't have any magic up my sleeve. Do you?"

"Not for this."

"We have limited options at this point," Bill said. "I suggest the next step needs to be non-technological and non-magical."

Miles replied, "What?" Even Rich had a questioning look.

"We need to buy us some time. So, let's bury the HGC chamber. Slow the enemy down long enough to find a solution."

"Bury. And how do we do that?"

Bulldoze the entire building on top of the HGC chamber.

"You are talking about destroying a complex worth billions of dollars," Miles exclaimed. "And it would cost twice as much to fix it later. If this turns out to be nothing, It would end my career."

"We can't take chances with something this dangerous. Doing nothing is just not an option."

"I can't believe this is happening. No... No. I can't. I won't do that."

"Then you'd better tell Bates to surround the rift with everything he has. If those Shadow demons break through, we won't survive."

Miles glared in frustration. "Why an invasion? According to Mr. Maeda, and I'm not saying I believe him, the only monster invasion of this world ended decades ago. Before any of us were born, that begs the question. Why are you so sure those creatures are about to come through my rift?"

"Because I have seen this same scenario unfold before. It didn't end well."

Miles shook his head. "Why should I believe you? How can I trust you when you are hiding something from me? Something pretty damn big. Tell me the truth. Where have you seen such an impossible scenario happen before? It wasn't on this planet, was it."

Bill looked at Rich for help but was busy with his problems. "Two parallel universes can be similar in so many ways. Except one has been fighting a war with monsters like these for almost a hundred years. The other just found out that such creatures exist."

"So, this is not your world."

"We are only trying to help," Bill assured him. "This is our world now. We live here. Our families and friends are here in this world. You must believe us. When this happened to our world, we didn't believe in demons, monsters, and magic either."

"Where is your world?"

Bill said, "Many interdimensional jumps away. We don't even know if it still exists. We couldn't save our world, but we can save this one." He took a deep breath. "Eugene, please. We are not the enemy."

******

Bobby couldn't wait for the fourth period. This new emotional connection between him and Sam kept surprising him. It amazed him that the thought of seeing her thrilled him as much as it did. When he saw her in the room, his heart skipped a beat. Her reaction was the same. She reached out to him and took his hand.

"Hi," she said with the cutest smile ever.

He felt the warmth of her power as he took her hand. The only reply his hormone-charged brain could come up with was, "How's it going?"

"Good. How about you?"

"Now that you're here, pretty good." He felt the muscles in his cheeks stretch to the fullest as he smiled. That made Sam smile even bigger. Lost in each other, they didn't notice that everyone in the room watched this unusual encounter with unusual interest.

******

Miles had activated all the fire doors throughout the control center to provide additional protection for his people should an invasion happen. A bang rattled the heavy door protecting the control room entrance. General Bates entered the room, followed by four military policemen. They made a direct line toward the two new members of Miles' team. The general stepped forward while the four soldiers grabbed and cuffed Bill and Rich. He looked at Miles with a smug smile.

Miles stood in shock. "What is the meaning of this, General?"

"Bill Williams and Rich Thomas, you are under arrest under the National Security and Antiterrorism Act of 2026."

"What are you talking about? These men aren't terrorists."

"They're not who they claim to be." Bates faced the two men. "You've lied to us. Remember what I said I'd do if I found out you lied?"

"We haven't lied to you, General," Bill said. "Everything we've told you, everything we've done is true."

"Yet, we now have the opposite of what you promised," The General barked.

Bill protested. "We told you it might be too late to stop an invasion. If you hadn't ignored our warnings, we could have better prepared for this."

"I have to wonder if this mess isn't exactly what you two wanted from the beginning."

Appalled, Rich protested. "Are you insane, General?" The man holding him wrenched his arms backward. Rich cried out in pain.

It was Bill's turn to protest. "What possible reason could we have for wanting this to happen?"

"General, I demand you stop this," Miles said.

"Shut up, Miles. I am in charge here. These men are spies."

"Nonsense."

"Sorry, Eugene, but according to the DNA test I ordered, these guys may not even be human. Can you believe that?"

"You took our DNA without our permission," Bill shouted. "You had no right."

"I don't know where you are from, but they tell me the odds are overwhelming against your ancestors evolving on this planet."

Miles raised his voice in frustration. "I know, General. I suspected it long ago. They have already admitted it to me. We have a crisis and can't handle this situation without their help."

"You should have informed me of your suspicions," the general barked. "If we weren't in the middle of a crisis, as you say, I would also arrest you."

"Oh, come now, General," Miles scoffed. "They explained everything, including their motivation for wanting to help us. Please stop this nonsense and let these men get back to work."

"Sorry, I cannot do that. These two may have come from the same world as those creatures. I cannot just take their word as proof. I am taking them into custody until this is over. Then we can sort it out." He turned to the guards. "I don't want them escaping out a window, so take them downstairs to a secure room. Hold them there until I can decide what to do with them."

"Yes, sir," the guards replied.

Bates refused to discuss the matter further. At least Miles got Bates to agree to establish a larger defensive perimeter around the HGC building. Fifty more soldiers and one armored vehicle equipped with a high-caliber machine gun showed up shortly after and surrounded the building. According to Bates, the situation didn't require any further action. The soldiers set up defensive barriers at all the building's exits. If they dared come through the rift, these creatures didn't stand a chance.

******

With a final power push, the witches opened and sealed the rupture. This time, it stayed open. The Shadows had total control. Twenty-one of the most prominent male warriors stood ready to enter the rupture. Their job was to punch a hole through the enemy's first line of defense. They knew they would probably die doing so, but they believed in a brave and honorable way to die. Behind the male Shadows waited High Overseer Strong and her forty-eight elite warrior witches. The faster, more agile witches would fly above the battlefield and destroy the enemy from the air. Aerial supremacy would ensure a quicker victory.

Above the massive staging arena, seven divisions of ninety-one male and female warriors stood ready. Among them were Fire Claws, Broken Fang, and several others of Claws' enforcers. This was a place of honor. They would lead legions of Shadow demons in conquest as overseers and sub-overseers. Each legion of three to seven thousand Shadows made this the most significant military force in the history of the empire.

Overseer Strong hissed as she entered the rift alone. Her staff illuminated the interior of the sphere. She looked up. She then looked to the right and the left. She touched the chamber wall with the raptor head on her staff. A rune appeared.

"Clear a pathway," she thought. "According to my will, so shall it be."

A flash of her magic made a hole through the metal structure. No one hindered the Overseer, so she stepped out of the sphere into the enclosed containment room. She planned to make four separate exit tunnels: one upward, two more directly to her right and left, and the final tunnel behind her. Not knowing the thickness of the surrounding walls, she would apply the full force of her magic.

The High Overseer touched the surface with her staff, where she wanted to create pathways. Four runes appeared.

"Clear these four pathways with the force of seven withes," she shouted. "According to my will, so shall it be."

The four openings exploded simultaneously. Metal, concrete, bricks, or anything else that lay in the path of her spell blew away hundreds of feet from the HGC building. The debris shredded personnel, equipment, and nearby buildings like cannonballs and shrapnel. When the dust settled, the Overseer smiled. She stepped back through the rupture and roared triumphally, "The battle begins." An army of tens of thousands strong roared.

Spine Back was the first through the openings. The center one led from the sphere up through the roof. Spine Back jumped from floor to ceiling and then up onto the roof. His final thought was, "Perhaps I become a hero today."

Spine walked to the edge of the roof. The human soldiers backed up before they opened fire. The armored personnel carrier with a high-caliber gun on top sat about fifty feet away. Spine Back leaped from the roof and tucked into a ball. Flaring his spines, he launched them at the APC. The shocked soldier manning the gun opened fire at a colossal monster hurtling toward him. The tracer rounds ripped through Spine Back before the Shadow's spines reached their target. The spines, ranging from six to forty-eight inches, flew like a barrage of arrows straight at the APC. It only took one to stop the gunner's heart. The rest disabled the vehicle. The APC's fuel tanks exploded.

Spine Back had done his duty and died a hero of the Shadow Empire. The rest of the advance force followed Spine Back's example. With equal determination, they exited all four fronts simultaneously, overpowering all remaining human soldiers.

Then came the warrior witches. Multiple blurred figures with magical wings wide emerged from the open tunnels. They launched in several directions. Blades of fiery magic slashed the ground, destroying buildings and killing people as they fled for their lives. The witches spread across the campus and out over the city.

High Overseer Strong appeared on the open roof, followed by Fire Claws, Broken Fang, and several other Shadow overseers. Each surveyed the rubble and strewn dead bodies. As far as they could tell, nothing remained alive within their view. Fire Claws growled with the pleasure of a quick victory. The others joined him. This was an excellent day for the Shadow Empire.

******

Everyone barricaded in the control center survived the first wave of the invasion. General Bates watched in horror as the assault proceeded. Security cameras provided them with front-row seats to the disastrous scene. Shaken, the General called for reinforcements. Ignoring all warnings had proved to be a tragic mistake. Air strikes would come from nearby bases. The army would airlift new ground troops. Bates knew he was responsible for this mess as the officer in charge. That would be the price of his arrogance.

Miles couldn't wait any longer. "General, I need Williams and Thomas."

"Don't be ridiculous."

"Me ridiculous? You colossal idiot," Miles yelled.

"I haven't forgotten your role as a collaborator with these men. I can also have you up on charges of insubordination."

"Haven't you made a big enough mess today? If you don't release them and let them help, I will ensure the world knows this happened on your watch. That is, if we don't die today. Those men may be the only people who can help me fix this."

"We can't..."

"And who cares where they are from? They can help us. Just get Williams and Thomas in here. Now, General, or I'll feed you to those monsters myself!"

The General ferocious glare made it clear he wasn't happy, but Miles stood his ground. Realizing Miles might be right, he backed off and nodded to the guards. They exited the room and soon returned with the two prisoners, the heavy fire doors closing behind them.

"Don't just stand there; cut them loose," Miles ordered. The guards looked to the General, who nodded.

Bill and Rich ran to Rich's computer station only to discover that things had worsened. "We have lost control of the rift," Rich told Miles.

"What do we do," Miles asked, desperate for a solution.

"Sorry. It's too late. We no longer can close the rift from here," Rich said.

"There is no way to close the rift? None?"

"I didn't say that. We can close it, but not from here. The only way to close it is from the other side."

"Are you saying I need to order men to go through the rift," The General said.

"Heavens, no," Rich replied. "I doubt humans would last ten seconds in that environment."

"Then who?"

"Only one being on this planet can get through that rift alive." Miles gave Rich a blank stare. "Cooper," Rich said!

Chapter 42

LET IT OUT

An animal acts on instinct. If threatened, it reacts. If hungry, it reacts. If afraid, it reacts. Every wild or domesticated animal will instinctively react when presented with a stimulus. Yet, Percy's specimen had remained stoic, ignoring all tests meant for studying animal behavior. Thus far, Percy hadn't even figured out what the creature ate. Considering the wake of the violent deaths the other creature had caused, he assumed his specimen was a meat eater. But when offered raw meat, the specimen turned up his nose like a finicky cat. So, he gave it live animals, thinking it might desire fresh meat, but even this offering proved unsatisfactory. The specimen either ignored the animals or played with them, petting, grooming, and licking the fury bodies in a rather maternal fashion. Percy considered the possibility of offering it human flesh, but he figured no one would agree. So, what did the stupid thing eat? The specimen was more interested in licking the walls of its shielded cage as though the cube-shaped prison was some kind of giant salt lick.

"What if the cage is like a salt lick to it," Percy said to himself. If so, then why?"

Then, the specimen's behavior changed. Earlier in the day, it had gone crazy and charged the walls of its cage.

"If it keeps this up, it may die before I get the necessary answers. Or worse, escape."

Percy thought of what Mr. Maeda had said. Studying this specimen would only prove that it could be killed. Because, in the end, all he would have learned was how to kill it. The old man's words haunted him. Percy knew it was true. He would study the alien creature for as long as possible. When the time came, if it hadn't died already, he would kill it. Then, dissect it with cold fascination. That made him feel a little sad.

Percy's experience with dissecting animals began in undergrad biology. Of course, that fetal pig was already dead. As a thirteen-year-old prodigy, he obsessed over what made things live. Since then, many creatures have died in his quest to understand the universal mysteries of life. The existence of life in this world, whether plants, animals, or people, was a miracle, yet all living things died. Paradoxically, studying life sometimes requires ending life. All to discover what made it alive in the first place. This paradox was hard to reconcile, even for Percy.

The creature, Cooper, as the kids had called it, came from another world. That made it a unique life form, but it, too, had to die someday. Percy would have the honor of picking that day in this particular case. It did frustrate him because, after ending a life, he had discovered that something significant and undefinable always went missing. Life was warm and vibrant. Death was cold and blank.

Percy asked himself, "Why do I always kill things?" Then he sighed. "Because my research requires it."

Percy had known for a long time that he was not like other people. He had several personality disorders, including an undeniable lack of empathy. He was a sociopath. He saw living things as objects to be studied. Feelings didn't matter. Feelings tended to get in the way of science. Percy wondered if ethics even mattered in the long run. This was his science. Cold fascination would always guide his choices.

Percy chuckled at himself, "I would probably kill and dissect my mother if I thought I could learn something from it." Fortunately for his mother, Percy didn't find her fascinating. They hadn't spoken in years.

The phone in the lab rang. The caller ID read Dr. Eugene Miles. "Eugene," Percy answered.

"Yes," the agitated voice on the other end said. "We're under attack, Percy. I need your help."

"Under attacked? By whom?"

"The Shadow creature that went back through the rift," he replied. "He came back with more of his kind. Williams, Thomas, and Maeda were right. What a horrendous mess."

"How fascinating. What is happening exactly? What are the creatures like?"

"Horrendous," Miles replied. "It's a nightmare. Everything happened so fast. The soldiers guarding the Center didn't stand a chance. As far as we can tell, the creatures now control the entire campus area. We barricaded ourselves in the control center. Fortunately, the creatures haven't discovered us yet. Probably the only reason we're still alive."

"Sorry to hear that, but I don't see how I can help."

"How is your specimen? I hope you haven't killed it yet."

"Of course not," Percy said, annoyed by the insinuation. Then he thought out loud, "That might explain this new behavior."

"What do you mean? What's it doing?"

"The specimen has been acting crazy since this morning. It's running around and banging against the cell walls. Maybe it senses something is wrong. Quite fascinating, really - for me, not for you. I had to evacuate the lab."

"Listen, Percy," Miles said, his tone urgent. "You need to let it go."

"Let what go."

"The specimen."

"What? Our only specimen? Why would I do that?"

"You have to, Percy. We have lost control of the rift. An invasion is underway."

"No, I won't do it. It's too valuable."

"Listen, the General himself has ordered its release. This is an order, Percy. The only way to close the rift and stop this disaster is from the other side of the rift. Someone has to trigger the rift's closure from there. This Cooper creature is the only being capable of doing that. It's the only way. Otherwise, we won't survive the day, and many more people will die."

"This is horrible. Where will I get another specimen?"

"There is no other way. I will explain everything later. Just do it."

"Look, it's not like I can put it on a plane and send it to you. It won't cooperate."

"It's the girl. She is the only one who can control it."

"Can we get her here?"

"Not possible, I'm afraid."

"Then what?"

"Let it out. Set it free. Considering how it responded to the girl, it will find its way to her. Then she will bring it to us?"

"How am I supposed to let it go?"

"Jeez Percy... Just open the damn door and leave it alone."

******

Little Toe's prison walls disappeared, and that change confused him, and he questioned the reality of this situation. It made no sense. Caution made him look around before acting. He couldn't see or smell any humans in the room but could smell the outside world. Looking up, he saw a large opening in the ceiling.

"Why would they leave such an obvious escape route?"

Toe decided he had to take this chance to escape. A terrible disaster had occurred. Sam would need his help. He climbed up to the opening in a few quick leaps and exited. In the empty hanger above, Toe waited, expecting his captors to stop him. They didn't, so he headed west at full speed toward Sam.

******

A distraught Percy walked back into the empty lab. At least he had been there to witness something extraordinary. The creature didn't just bolt for freedom. It thought about it. Then, it determined a logical course of action. "Intelligent. Fascinating," Percy said. "But I better get the specimen back when this is over, or another just like it."

Chapter 43

CASUALTIES OF WAR

The air attack began as the first wave of army Apache and Blackhawk helicopters roared over the quiet El Palmar community. Lieutenant Heart, call sign *Papa*, had flown his Apache into combat many times before, but his co-pilot and gunner, Lieutenant Parker, call sign *Firefly*, was new to the aircraft. That didn't mean he lacked skill. What the kid lacked in experience, he made up in situational awareness, quick wit, and accuracy. The kid could shoot like the best of them.

"The UCEP campus lays dead ahead," Heart said.

"Okay, Papa," Parker replied. "I'm ready to slice and dice whatever is out there."

"That's the attitude, Firefly. Let's kick some enemy butt."

"That's assuming the enemy has a butt, Papa."

"They got to have a butt of some kind. Every living thing has to take a crap somehow. Well, if they don't, we just kick some other part."

Parker laughed. "Roger that, Papa. Let's rock and roll the night away."

Lieutenant Heart's mind flashed back to the bazaar briefing when their commander explained their mission's unusual and grave nature.

******

"This is no ordinary act of terrorism," the commander told them. "Terrorism has little to do with this. We are being invaded. I can't think of another way to break this to you, so I will just say it. The enemy is of a non-terrestrial origin."

"Wait," Parker said. "You mean... like an alien invasion?"

Harris, another pilot, said, "This has got to be some kind of joke, sir."

"They are probably talking about undocumented aliens," said Hernandez. "That's just damn racist, man." A few chuckles around the room.

"You heard what I said. No joke, these are non-terrestrial; our orders are to refer to them only as the enemy. So, no loose talk about aliens. Understood?"

"Yes, Sir," they all barked.

Lt. Heart thought out loud, "Why would little green men want to invade a quiet university community like El Palmar?" Some of them gave a nervous laugh.

"This is serious, Lieutenant. No laughing matter," the commander rebuked. "A contingent of Army National Guard and some Special Forces soldiers were already on the ground when the attack began, so someone must have expected something was up. From what I understand, the aliens killed them all." An unsettling silence fell over the room.

"What do we know about these... aliens?"

"Enemy."

"Okay, enemy."

"You know what I know. Everything about this mission remains highly classified. All Command told me was that you will have no trouble identifying the enemy."

A pilot gulped. "What's that supposed to mean?"

"My guess? The enemy looks nothing like us." Discomforted by that answer, the pilots shifted in their seats. "As I said, casualties on the ground have been high. That includes citizens. Look for survivors. Rescue when possible. Otherwise, once you identify the enemy, fire at will. This is an attack on the US of A. We cannot let this stand no matter who or what the enemy is. Be smart, be safe, and please come home."

"Yes, sir," they trumpeted in unison!

******

Before they reached their target, Heart saw what appeared to be incoming air-to-air missiles trailing fire.

"Incoming, Firefly," he yelled.

Firefly opened fire as Papa performed evasive maneuvers. The incoming fire missed them. Half of the helicopters went down within a few minutes of engagement.

"Holy crap, what was that," Firefly squawked? "Where did those missiles come from?"

"It must come from an enemy aircraft of some kind. I didn't see anything. Did you, Firefly?"

"Not a thing."

The surviving aircraft passed over the Center for Interdimensional Physics. That's when the remaining pilots got their first look at the enemy. They opened fire. The blaze of fire shredded several large Shadows into dust. Explosive fireballs incinerated more of the monsters.

Papa swooped in for a closer look, and Firefly opened fire at the gaping holes filled with oncoming Shadows. The previous bombing run had done little to stop the flow of alien creatures.

"Okay, you ugly, crap holeless freaks, come to Papa," said Lt. Heart. "Come to Papa." The pilot's signature line that got him his call sign.

Keeping Firefly's gun pointed at the building, Papa rotated around ground zero while Firefly let his guns and missiles blaze away. He killed the creatures by the hundreds. But even more of the horrifying monsters appeared out of the fire and smoke.

"I'm pulling up for another run at these things," Papa said.

"Okay, Papa. These darn things are everywhere. We need a new strategy," Firefly said. Out of the corner of his eye, Firefly saw something move. "Look out," he yelled.

As the Apache pulled up, one of the monsters, this one with long clawed hands, leaped off the ground and slashed through the front cockpit. The Apache spun out of control and crashed into a nearby building, sending a ball of flames high into the air. The two remaining aircraft retreated, but the Shadow Witches pursued and destroyed them.

Back at the airbase, the brass watched the sortie's real-time transmission. The mission had failed on every level, except maybe reconnaissance. Although they still didn't know what the enemy was, they now knew what they looked like and how dangerous they were.

Then came the news that the invasion had trapped several important scientists and military personnel inside the Center for Interdimensional Physics command center. The next sortie received orders to locate and rescue General Alfred Bates and Dr. Eugene Miles and, if possible, any other survivors at the site.

******

Alarmed residents came out of their homes to investigate the cause of thunderous noises. After the low-flying military helicopters had passed over, gunfire and explosions followed. The sounds of war seemed way out of context for El Palmar. Sirens blared as police and other first responders took action. Police cruisers appeared in the residential neighborhoods, broadcasting a Department of Homeland Security message that a real emergency existed. The police warned people to stay off the streets and to remain in their homes until further notice. Of course, when people fear for their lives, they don't always obey. Thousands of panicked residents made the situation worse by trying to leave town. Cars soon clogged all the routes in and out of town, delaying the arrival of Army National Guard troop reinforcements. Personnel choppers began carrying troops into the city. The strange creatures in the air attacked and destroyed. The troops made their way to the battle on foot.

A bloody feeding frenzy led the Shadows to the nearby homes and businesses.

Chapter 44

THE VENGEFUL DEMON

The school had already let out before the invasion started. Bobby sat in the hall waiting for Sam, who was at another one of her meetings. These meetings went on forever. He wondered what they could be discussing. Not that he minded waiting for Sam. No matter, he would use the time to daydream about her. He had never felt like this before. Just thinking about her gave him a rush. He thought about holding hands, going on walks, swinging in the park together, and kissing. Why hadn't he tried to kiss Sam sooner? He had wasted so much time.

Bobby daydreamed away until he fell into darkness. All thoughts of happiness left him, and something horrible replaced it. An unrelenting panic doubled him over. He felt physical pain. Struggling to breathe, he rolled onto his side, curled up into a fetal position, and passed out.

"Bobby... Bobby," Sam's voice echoed inside his head. He awoke to see her and three other students looking down at him. It took a minute for the terrible feeling to subside. Shaking, Bobby said, "The Shadow demons. They're back." Another intense anxiety attack hit him, and he cried out in pain.

"What did he say," asked one student.

All their phones chimed off with text messages and calls. Sam looked at her phone. It was her mom, but she needed to tend to Bobby first.

"What are you talking about, Dad," a boy said into his phone. Then, they all heard the sounds of explosions in the distance. "Yeah, okay. I'll come straight home."

"My mom texted me. There has been a terrorist attack or something," a girl said.

"Yeah, that's what my dad said, too. I need a ride home," the girl said.

"Okay, I'll take you home," said another. "It's on my way."

"Thanks," she replied. "You're the best."

Sam turned to her friends. "Yeah, you guys better leave. I'll take care of Bobby and make sure he gets home safe."

"Are you sure," one of them asked.

"Yes, we will be fine. Don't worry. Get going." The other teens ran. Sam turned to Bobby and asked, "Do you mean the one who attacked us has returned?"

He struggled to say, "Yes... I think so. It feels the same as that night, only a hundred times worse. Sam, I feel... sick. I think I might throw up."

"Oh no! Don't... I mean.... What can I do? Can you get up?"

"Yeah," he said. "I think so." She helped him to his feet. "Man, if this happens every time I sense danger, I'll be useless."

"Maybe it takes time to get used to the side effects."

"Sam, something is happening. Here in town. Maybe we should leave, too."

"Okay," she said. "Let's get to my car."

Sam supported Bobby as they headed to the parking lot. But when they reached the car, Bobby doubled over again.

"No, wait," he said, shaking. "We can't go yet."

"Why?"

"It's too dangerous out here. We need to hide."

"Our moms will worry if we don't come home."

"Call your mom," Bobby suggested. "Believe me, Sam. We need to stay off the streets."

"Why not go home as fast as we can?"

"It's hunting you, Sam."

"What's hunting me?"

"That bad Shadow demon. It's out there," Bobby continued. "I can sense it better now. There are a lot more of his kind as well. I can feel their hunger, but the one who attacked us is pissed off. It is looking for you."

Shaken, Sam agreed. "Okay... okay. We will need help. You call for backup while I call our moms." They both retreated to the campus complex, hoping to find a good place to hide as far away from the danger as possible.

******

Broken Fang left the battle to begin his search. Fire Claws and the others had gotten lost in a feeding frenzy. They wouldn't miss him. Although as hungry for human blood energy as the other Shadows, at the moment, the desire for revenge motivated far more. He would return to the battle once he killed and ate the little witch. The scent of her magic hung in the air. All he had to do was follow that scent.

******

Anne and Kevin waited with Sarah at the Williams' home for Sam and Bobby to arrive. Urgent texts from their husbands had said, "Get to the safe room with the kids! Now!" But neither Sam nor Bobby had answered their phones.

"Where are they," Anne said. "Why is it whenever an emergency arises, our kids are never where they need to be?"

"I'm here, Mom," Kevin replied.

Anne looked at him. "Yes, Kevin, I know, and I'm glad."

"What's going on, Mom," Kevin asked.

Anne's phone rang. "It's Sam," she said, answering. "Sam, where are you?"

"We're still at school," Sam replied.

"Is Bobby with you?"

"Yes, but..."

"Get home," Anne ordered. "Your dad sent a text. We must go into the safe room as soon as you arrive."

"We have a safe room? What the heck, Mom? Are there any other bits of information you would like to share?"

"Sam, just get home... please. I'm worried sick."

"Bobby says it's too dangerous to be on the streets right now."

"It's dangerous everywhere. I want you home. Our safe room is the safest place on the planet."

"I'm sure it is, but Bobby felt something awful coming. It was so strong he passed out. Tell his mom not to worry. He's okay now. We will hide here at school until Bobby feels it's safe to leave."

"Sam!"

"I promise we will get home as quick as we can. Bye. Love you." Sam ended the call.

"Sam! Those two..." Anne exclaimed.

"What did she say?"

"They are still at the school because Bobby had one of his feelings."

"Oh, I see, and she won't leave until he says it is okay."

"Exactly. We have created monsters."

"We can't lock ourselves in until they get here. They won't know what to do. What choice do we have? We have to wait for them."

"Have we kept too many secrets from them?"

"Call her back and tell them to come directly to this house. That will save time."

Anne tried to phone. The screen read, No Service. "Oh, great. Now, what do we do?"

"Let's put notes on your doors so she will know to come here."

"Yeah... alright."

"Try not to worry," Sarah said, knowing how impossible that would be. They turned off the lights and returned to the dark house, preparing for the worst while hoping for the best. They had done that a lot over the last few weeks.

******

Fang's nose led him straight to El Palmar High School, where the witch's scent permeated the place. The campus had several structures with courtyards and green spaces between them. Fang began a destructive search, going from building to building and classroom to classroom.

Bobby and Sam ran across the open gymnasium, then into the men's locker room.

"Is it okay for me to be here," Sam asked.

"Under the circumstances, I'm sure no one will complain." Bobby listened at the door. "Quiet so far," he said. "Maybe we lost it this time."

Sam said on the edge of tears, "How does it keep finding us?" Her whole body trembled. "Bobby, I'm so scared. Hold me."

He put his arms around her. "Yeah, I'm scared too." A loud crash of broken glass and metal came from somewhere close. "Crap! It's like a freaking bloodhound."

Sam relied on Bobby's senses to get them out of this, but the determined Shadow still managed to stay on their heels. "Should we hide in the lockers?"

Bobby looked around for an exit. "No, we need to keep moving." The frosted windows in the outside wall above the lockers looked to be the only way out. He stacked several benches next to the lockers and climbed up on top. Twisting the latch at the bottom of the window, he pushed. The window pivoted outward. The opening gave just enough room to wiggle through one at a time. A good reason for eating healthy food is to stay thin.

"Climb up, Sam. You go first." He gave her his hand and helped her up. Sam climbed on top of the lockers. "Go out feet first. Be careful how you land. This would be a bad time to twist an ankle."

She poked her head out the window. "There's a dumpster right below us."

"Perfect." Another loud bang. "Go." Sam stuck her feet through the window and inched backward until her feet dangled. The final push put her on top of the dumpster. Another loud crash came from outside the locker room.

"Hurry, Bobby."

It was Bobby's turn. He had just got his feet and legs through when the locker room door and part of the wall crashed open. The angry creature entered the room. With Sam's help, Bobby slipped the rest of the way out and landed on the dumpster. Looking back through the window, he saw the giant ripping through the locker stacks.

"It's good we didn't hide inside the lockers," Bobby told Sam while closing the window behind him. They ran on to the next building.

In fury, Fang threw lockers and benches around the room. His hatred pushed him onward. The search led him to another large building. The building's roof sloped upward from the front entrance, forming a mountainous roofline that leveled off two stories up. The sign out front of the building said, *EPHS Theater Center, Opening soon: Shakespeare's Tempest, November 16 thru 18*. Not that Fang could read or cared what the sign said. As soon as he broke through the front glass doors, he knew he had found them. Scurrying across the entryway lobby, he charged through another set of doors and into the empty auditorium.

A single bare sixty-watt light bulb on a six-foot-tall movable stand cast shadows across the stage. The light, however, did little to illuminate the auditorium itself. The drama students had constructed scenery for the upcoming play, so there were platforms at various levels with steps and ramps connecting them. Above the platforms hung several painted backdrops and portal drops depicting the play's various scenes. Usually, the theatrical setting would have fascinated Bobby, but the colors and dark shadows looked downright creepy right now. This had to be the worst place in the world to get cornered, but the insane creature was relentless. They had to keep moving. In the backstage right corner, they found stairs. They climbed several flights to a metal catwalk high above the floor. Bobby felt dizzy looking down through the scenic drops to the platforms below. The catwalk led to a fire door in the proscenium wall, the main wall that separated the stage from the auditorium. On the other side of the fire door, the catwalk continued above the seats.

Trying to be as quiet as possible, they crept past two perpendicular catwalks leading to the banks of lighting equipment. The two frightened teens continued to the back of the auditorium to the sound and lighting control booths. Fang's large, dark figure searched through the seats below. Bobby tried to open the booth door but found it locked. Several choice words nearly left his lips, but screaming out swear words wouldn't help. Neither of them felt ready to fight this Shadow demon, but it looked more and more like they would have to. For now, they just needed a place to think and plan.

The smell of the witch was everywhere now, and it confused Fang. He searched the seats row by row, ripping seats out of the floor. When he finished with the seats, the Calibanian figure, looking *"as wicked dew,"* took his place on stage for Act I, Scene II.

Bobby glanced across at the wall of glass windows in front of the control booths. A sliding glass panel in the middle section was open. He pointed to it. Sam looked at him as if to say, *you've got to be kidding me*. Through impromptu signing, he laid out the plan. He would inch along the twelve-inch wide ledge across the windows until he reached the center window. The ledge hung about fifteen feet above the back row of seats. It would be a simple enough task if not for his shaking arms and legs.

He climbed out on the ledge. Hugging the glass, he crawled on his hands and knees toward the opening. The ledge lay in a dark shadow. He prayed nothing hidden in the darkness that he might accidentally knock off the ledge, which made him think of rats. He hated rats. It's a stupid thing to worry about, considering the monster after them. When he reached the open window, he looked inside. The room was dark. He climbed through the window onto a table covered in black electrical extension cords. That instantly made him think of snakes. He didn't much like snakes either. Untangling himself, he shook off the creepy sensation and reached the access door. It opened with a swish, and Sam slipped into the room.

"What do we...?" Bobby put his hand over her mouth. He made his way back to the open window and slid the window panel closed. The window latch made a "click". Not the loudest click in the world, but loud enough to make him gasp with fear. The small but audible click seemed to echo through the empty auditorium.

Fang stood mid-stage on top of the highest platform. He heard the sound and turned to find the source. His eyes narrowed on the windows at the back of the auditorium. "I've got you now, witch."

"I'm so sorry, Sam," Bobby whispered. "My decisions have only made things worse."

"We'll think of something. We have to." Tears filled her terrified eyes. They held each other tight. Sam buried her face in Bobby's shoulder to muffle the sobs slipping out.

"I've got an idea," Bobby said. He found the lighting control console and turned the power switch to the on position. As Fang crouched, ready to charge, bright lights flooded the stage from all directions, dazzling his eyes. The demon's shadowy body blurred as he turned and twisted in blinded confusion. The last lighting cue of the previous night's rehearsal had been the curtain call - all instruments set to one hundred percent.

"Thank you, Drama Club," Bobby whispered.

Fang roared in anger. "Enough of your witchy tricks," he thought out. "I will enjoy killing you!"

From the back of the auditorium, two voices, one old and one young, chanted in unison, "Rin pyō tō sha kai jin retsu zai zen... Destroy this demon!" Grandpa Maeda and Jeff entered through the two opposite side aisles. Their hands were in front of them, making the hand seal that Grandpa had used the first time he met Cooper. "Rin pyō tō sha kai jin retsu zai zen... Destroy this demon! Rin pyō tō sha kai jin retsu zai zen... Destroy this demon!" They repeated the chant again and again. To help Jeff remember, Grandpa had written each syllable on the boy's arm with a black Sharpie. There hadn't been time to memorize. Jeff's spell casting was weak but added some strength to Grandpa's spell. Fang stood dumbfounded by the unexpected attack of magic. He felt dizzy as the spell drained him of strength.

Sam ran out of the control booth onto one of the two main lighting catwalks. "Sam, wait," Bobby yelled as he followed her.

While Grandpa Maeda kept chanting, Jeff called out to his friends, "You guys okay?"

"Does it look like we are okay," Bobby said. "What took you so long?"

"We are okay for now," Sam said. Jeff returned to his chanting. "But what should we do?"

This time, Grandpa answered. "Attack the creature while he's vulnerable. You can do it, Sam. Just like you did the first time." He returned to chanting.

"Sam," Bobby said. "We have to do something. Ready or not, it's time to fight. This monster has to die because I don't want you to die."

Sam stood firm, extended her arms in front of her, and concentrated. Her hands began to glow. An energy ball flashed from her hands and struck Fang in the leg. Unharmed, he growled in defiance.

The old man called out again. "Again, Sam. Hit him in the head. Just keep doing it until it kills him."

Sam hit Fang with another bolt of energy higher in the chest. She must have hit something this time because Fang let out a horrifying scream.

"It's not enough," Sam cried out.

"Lend her your strength, Bobby," Grandpa yelled.

"Yeah, that's it," Jeff yelled. "The coupling thing. You two have always been strongest as a couple." The two spell chanters had reached the stage front as the mantra of mind-numbing magic held the Shadow demon confused.

Sam looked at Bobby. He stepped up behind her, put his arms around her waist, and embraced her. Then he whispered in her ear the perfect magical charm. "I love you, Sam. You can do this." With Bobby holding her, Sam refocused.

Fang managed to break free of the spell and launched toward Sam.

Sam screamed, "Stop it. Just die already!"

The Shadow was halfway to Sam when the fiery blast hit him. The intense blue and white energy lit up the auditorium, incinerating Broken Fang instantly. A cloud of black dust fell to the floor.

In newly found bravado, Sam said, "That's what I'm talking about. You big, ugly dust bunny!"

Sam then turned to Bobby and threw her arms around his neck. Still shaking from the adrenaline rush, she held him tight. Her powers had worked—they had actually worked.

"Thank you," she said breathlessly into Bobby's ear. "I love you too."

Jeff whooped with laughter. "Ugly dust bunny? That's all you had? I love it. That was so you." He turned to his grandpa. "She called it an ugly dust bunny."

"An apt description," the old man said. "And I gather she didn't like the demon's performance." Grandpa had a mischievous grin.

"Gee, I thought he was on fire," Jeff laughed.

"Yeah. One hell of a performance." Grandpa chuckled.

"Everyone's a critic these days," Jeff called out. "Sam, you were amazing."

"Come on, you two," Grandpa called to Bobby and Sam. "We won this battle, but the war isn't over yet."

Chapter 45

RUN THROUGH THE NIGHT

Little Toe felt powerful as he ran through the Southern California landscape. This world had changed him in so many ways. He ran faster, leaped further, and moved with more fluid motion than he ever thought possible. He was a new Shadow. His prison cell walls tasted bitter, but the energy emitted enhanced his physical strength. Although he believed that captors should treat all prisoners with a degree of mercy, his captors seemed quite generous. The prison walls provided him with more than enough nourishment.

For some inexplicable reason, his captors kept bringing strange offerings to him. He got the impression they wanted him to eat the offerings. They offered him the meat of dead creatures, completely useless for food and thoroughly disgusting. When a creature dies, the energy leaves the body. He ignored the gross meat. His captors finally stopped bringing it to him.

Then, one day, they placed small living creatures in his cell. He liked these creatures. They made good company for him in the long, lonely hours. Toe wondered why his captors had imprisoned these cute little creatures. He understood why he was there, but what had these little ones done to deserve imprisonment?

When the invasion started, Toe had felt it. Afraid for Sam, he tried desperately to escape. The harder he tried, the more desperate he became. The strong walls kept knocking him back, but he had to keep trying. He had to get to Sam.

His journey through the night took him from the eastern California desert bowl, up and over the rugged desert mountains with its rocky peaks and deep canyon gorges, down into the rural inland valleys and coastal foothills. Finally, he reached the coast, arriving at El Palmar before sunrise. The urgency to find Sam drove him all through the night. He needed to be at her side, but not just to protect her. She had already proven she could take care of herself. But Toe wanted to fight alongside her and his other friends.

******

Sam pulled her car up in front of the William's house. Leaving the car doors open, they ran to Bobby's front door. Bobby entered first and turned on the entryway lights. "Mom. I'm home. Where are you?"

"Bobby," his mom called from the kitchen. "Thank heavens you are alright. Turn the light back off. We heard on the emergency radio that these demons have attacked some homes." He hit the switch. In the dark, he gave his mom a big hug.

Anne and Kevin came up behind Sarah. "Where's Sam," Anne asked.

"Mom, I'm right here."

They found each other. "Thank God," Anne said as she held her daughter tight. "I was so worried."

Grandpa Maeda pulled up out front. They, too, ran to the front door and knocked.

"Who's there," Sarah asked.

"It's me, Mrs. Williams, Jeff... and my grandpa." Bobby opened the door for them.

Sarah said, "Are your parents okay, Jeffrey?"

"I don't know. Grandpa and I went straight to the school to help Bobby and Sam. I haven't been home yet."

"Unfortunately, the phones are out of service. You can call them later and let them know you're here with us," Sarah said. We have a room downstairs that will keep us protected until this is over."

Grandpa Maeda said, "Thank you for your concern, dear lady, but I must continue to fight. There are too many people in danger."

"He's right, Mom," Bobby said. "People need our help. We should go with Mr. Maeda and help anyway we can."

"Absolutely not," Anne Thomas ordered!

"Mom, we have to," Sam insisted.

"You're not ready to fight these monsters. Sarah, back me up here. It is too soon."

"She's right," Sarah said. "You are not ready to fight. Not yet."

"Too late on that one," Jeff said.

"What," Anne asked. "What happened?"

"We just finished our first real battle, and Sam fried that demon to dust," Jeff told her.

"Mom, please understand. There is no more time to prepare. Ready or not, we have to fight."

"No," Anne pleaded. "You don't realize how dangerous these things are. They aren't like your Cooper."

"I know that, Mama."

"Ladies," Grandpa Maeda interrupted. "No mother wants their child, whether young or old, to go to war, and you are right, there is considerable danger. If we don't act now, everyone in El Palmar could die before tonight is over. When has danger ever waited for the world to be prepared? Danger doesn't care about convenience." He stepped up to Anne and Sarah. "You knew this day would come. It's time to let fate run its course. Sam and Bobby must fulfill their destiny."

Mr. Maeda had spoken the truth, but those agonizing words filled them with dread. So they cried and hugged their warrior children, hoping this wouldn't be the last time.

"Wait," Bobby said. "Where is Dad?"

"As far as we know, your dads are still on campus."

"But that is ground zero of this invasion," Sam said. "Why are they still in there?"

"Sorry, Sam," replied her mom. "I wish I knew. The last we heard from your dads, they were okay. It scares me that they haven't come home, but what can we do but wait?"

"We get them out, that's what," Bobby said. "Geez, dad could…" The words caught in his throat.

"I agree," said Sam.

"I'm in," said Jeff.

"Hold on, my young friends," the old man cautioned. "That is the most dangerous place on earth at the moment. I doubt your fathers want you charging in to rescue them."

"We have to do something," Bobby replied.

Sam said, "We should call them?"

"The phone service is still out," Sarah said.

"What about the internet," Jeff suggested. "If the power is still on, we could text or email."

"Brilliant," said Bobby, lifting his phone to find the wireless connection. We still have the internet."

"I'll check my email," Sam said. Maybe there's a message from Dad," Sam got excited. There is."

"Open it," Anne told her. "What does it say?"

She read. "It says, 'Sam, held up in the HGC control center on campus, but safe for now. Need your help. We let Cooper go, and he is undoubtedly on his way to find you. Don't know when he will get to you, but when he does, you must bring him here at once. I hate asking you to do this, but you must get Cooper to the rift as soon as possible. He is our only hope for ending this nightmare. Please be careful. Love you, Dad.'"

"When was it sent," Bobby asked.

"Almost three hours ago. What should we do?"

"Let's head toward campus," Jeff suggested.

"What about Cooper," Sam asked.

"Like your dad said," Bobby replied. "He will find you."

Mr. Maeda said, "We should go now." Without another word, they ran to their cars and drove away.

"I don't like this," Anne said.

"Me too, me too," Sarah answered, embracing Anne.

******

Toe ignored any Shadows he sensed as he entered the city. It was unlikely any of them would see him as a threat. He needed to focus on finding Sam. He sniffed the air. It alarmed him that so many Shadows had already come through the rupture. That probably included Fire Claws and his enforcers. Toe worried about the Shadows seeing him and recognizing him. Then what? He worried that Broken Fang would be back seeking revenge.

He also detected the scent of warrior witches. Shadow Witches were insane.

Chapter 46

GEEKS SURVIVE

The two cars raced to the Maeda home. Several more military helicopters flew overhead, followed by more gunfire, bright flashes, and explosions. When they arrived, Grandpa hurried into the house, returning with a katana and a wooden fighting staff. Grandpa's weapon of choice was already strapped to his waist.

"We can leave the cars here," Grandpa said. "It will be safer to proceed on foot."

Seeing the second katana, Jeff got excited. "You want me to use a real katana? With a real blade?"

Grandpa looked at Jeff and said, "Don't make me regret it." The skinny geek almost peed his pants when he tied the belt with the sword around Jeff's waist. "This katana was made in America. It's not as sharp, and if you break it, I won't cry as much. Please, don't cut off anyone's arms. I taught you the basics, so stay focused. Use what you have learned. I am counting on you, Jeffrey." Jeff gave a sober nod.

He turned to Bobby and gave him the six-foot-long staff. "This is a *bo*. I wish I had time to train you and Sam in a few fighting techniques. Use it the best you can to deflect any blows coming at you and Sam. I made it from a three-hundred-year-old red oak tree so it can receive and give a mighty hard blow. Jeff and I will watch your backs while we cast spells. Remember, our spells might only slow the enemy down. Be ready to defend yourselves at all times.

"Sam, do what you did in the school auditorium. That power will defeat anything we encounter." He put his hand on her shoulder. "You must believe in yourself, dear girl. Can you do that?"

"Yes, sir."

"Oh, and boys, Sam is our ace. Protect her with all you've got."

"Yes, sir."

"Bobby, the best way to survive is to avoid any Shadow demons in the first place. Your primary task is to help us do that. If you sense anything, tell us at once."

With those final words, the odd band of warriors headed toward campus.

They hadn't got more than a block when Bobby sensed the first Shadow.

"Up ahead." He pointed at a local market halfway down the block. "I think it's there."

They ducked through the nearest side yard into a back alley. The alley led them behind the store. As they passed, one of the store's rear exit doors slammed open, and two terrified individuals, a man and a woman, ran out into the alley. When they saw Grandpa Maeda's drawn katana, they stopped and backed away. Orange light from a power pole reflected off the shiny blade. The old man relaxed and sheathed the sword. The couple ran off without a word.

Before the back door closed, they heard screams coming from inside the store. Grandpa looked at his three worried companions. "I know that sounds bad, and I wish we could help them, but we mustn't forget our mission. Best we keep moving."

Bobby found it easier to sense the Shadows as they moved toward campus. He felt their dark nature. He also sensed something else. A new type of Shadow had appeared on the scene. These were smaller, but whatever it was, it was far more unsettling than the big guys. Its movements were much faster. One minute, it was there, and the next, it wasn't. Or worse, it wasn't there one minute, and then it was!

"Mr. Maeda," Bobby said. "I am sensing something new." At that moment, a warrior witch flew over their heads. They only got a glimpse of it. Bobby pointed. "There, see that?" The black specter slowed as it flew across the sidewall of a nearby building. The dark, distinctive silhouette appeared to have wings.

Grandpa nodded. "Yes, I did."

"Oh, great. Shadow demons can fly," Jeff asked.

"That one can."

"There is more than one of that type. There are a lot of them. The new type of Shadow feels more dangerous," Bobby explained. "They move so fast. That makes it harder to sense them."

"Everybody, keep an eye on what's above."

The band of warriors darted across a wide street. The green street sign at the intersection said University Ave.

"Something is close by," Bobby said. "We need to get out of sight."

They were about to run down the avenue when a big red pickup truck approached them. The unseen Shadow stood atop a two-story bank building across the street. Hearing the roar of the truck's engine, it came to the edge of the building.

"Shadow demon," shouted Bobby. He ran, leading them away from the threat.

This creature had a long blade-shaped horn sticking out of its forehead. Spike had made it farther into the city than any other of Fire Claws enforcers. He leaped from his position on the roof and landed in the path of the oncoming vehicle. The truck driver tried to swerve around the monster, but the maneuver didn't work. Spike gored the side of the truck. The driver lost control and drove through a storefront. An explosion followed.

The four warriors ran away from the burning truck as fast as they could, but not quick enough to avoid detection. Bobby didn't need to look back. He felt Spike's lust for blood. "It saw us," he yelled.

"Run faster." Spike charged after them. The distance between them quickly disappeared.

Sam looked over her shoulder only to see Bobby stop and turn to face the charging monster. "Bobby!" she screamed, raising her hands and preparing to attack. "Run!"

Bobby didn't hear her because the Shadow's thoughts had captured his full attention. The Shadow's hostile intentions sent chills through him. Spike planned to lower its head at the last minute, gore Bobby, and then ram its horn through Sam's back. Bobby understood it all.

All logic told Bobby to keep running, but his legs wouldn't cooperate. Instead, he held the fighting staff out horizontally in front of him. Then, in a moment of pure insanity, he charged the Shadow.

Surprised, Spike lifted his head momentarily. Bobby's staff hit Spike in the head just below the base of his horn. Bobby pushed the staff upward with all his strength, but his sneakers lost traction. The soles of his shoes started to burn as Spike pushed him backward across the pavement. Bobby's legs gave out. His knees buckled, and he fell back onto the pavement. The lethal horn missed Bobby's head as it gorged deep into the pavement. The stuck horn stopped the Spike's forward thrust, but his momentum launched him into the air, feet overhead.

Sam dove to the ground and twisted onto her back. The out-of-control creature passed over her just as she released intense energy. Spike burst into flaming dust and fell to the ground, missing Sam. Her arms drop to her sides in pure relief.

After the adrenaline subsided, Bobby gasped for breath. In shock, he began to shake so much that he had trouble getting to his feet.

"God is truly on your side," Grandpa said out of breath. "I can find no other explanation for what just happened. Now, everyone, breathe and clear your minds. We have a long way to go. You are getting stronger, Sam. I know you're afraid, but you are stronger than you think."

Bobby yelled out, "Behind you, Jeff." Startled, Sam screamed.

"Jeffrey, get behind me," Grandpa yelled out. The old man drew his katana.

Jeff didn't even look. He ran past his grandpa like a scared rabbit. Once past his grandpa, he turned and drew his blade. This Shadow was about Little Toe's size. Focused on Jeff, it ignored everyone else. Grandpa stepped forward and sliced his blade through the oncoming Shadow's shoulders right below the Shadow's toothy mouth. It had no neck. The head lifted off the body. It fell and bounced. The creature's lower body fell, but the separated head remained alive and focused on Jeff. It bounced and rolled, mindlessly chomping its sharp teeth at the boy. Jeff backed away as fast as he could. The boy slashed his blade back and forth. Finally, the head rolled to a stop and died.

"Holy, freaking, creepy, decapitated...," Jeff yelled, trying to shake off the near-death experience. "That was freaking terrifying."

Bobby leaned on the staff to take a deep breath. Somehow, they had survived two Shadow attacks in less than a minute. "I hope... that was... the last one... we run into," Bobby said, breathing hard. He smiled at Sam. "You are getting good at this, sweetheart."

She flushed at her boyfriend's endearment. "Thanks," she replied, quite delighted. "You were pretty awesome yourself, lover boy."

Grandpa rolled his eyes. "Will you two lovebirds pay attention? For all we know, these are the dumb ones, so don't get too cocky. Good job protecting Sam, Bobby. But maybe you should let her do the attacking."

"Yes, sir," he replied. "No problem."

"I can't believe we survived that," Jeff said.

Bobby replied, "That's what geeks like us do. We survive. Right?"

"Where do we need to go," the old man asked. Bobby pointed at a side street.

Chapter 47

ANTI MAGIC

Rich made the device with ease of activation in mind. A simple button on one end of a twelve-inch long by two-inch diameter, clear plastic pipe. It looked crude, duct tape and all, but the high-tech, anti-magic device hidden inside was anything but crude. Rich had no doubt Cooper was smart enough to operate the device, but getting him to understand what he needed to do for them was another thing altogether. He hoped his daughter could communicate with him well enough to make him understand and cooperate. Considering how badly humans had treated him thus far, he might just tell them where to go.

No, Rich thought. Cooper will help Sam. He would bet their lives on that fact.

Chapter 48

THE BATTLE GOES ON

After running across the open green space that encircled the UCEP campus, they huddled in the shadow of a campus building.

"What are you sensing now," Grandpa whispered to Bobby.

"They're everywhere," Bobby said. His three companions looked at him. "Sorry, but they really are everywhere. Finding ways around them from here on out will get harder."

"What if we used the buildings as shields," Jeff suggested.

"What do you mean?"

"You know, go through the buildings instead of around them."

"I see," said Grandpa. "Then we would only need to run from building to building."

"What if some Shadows got inside the buildings," Bobby argued.

"That's where you come in," Jeff reminded. "You decide which buildings are safe and which ones have an infestation."

"Okay, that sounds like a good plan," Bobby agreed.

"More places to hide inside, I suppose," Sam said.

"Yes, but less room to run," Grandpa cautioned. "Easy to get trapped in a corner." The old man thought for a minute. "Still, Jeffrey's idea is the best one."

Jeff looked around the corner. A courtyard garden was up ahead. "If we just had a...." He spied a three-sided kiosk through the raised flower beds at the intersection of several pedestrian walkways. "That's what we need." He pointed at a sign that said Campus Information. "I'll be right back." He ran off toward the kiosk.

Bobby hissed, "Where are you going?"

Jeff just waved him off and kept going, only stopping to look around after he reached the kiosk. He crouched and circled behind the signs. After a minute or two, Jeff to come running back, his phone in hand. "Here we go," he said. "Just what we need. I took a picture of the campus map."

Grandpa Maeda scowled and smacked Jeffrey on the back of the head. "Baka! Don't run off by yourself again."

"I'm Sorry," Jeff said, "but this will help us figure out the best path."

After looking over the map, they ran across the courtyard to the building on the opposite corner. They huddled in the bushes next to the building's entrance. Bobby tried to sense any unwanted inhabitants. He felt nothing.

Jeff grabbed a stone from the garden. "The perfect tool for getting past the locked doors."

Using this method, they moved further into the campus. The closer they got to the Center for Interdimensional Physics, the campus looked more like a bombed-out war zone. Damaged and burning buildings lined the once-peaceful campus walkways. They discovered the wreckage of a couple of downed aircraft but no signs of survivors. The smell of aviation fuel burning assaulted their nostrils.

Dead shadows and human bodies covered the open spaces, a gory display of the realities of this invasion. It had produced a slaughterhouse. Although they had only come across a few gruesome human remains. Such discoveries conjured images of horrific encounters that none of them wanted to contemplate.

"Geez," Jeff said, stunned by what he saw.

Grandpa expressed his nervousness. "Judging from what we see now, we are lucky to be alive. What are you sensing, Bobby?"

"Something wicked this way comes," Bobby replied. "And it's somewhere close."

"Okay, my young friends," Grandpa said. "Keep your wits about you and your eyes open."

Bobby piped up again. "Wait. I feel something else. I think it's people. Sam, our dads must be nearby."

Sam, eager to get to her dad, asked, "Can you tell which way to go?"

"That way," he pointed at a long campus corridor lined with buildings in various degrees of rubble.

Jeff looked at the map on his phone. "If we are not completely lost, the map says the Center for... something... Physics is three more buildings from here. That has to be it."

"Not much cover for us," Sam said.

Three Shadows came into view at the far end of the walkway, right where the warriors needed to go. The four warriors ducked behind a concrete retaining wall. They could hear growling and loud noises. Grandpa peered over the wall.

"It looks like they are fighting each other. One has something the other two want. It's a... Oh." He didn't finish. His face went pale as he sat down. "A Shadow demon just ripped the head off the other," Grandpa said.

"What is going on, Grandpa? Why are they fighting each other?"

"I don't know, but that's better than fighting us." Grandpa peeked over the wall. "They are gone." He stood. "We've been very lucky.

Things could have gone much worse." He looked around at the carnage. "A lot worse." The old man's words came true immediately when the biggest creature they had encountered thus far stumbled out of a nearby building. It had massive hands with long clawed fingers.

Fire Claws staggered a few more steps, acting strange, as though drunk or on drugs. That was close to the truth. He was high on human blood energy.

The four warriors froze. "What should we do," Jeff whispered.

Sam whispered back, "Maybe if we stand still, it won't see us."

"I doubt that," Bobby said.

Fire Claws had something dangling from his mouth. The dazed Shadow shook his head. The dangling bit came loose and landed on the ground in front of Sam. She gasped out loud. The human leg with a booted foot was unmistakable. Sam put both hands over her mouth to stifle the desire to scream.

Sensing that the Shadow saw them, Bobby yelled, "Run."

As soon as they moved, Fire Claws reacted. Everyone followed Bobby. Grandpa, who was not letting his age slow him down at a time like this, kept close behind. They ran toward the nearest building. The missing doors at the end of the building gave them a clear path for entry. Running through it, they dodged the shattered glass and chunks of ceiling tiles covering the floor and kept running.

Fire Claws launched into a full power run, reaching the building entrance seconds after the four humans disappeared through it. The small double door opening didn't stop Claws. Crashing into the doorway, he made the opening bigger. Interior walls and ceiling tiles exploded in the wake of his charge. Fortunately for his fleeing prey, the cramped space slowed Claws down enough for them to get further ahead. The four turned down another hall and kept running. The ninety-degree turn slowed Claws even more. His large body slid into and through a wall, sending walls, desks, and chairs flying.

At the end of the hall, the desperate warriors found a set of double doors that opened into a large lecture hall that spanned across the entire end of the classroom wing. The floor sloped downward to the back wall and a set of exit doors. Relieved, they darted for safety. But when they pushed the hand bars, none of the doors opened more than an inch. Outside debris blocked the only exit.

By the time Fire Claws recovered, the humans had disappeared. He followed their scent.

"Push," Grandpa yelled. They could hear the Claws getting closer. "Push harder."

Jeff grabbed hold of the vertical bar that formed the center door jamb and pushed on the bottom of the door with his legs. Bobby pushed with his back against the door while Sam and Grandpa pushed with their arms. This combined effort opened one door wide enough for them to squeeze through.

Once outside, they ran again. Seconds later, a loud crash came from behind them. The pursuing Fire Claws had made his own opening. Nobody wanted to look back, so they kept running until the giant Shadow leaped over their heads and landed in front of them. They slid to a halt as Fire Claws turned to face them. A creepy smile spread across the Shadow's face.

"Be strong," Grandpa called out while drawing his katana. Jeff did the same. "I know you are afraid, but this big fellow is in our way. We need to do something about that."

Sam raised her shaking hands. An energy ball shot straight at Claws, but he sensed her magic and dodged the strike. This Shadow was smarter than the others. Claws swung his right arm over his massive shoulder. Bobby grabbed Sam and pulled her back. The long claws landed inches from where they had stood. Sparks exploded like fireworks.

Grandpa Maeda yelled, "Start your spell, Jeffrey." Jeff responded and recited the mantra, katana in hand. The old man took a position in front of Sam.

"Bobby, watch Sam's back," he yelled over his shoulder.

"Rin pyō tō sha kai jin retsu zai zen... Destroy this demon," Jeff shouted. Fire Claws looked dazed. Jeff hoped that meant the spell was working. Claws blinked and backhanded Jeff and sent him flying. The katana hit the concrete with a clang. The nearby bushes softened the blow to Jeff's tumbling body. Bruised and body aching, Jeff climbed out of the bushes. Blood dripped from the boy's nose and a gash on his forehead.

Once again, they watched Grandpa move surprisingly fast. "Sam... Now Sam," the old man said as he ran toward the Shadow. He slashed the sword forward at the creature's clawed fist. The blade made contact but glanced away with a burst of sparks. Sam's fiery flame hit the Shadow in the chest, but once again, Claws anticipated the attack. A large hole appeared in the giant's chest, and the flame went right through him without hurting him.

"See what it did," Sam shouted. "How do I fight against that?"

"Jeffrey. Are you okay," Grandpa cried out.

"Yeah, I guess," Jeff coughed. "That blow knocked the air out of me, but I..."

"Then get up," Grandpa yelled. "Sam needs us!" Grandpa moved to the Shadow's right while Jeff stumbled up and took the left side. They chanted together, "Rin pyō tō sha kai jin retsu zai zen... Destroy this demon!" And again, "Rin pyō tō sha kai jin retsu zai zen... Destroy this demon!" Fire Claws reacted to the spell and roared. "Again, Sam," Grandpa ordered. She hit him again. This time, the bolt of energy did some damage.

Fire Claws roared, grabbing at the wound. He twisted and slashed the ground to his left and then right, sending fiery sparks at the two spell casters. That broke their concentration. The angry Shadow lunged at Sam and Bobby, desperate to sink his teeth into the little witch.

A blur of black came charging out of the night and tackled the Fire Claws by the head, sending him rolling away from Sam.

"COOPER," Sam shouted.

Little Toe recovered and gave an uppercut to Claw's head. He made sure his fist was extra hard. The blow knocked Fire Claws back.

Fire Claws blinked in disbelief at who had tackled him. "Little Toe," he thought. "What are you doing?"

Toe replied. "I am here to stop you and this invasion."

"How are you going to do that? You are no bigger than my little toe. Bruff, bruff, snort."

"I am not your Little Toe anymore!"

Claws stood, regaining his stature. "So, just what are you, my small friend?"

"I am not your friend." He roared in defiance. "I am stronger and braver. I will prove it today when I kill you."

Claws smiled at this challenge. "I see. You got yourself some courage. I should have squashed you long ago." He smashed his fist down at Toe but hit nothing. Toe had darted out of the way and was now behind Claws.

"Over here, dumb as a rock," Toe mocked. "That will be your new name on Tiarnas when we get home. I will tell them how easily I beat the once-feared Fire Claws." Claws twisted around and slashed at him again, but Toe evaded his attack once more. "Missed again, slow as mud. Bruff, bruff, bruff, skree." Toe laughed.

Enraged, Claws took another swipe with his right fist, but this time he fooled Toe with a sucker punch from the left. Toe rolled backward from the impact. Fire Claws roared with delight.

Toe recovered. "I guess I better finish this before you kill me." His next move needed Sam's magic. If this fight was to end in a victory, he had to make her understand. It would be difficult to get close enough to strike a fatal blow. Claws was cunning but vulnerable where his body was most solid. Toe created a specific image in his mind. Then he looked directly at Sam, who stood on the other side of the enemy Shadow demon. As soon as he made eye contact with Sam, he thought clearly and hard, sending a mental message. Sam's eyes grew large as their two minds connected. She understood and confirmed it with a nod. Toe looked straight up into Claws' blazing eyes to make sure he had the enormous Shadow's full attention. "This ends now." Then he charged.

Fire Claws raised his right arm high above his head, ready to slash through Toe's forward assault, but an unexpected fiery flash came from behind him. The blade-shaped energy sliced through the Shadow's clawed right hand, severing it from his arm. The hand fell to the ground uselessly. The pain must have been intense because Claws screeched an ear-splitting scream. He turned with a fierceness that he was sure would put pure terror in the heart of such a little witch. He made eye contact with her and, in a blind rage, thought, "You cowardly little witch."

Sam understood the emotional venom the Shadow sent her. "That big jerk just called me a witch."

Bobby thought of the flying Shadows. "I suppose to him, you are a witch," Bobby said. "It makes sense. Those flying Shadows must be witches."

"Yeah, well, I am not a witch!"

"In a way, you are a witch."

"Sam is a witch," Jeff asked. "Really?"

"Excuse me, I am no witch."

"I'm just saying that you and I have the magic gene. That makes both of us witches of a sort. In my case, maybe a wizard."

"That's just stupid," Sam said, facing Fire Claws again, incensed by the insult. "Take it back, you ugly demon, before I cut your nails for you."

Fire Claws blinked several times, stunned by what he saw. Expecting to see a scared, cowering little female pleading for her life, he found a fearless, powerful witch instead. Next to her was a young male who had his own powerful magic. He saw the magical aura surrounding the two humans for the first time. Such an aura wasn't possible. It only existed between a Shadow Lord and a coupled Imperial Witch.

"Who are these two creatures," he thought, stunned by their magic.

Bobby sensed the Shadow's moment of confusion. "Now, Sam," he yelled. She released another bolt of energy, this time wounding the monster's left hand.

Fire Claws screeched in pain and backed away. A loud, crunching sound came from inside his head. He tried raising his wounded left hand to his face, but inexplicably it didn't move. Even the pain from his severed right hand had stopped. The only part of his body he could still move was his eyes. Looking down, he saw five long claws protruding out of his mouth.

When Fire Claws had turned to face Sam, Toe grabbed the severed right hand, leaped onto his nemesis' back, and rammed the five-clawed fingers through the back of the Shadow's head. Fire Claws fell forward stiff-legged. Dead before he hit the ground. He had used those long claws to torment, oppress, and kill weaker Shadows. They had been the source of his power and malicious pride. The irony of the Magistrate's death struck Toe as profound and pitiful. Fire Claws' death had come by his own hand.

Still panting from the fight, Sam walked up to the big body. This long night would forever change her. In the beginning, fear had awakened her power, then love had activated it in the school auditorium, but courage had empowered it while fighting this monster alongside her friends. Sam, the girl, was born again as Sam, the guardian, protector, and warrior.

"Okay, let's go get our dads," she said. Walking away, she took the lead. Bobby and the others, including Little Toe, followed.

Grandpa Maeda had never felt prouder of Sam, Bobby, and his favorite grandson Jeffrey.

Chapter 49

REUNION

"Sam, over here," Someone called out.

"Dad?" Overjoyed, she ran to him, threw her arms around his neck, and held on tight.

Attracted by Sam's magic, the Shadow witches gathered overhead. Overseer Shadow Strong slowed to look at the six individuals, including one male Shadow, grouped together below her.

"Who is this traitorous Shadow," the Overseer thought. She reached out to the Shadow's mind.

Little Toe felt her thoughts and looked up. "Warrior witches," he thought. "This is bad." He shut her out of his mind and gave her a defiant roar.

"Traitor." The Overseer seethed in anger as she prepared to attack.

"Above us. Sam," Bobby said, jumping back. Sam reacted fast and blasted a fireball at the Shadow hovering above them.

The Overseer evaded the attack easily. "So, this is the cause of the unknown magic." Then she noticed a magical aura now engulfed the six individuals. She called out to her fellow witches, "Quick, kill them all."

Bobby said. "We need to take cover. Now."

"Quick, everyone inside," Rich said. They followed him into the building and then into the control center. The outer entryway exploded into flames as the big fire door closed behind them.

"Bobby," Bill called out.

"Dad." Bobby pushed through the crowded room to get to his dad.

"I am so glad to see you're alright." They hugged. Bobby winced at the firm bear hug

"Me too, Dad. Me too."

"You are okay, aren't you?"

"I expect to be covered in bruises for weeks, but thanks to Sam, I am still in one piece. Dad, those flying creatures outside know that we are in here. They are angry. We all need to get out of here."

"We've got a plan. Hopefully, this will be over soon."

It took a minute for the humans to recognize the non-human presence in the room. They turn their attention from the hopeful reunion to the black Shadow demon who stood by the fire door. The two soldiers guarding the door had already backed away. Their weapons were pointed at the floor as ordered by General Bates. Still, the big creature made them plenty nervous. Dr. Miles had wisely backed away to the far side of the room.

Toe remained calm as he looked across the room at Miles.

"It seems recent events have put us on the same side," Toe thought. In spite of his distrust of that particular human, it was time for a truce. Toe remained at his position by the door.

Sam led her father by the hand to meet Toe. She made a mental image of the man from her memories of his loving and gentle ways as a father. As she looked into Toe's eyes, the way he had done during the battle, she said, "This is my father." Toe saw the love she had for the male.

Rich extended his hand. "Thank you for protecting my little girl." Toe responded by taking Sam's father's hand. He licked it. The hand tasted of Sam. That pleased him.

Bobby introduced his dad the same way. Grandpa Maeda and Jeff gave their Shadow comrade a warrior-sized hug. The old man chuckled. "I never believed the day would come when I would be so happy to see a demon. Your timing, my friend, was perfect."

Rich took his daughter aside to show her the device he had made for Little Toe. He handed it to her. "This," he said, "is for Cooper."

"Why? What do you need him to do?"

"If we are to save lives, then we have to close the rift." Rich paused before giving her the bad news. "But... we can't close it on this side. Cooper needs to close it from the other side. I am sorry, Sam, but Cooper is the only one of us who can do that."

Sam held back her emotion. "I see... but when you say explosion... will it hurt Cooper?"

"I don't believe it will, but to be honest, honey, I don't know how it will affect these Shadow demons."

"Shouldn't we test it first, not on Cooper, but on another Shadow demon?"

"I'm sorry, sweetie. This might only work once. Besides, Cooper will need the element of surprise if he is to fulfill this mission. I am sorry, but since you can communicate with him, we need you to ask Cooper to cooperate. I know this is a hard thing to ask of you, but can you do it for me, your family, and this world we've come to love?"

Grandpa Maeda, who had overheard the conversation, stepped up behind Sam and put his hands on her shoulders. "You are a warrior now, Sam," he said. "And so is Cooper. Warriors are called to go on missions like this. Your dad is asking Cooper to do a noble thing. He will do it."

Reluctantly, Sam took the apparatus to Toe. He smiled and took her hand. She created mental images while she spoke. "Cooper," she said. "We need you to take this device, this tube thing." She handed it to him. He took it with great interest. "You need to take it back through the rift to your world." She envisioned Toe going back through the hole to his world. Toe's smile faded. "When you push this button at the end." She imagined him holding the device in his hand. "It will explode with anti-magic light." She imagined him pushing the button and a blinding explosion of light. Toe's eyes narrowed with concern as she explained. "It will stop the magic and allow the rift to close." She imagined the rift closing behind him. "You won't be able to come back to this world... to me... us." Tears filled Sam's eyes and dripped down her cheeks. "It's the only way to save my world. To save me." She remembered how he tried to defend her against Fang, stood up to Dr. Miles and the armed agents, and killed Fire Claws to save her once again.

Toe understood. He smiled at her and nodded yes, but his eyes were sad. A drop of fluid fell from one of his eyes.

"I don't know what will happen to you when you go back home," she said. "I don't want you to get hurt. I don't want you to die." She put her arms around his big head.

Toe gently patted her back. "I will do anything for you, Sam," he thought. "Even give my life for yours because you have made me happy. I have felt love because of you." The image of him being happy and content entered Sam's mind. A deep connection had already formed between the two of them. Now, that connection would be eternal. A kind of trust and love that was rare, not just in this world but throughout all the numberless universes.

She let go of him and smiled, "Thank you, my very best friend." She looked at her dad and said, "He will do it."

"Good," her dad said, relieved.

They said their goodbyes once they completed the preparations for Toe's heroic mission. Grandpa Maeda faced Little Toe as if before a great nobleman. "Cooper," he said. "You are a creature of great strength and honor. I am honored to be your comrade and stand with you in battle." The old man gave a deep bow. The image of them fighting side by side appeared in Toe's mind. It was a gratifying image.

Rich thought of one more thing he could do for Cooper. At least, he hoped it would work on the Shadow demons. He pulled his special smartwatch out of a duffle bag in which he kept his tools. The DoD had confiscated the first one. This one was for an emergency escape if things got too dangerous. He showed it to Toe.

"Cooper," he said. "Watch me." Rich touched the screen and disappeared from view. Toe's eyes went big and round. He looked downright baffled. A second later, Rich reappeared. Toe jumped back. Rich did this one more time. The trick delighted Toe. Rich looked into the Shadow demon's eyes, and as he had seen Sam do, he said, "Touch to disappear... touch to reappear. Do you understand?" Although mystified, Little Toe nodded. Rich strapped the watch to the anti-magic device. "Don't lose it, my friend. You can use it to get out of trouble."

Toe turned to the human's present. He looked at Sam, Bobby, Jeff, and old man Maeda. The thought of seeing them for the last time ignited something dormant deep inside his soul. He saw a profound vision. In it, he saw what his species had once been and how his world had fallen into awful darkness. So dark that darkness became their story for a thousand years. He saw in that vision that a small but brave warrior would someday come to reclaim his world and free his fellow Shadows.

Moved by the emotion of this powerful visionary experience, Little Toe raised his head upward and did something no one expected. He sang, not with words, but with his voice and mind. It began as a mournful howl, not the high shrill of the wolf, but in haunting baritone. The tones resonated and filled the room with a magical tale that was as beautiful as it was sad. Toe had heard this song only once as an imp, yet the notes came to him in perfect remembrance. Then, Toe allowed everyone present to see what he saw.

The ballad tells of a warrior who, in the aftermath of a great battle, stood among the fallen to say goodbye to his comrades. Bodies of dead warriors from both sides of the conflict spread across the landscape. He knelt at the side of his dearest friend to comfort him in his final moments of life and said these words. "To you, freedom did call," the lyrics went. "And for freedom, you did fall." Toe looked around the room one more time as if to say goodbye. He will go home now. If he survived, he would fight to make his world a better place for all Shadows because, to him, freedom did call, and for freedom, he would willingly fall. Then he touched the watch and vanished. The main door opened and closed, signaling that Little Toe had left the room.

Chapter 50

TIARNAS

Little Toe reappeared inside the HGC chamber next to the rupture. Stepping into his world, he stood face to face with seven imperial witches and seven Shadow Lords. Thousands of Shadows were present, still waiting for their regimental overseers to order them to join the battle. News from the war was far overdue, so when a Shadow like Little Toe stepped through the rupture, it surprised those present.

"Who are you," demanded an Imperial Witch.

"Isn't that the little imp that found the rupture," another Shadow thought. "The one Magistrate Fire Claws called Little Toe." The Shadows all laughed.

"Then why is he here?"

"Because he is a coward." They laughed again. "The little freak has run away from the battle." More loud laughter.

Toe remained calm. Such mockery no longer hurt him. He knew who he had become; soon, these fools would know, too. He looked at the noble lords and witches and proclaimed, "The time for a change has come, my lords. I have come to free this world from your tyranny."

They would have laughed again, but Toe's ludicrous declaration left them speechless. Some got quite angry. A Shadow Lord thought, "Kill this imp and get his body out of our sight."

Toe raised the anti-magic device high, ready to push the button with his thumb. Then, to the shock of Shadows present, he spoke in an audible voice for the first time in his life. "I KUPOR. RE MEMBUR THA NAME" Pushing the button, he released the blinding anti-magic light.

Chapter 51

WAR'S AFTERMATH

The death toll reached 3,537 humans - a terrible loss of life. Still, it could have been much worse. Considering the aggressiveness of the enemy, that number seemed low. Most of the invading Shadow creatures, estimated at five to six thousand individuals, hadn't advanced that far from the campus. The lust for human blood had caused a mindless feeding frenzy. Chaos among the Shadow leadership left the Shadow warriors without direction. The intoxicated Shadows kept searching the campus area for more food, even after they had decimated the remaining campus population. Autopsies performed on the creatures' bodies showed that as many as one-third of the Shadows had died at the hand of another pillaging comrade. This chaotic battle environment was a miracle. It saved the local population from further loss of life.

From the White House rose garden, the President of the United States declared, "The worst act of terror since 9/11 is over. I promise to bring those responsible to justice. The chemical weapons used in this cowardly attack caused mass hallucinations, killing over three thousand innocent citizens. We will not forget them, nor the sacrifice of the hundreds of military personnel who gave their lives defending innocent Americans. We will not forget."

"As a precaution, I have ordered the quarantine of the area closest to ground zero and the cremation of the bodies to eliminate any trace of the weaponized hallucinogen. We must also thank local, state, and federal government agencies whose prompt response to the crisis saved thousands of lives. To them, we owe a debt of deep gratitude."

Much of the original campus site ended up behind a tall stone wall.

Since a significant terrorist attack had occurred on home soil, the country demanded answers. The President demanded answers from the DoD. The DoD demanded answers from General Bates. Someone had to take the blame. That someone was the now-retired Andrew Bates.

Few knew what happened in El Palmar that late September day. Those who did know had plenty of reasons for keeping it secret. For now, the Williams and the Thomas families' secrets remained safe, but now that others knew their secrets, danger would always be nearby. Wisdom teaches men to err on the side of caution. In the long run, sustaining trust would be difficult, if not impossible. Demons come in many forms, and many are in the form of human beings.

******

Although forced to grow up too fast, Bobby, Sam, and Jeff regrouped as friends. They coped with their new reality the best they could. Their role in the nightmare would remain a secret. For that reason, they signed a document promising to keep quiet. They decided to focus on salvaging as much of their young lives as possible. Life goes on.

"It's interesting," Bobby said one night as the three were swinging in the park. "Sam and I came together by a mix of science and magic. But Jeff, you came to us by what I would call random circumstances."

"Yeah," Jeff replied. "So, what are you saying?"

"It's interesting that you became our friend out of the billions of people on this planet. You were there for us when we needed you the most."

"I didn't do that much," Jeff said, embarrassed by the praise.

"Think about it, Jeff," Bobby continued. "If it hadn't been for you, the favorite grandson of the coolest old guy in Southern California, maybe the whole world, the outcome of the recent events might have been different. Your grandpa had survived the first demon war. Because of you, we met him. Because of him, the three of us survived. Was that a matter of incredibly good luck or something else?"

Sam understood. "Too lucky to be an accident."

"It makes me think about how important personal relationships are. We should never take family and friends for granted. By treating those relationships with love and care, we may be ensuring our survival. The day might come when everything we hold dear and value will hang in the balance. At such times, help will most likely come from that perfect person already part of our lives." Bobby paused. "So, is that by accident or by divine design?"

"Do you guys believe in God," Jeff asked.

Bobby thought about it. He said, "I think I do."

"I do," said Sam.

The three teens continued swinging together without speaking.

Epilogue

SHADOW STRONG

High Overseer Shadow Strong earned her title and fame through years of supremacy in the battle arena. No witch could match her strength and cunningness. No male Shadow had ever defeated her. Not an ounce of weakness held her back. Fast, agile, and observant, she always controlled her fate. That is what kept her at the top of Tiarnas' food chain. Although fate had dealt her this unexpected blow, she considered this situation an opportunity. She and thirty-seven known Shadow witch survivors, found themselves stuck in this strange world without an army or orders for how to proceed. Thus far, they had escaped detection. She vowed to keep it that way until she found a way back home. Until then she would rule over her sisters in secret.

******

Blending into this world population would be easy for a Shadow witch with powerful magic. Shadow Strong had used the *soul eater* spell many times before. It would serve her and her sisters well in this world. Tonight, for the first time, she stepped out of the early evening shadows of Balboa Park wearing her new five-foot-ten human female body. The original owner was Kylie Harrisford, the daughter of one of the wealthiest men in the world. She had given little protest when she died. Not that Shadow Strong had given her a chance to object. Now, the young woman's body, life, knowledge, and memories belong to the Overseer. Shadow Strong had picked this body because of the way it moved with confidence and entitlement. The fact that it came with so much of this world's wealth was a stroke of pure luck. This body pleased Shadow Strong, as did the soft fabric garment she picked to drape over it for tonight's event.

As she walked through the park toward the evening's event, she noted that others glanced and smiled in her direction. Such a reaction confirmed that she had chosen well. Shadow Strong disappeared into the crowd of humans gathering for a gala event at the elegant Botanical Gardens.

The Overseer's next move will be shrouded in mystery.

Author's Final Thoughts:

I hope you enjoyed reading **Shadow Invasion: Shadow Demon** as much as I enjoyed writing it. A lot of love went into creating the characters and the story's universe, especially the Shadow named Little Toe. As you finished the last chapter, I am sure you noticed there are a couple of loose ends unresolved. High Overseer Shadow Strong and her Shadow witches are still trapped in this world. What will Shadow Strong do next? Little Toe, a.k.a. Cooper, returned to his world vowing to bring freedom to his kind. What will happen to him, and will he be able to return to our world to fight alongside his human friends? Will Bobby and Sam grow as a coupling? Will Jeffrey finally become a Jeff and find a real girl to love?

The answers to these questions and more await you in the series' next book, Shadow Invasion: Shadow Witch, promising an exciting continuation of the story. Now two years older, Bobby's and Sam's discover their world has become far more dangerous.

www.ingramcontent.com/pod-product-compliance
Lightning Source LLC
LaVergne TN
LVHW061034070526
838201LV00073B/5030